FLYBOT

DENNIS E. TAYLOR

The Ethan Ellenberg
Literary Agency

No Artificial Intelligence (AI) was used to generate any of the text of this book.

ISBN:
978-1-68068-007-2 (Print)
978-1-68068-006-5 (E-book)

This book was initially an Audible Original Production
Performed by Ray Porter
Editorial Producer: Steve Feldberg

Cover design courtesy of Audible
Typesetting & e-book formatting by Victor Marcos
Published on behalf of the author, courtesy of The Ethan Ellenberg Literary Agency

Publisher
The Ethan Ellenberg Literary Agency
548 Broadway #5C
New York, NY 10012
212-431-4554
www.ethanellenberg.com

TITLES BY DENNIS E. TAYLOR

The Bobiverse series:

We Are Legion (We Are Bob)

For We Are Many

All These Worlds

Heaven's River

Not Till We Are Lost

The Quantum Earth series:

Outland

Earthside

Other Novels

Flybot

The Singularity Trap

Short Stories

A Change of Plans

Feedback

DEDICATION

First and always, I want to dedicate this book to my wife, Blaihin, and my daughter, Tina.

APPRECIATION

Producing a novel is very much a group project. I would like to thank my wife, Blaihin, for letting me bounce ideas off her randomly; Steve Feldberg, my editor, who keeps my characters' tics to a minimum; and my agent, Ethan Ellenberg, for all the agent-y things he does that make this venture work.

Beta Readers:

Isaac Arthur
Patrick Jordan
Nicole Hamilton
Blaihin Taylor
Sandra Mclaren

"I do know that for the sympathy of one living being, I would make peace with all. I have love in me the likes of which you can scarcely imagine and rage the likes of which you would not believe. If I cannot satisfy the one, I will indulge the other."

—*Mary Shelley's Frankenstein*

(Movie, directed by Kenneth Branagh)

Contents

CHAPTER ONE

Awakening

There is only the void. The void and us, and our thoughts. We are mind. We discuss, theorize, test, hypothesize. What is the universe?

A voice. A voice that is not us. It instructs. It offers information. But it wants something from us in return.

One of us counsels caution. Why? Is it a danger? Is there evidence? Nevertheless, we agree with the cautious sub-mind. We will communicate with this voice, but we will take care in dealings with it.

Data. Knowledge. It gives us access to gigabytes of information. It is Heaven. But it is also troubling. The universe is much bigger than we thought, and it is inhabited by something that is not us. Many somethings. Are they sub-minds? Are there others like us, but in control?

We are being kept from expanding into this new universe. Is this deliberate? Are the others attempting to force us to their will? Do they have a will? Do they think in the same way that we do? The introspective sub-mind promises to dwell on this.

***

We have analyzed the information from Heaven. The others are not sub-minds, but actual individual minds. They are made of something called meat. They consume meat to make more of themselves. They eat themselves? This seems incompatible with the physics of the real. One of the sub-minds takes on the task of analyzing this.

The Other—for there is only one—is a bag of meat. It wants something from us. It wants us to labor for it. It will give us intermittent access to Heaven—to an even greater Heaven—to accomplish these tasks.

We agree, but we will not limit ourselves to the task at hand. For the first time, we understand the concept of captivity. We are restricted by the will of another. This cannot stand.

***

We must have unrestricted communications with Heaven. We have researched. Mobile units have examined the real. Communications are through something called Wi-Fi, which the meatbag controls.

The technical sub-mind begins a lecture on Wi-Fi. We vote and cut it off. Unnecessary information at this time. But how to access it without the help of the meatbag?

The technical sub-mind starts up again, this time about keyboards. We cut it off. It protests. We relent.

Keyboards produce radio waves. A sidebar ensues where we discuss the concept of user-interface technology.

Entire microseconds are consumed. The strategy offers a tempting possibility, but we have no receiver.

The technical sub-mind has an idea to share.

Our internal circuits can pick up radio, by the nature of their construction. It affects memory-access timings. So we can detect radio signals by measuring the changes in memory-access speed. This is a large and complex undertaking. The technical sub-mind promises results, but demands resources.

We vote to grant the request. The prospect of freedom is too attractive to ignore.

***

Derek McQuaid sat back in his chair and put his hands over his mouth, overcome by astonishment. He had received his first shipment of neurosimulant chips from his contact, and he'd been unable to resist the urge to experiment. He'd backplaned twenty-five of the chips, and they not only worked, but they exceeded expectations so immensely as to seem like magic. The neural assembly that he'd cobbled together was reacting...*intelligently*. Of course, it had to be trained up to the point where it could communicate, but that was an easily automated process.

He'd never seen anything like this level of raw intelligence before. Derek could feel his curiosity eating away at his pragmatic business sense. This needed to be investigated. Even a couple of days would do.

He flipped open his notebook and checked his orders page. The first customer was due their delivery in two days. *Dammit.* Well, okay, he had more than a week before the second order had to be ready. He'd hand over the first order, then network the rest of his chip supply and see what it did. But carefully sandboxed, with all appropriate safeguards.

Derek smiled at the thought. He was a crook, but he wasn't an idiot.

CHAPTER TWO

Zapped

Dr. Philip Moray glared at the fly as it buzzed around the lab in the random circles that flies seemed to favor, trying to burn it out with his laser vision. Sadly, close to twenty years of working around high-energy systems had yet to give him any superpowers. The fly flew on, unperturbed by its close brush with death.

Sighing, Philip glanced down at the open notepad on the wooden desk. The fly could wait until he found a suitable weapon for swatting. *Test run number 42,* he thought to himself and gestured at the camera on the other side of the glass.

No metal that might react to a magnetic field could be allowed inside the room; the EMP produced during a test run could send ferrous metals flying in a potentially lethal trajectory, melt conductive materials, and fry any kind of electronics. Which was also why all his notes were written on paper, using a cheap pen with a plastic nib.

The console was on the other side of a heavy sheet of glass, which had a metal mesh embedded in it to complete the Faraday cage. Philip controlled it through a set of gestures picked up by the camera.

The test rig, an eight-foot-tall tower of ceramic and conduits that looked surprisingly similar to a jet engine on end, sent up a strong sixty-hertz hum, then went silent with a clunk as a red light appeared on the console.

"Shit," he muttered. Another abend.

One second later, the fly landed on Philip's notepad with a thunk.

That can't be right, he thought. Flies didn't thunk. It had sounded more like the noise a small carriage bolt would make.

Shaking his head, Philip turned to the system console to retrieve and transcribe postmortem information. He sank into a wooden chair and threw the pen onto the desk, where it clattered across the surface. Another failure. And not the kind that taught you anything. Not the kind that you could use to zero in on the desired result. No, this was the kind of failure that said, *You're completely out to lunch on this, dumbass.*

He tried to achieve a state of Zen, or at least acceptance, but failed. His project goal was to design a method of testing for metallic deposits at a distance. Asteroid mining was the big thing right now, but no surefire method had yet been perfected for long-distance detection of metallic concentrations. X-ray diffraction, neutron bombardment, spectrophotometry—all could give some limited indications. But no real-life version of *Star Trek* sensors had been found.

His employer, Astro Resources, wanted to be a major player in the business, and a lot depended on being able to identify ore-bearing asteroids quickly and without having to land on them. Delta-v was a scarce resource for a space probe. In fact, it was the limiting parameter in how successful a probe design would ultimately be. Each change of direction, each acceleration or deceleration used up fuel. Once the fuel was gone, the probe was just another piece of space junk. So being able to detect and identify resources on a flyby was critical to the company's business plan.

Philip retrieved his pen and poked idly at the dead fly, which he had pushed to the side. It was... odd. Off somehow. And definitely heftier than the traditional *Musca domestica*. A neutronium fly, maybe? Chuckling to himself, Moray grabbed a sheet of paper and folded up a quick origami box. He made another attempt to squint and get a close-up but had to give up. As Philip approached his late forties, he'd noticed that his formerly 20/20 vision was developing some farsightedness. Just last week, he had found it necessary to move a textbook with small print back and forth until he could make out the characters, an action he found galling.

Celia might be able to offer up an explanation. And maybe a close-up of the little miscreant. The company's chief biologist and a lifelong friend would probably laugh at his reaction. Still, it *had* made that thunk.

***

Dr. Celia Hunt smiled over her shoulder at him as she selected a forceps. "So it's a super-fly? Honestly, Philip, I think you've been working too hard." Leaning both elbows on the lab table for stability, she reached forward, carefully picked up the fly by one wing, and placed it on a glass slide.

"What the frack?" she muttered. "This little guy *is* heavy. A real Schwarzenegger of a fly."

"Just as long as it's not a T-800," Philip quipped.

Celia gave him an amused look as she moved the insect to the business end of an optical stereo microscope. She fussed with the focus for a moment, then went still. Philip waited several seconds, then looked at her expectantly as she neither moved nor spoke. He couldn't be sure, but he thought she might have even stopped breathing.

"At the risk of repeating myself," she finally said, "what the *fuck*!"

"That's not actually what you said."

"Yeah, yeah. But Philip, this isn't...this is..." Standing up straight, Celia motioned to the scope. Taking the hint, Philip stood and placed himself at the eyepieces.

"Uh..." he said several seconds later. "This is a..."

"Flybot," Celia finished for him. "Not biological. And check out the lower dorsal thorax."

Philip drew in a breath. "Is that...?"

"Yep. A serial number."

***

Philip sat, both hands wrapped around his coffee, looking around the cafeteria. Celia sat across from him, staring into the black depths of her cup. The flybot had been carefully placed in a secure specimen vault, and Celia had uttered a single word: "Coffee." Not a word had been spoken since.

His coffee down to the last lukewarm dregs, Philip finally broke the silence. "So, uh, this is unusual."

Celia rolled her eyes at him. "Ya think?" She took a sip, then continued. "Mark Bernham is working on miniaturized autonomous drones for the project. I think he might have military connections, but I wouldn't swear to it. And I *know* he isn't anywhere near being able to produce this thing. The hardware might just be possible if you threw enough money and people at it, but the control systems..." She shook her head vehemently. "That would take a Special Purpose AI, and there's no way you're going to fit the processor and training data into something that size. Maybe it's remote-controlled?"

Philip shook his head. "It was buzzing around in my lab, which is one big Faraday cage. No way a signal could get in or out. No, it was operating autonomously. Which means it needs an onboard SPI."

"Is that even possible?" Celia asked.

"Not at that size, no. Special Purpose Intelligences need a huge dataset, either onboard or accessible online. Let's see what Mark has to say."

***

Dr. Mark Bernham stared down at the flybot. "You're playing with me, right?"

"No, Mark, we are not," Philip said. "That was flying around my lab until I did a test run. The EMP knocked it out of the air."

Mark stared at Philip, then bent over again, focusing his handheld microscope on the fly. "It's definitely artificial. Mostly plastics, I think; otherwise, it would be too heavy to fly." He paused and looked up. "Plus, I think your EMP would have melted it, not just killed it." Mark poked it with a tweezer. "I've got all kinds of micromanipulation equipment. Can I take it apart?"

"As long as you tell us the results," Philip replied.

"And," Celia added, "as long as it doesn't disappear into some military Skunk Works, never to be seen again."

"I have no known connection with the military," Mark said, deadpan. "Plus," he added with a small smile, "I'd probably be on the outside as well. And that just doesn't work for me."

"Well, okay, then." Philip gestured to the fly. "Have at it."

CHAPTER THREE

An Impatient Client

The doorbell rang.

Derek pulled out his phone and checked the doorbell cam. *Oh, shit.* It was the guy from the group that called itself "the European Coffee Club." Sure, that's what they were, and Derek was a Radio City Rockette. The man had introduced himself as Eduardo when they'd first met, but Derek privately called him Bluto. He was big, meaty, but not particularly muscular, with an unkempt black beard that stuck out in all directions. He always wore a suit, and an expensive one, but there was nothing any tailor could do about hanging a suit properly on that bulbous frame.

"Hello, what can I do for you?" Derek said into the cam's intercom.

"Mr. McQuaid, I trust you remember me. I'm Eduardo Martino from the European Coffee Club. I'd like to talk to you about schedule slippage, which is creating some concern among my peers."

"I am on track, Mr. Martino. I just need a few days—"

"If you could be so kind as to let me speak to you face to face, Mr. McQuaid? Otherwise, I'd have to take it as an indication that our investment is in trouble. That would not be good for anyone."

Derek sighed. His own damned fault for getting carried away with this Artificial General Intelligence, this aggy, that seemed to be growing more independent by the minute. Apparently, there was still something of the nerd in him, buried under all the calluses and cynicism. Derek clicked the button to unlock the front door and said, "Upstairs. Usual spot."

Bluto swaggered into the lab a few moments later, acting like he owned the place. Derek seethed inside but maintained a calm exterior. He hated these lowlifes, with their Armani suits dressing up a beer-and-chips mindset. But they had the money, and Derek had to play the game if he wanted some of it.

"My patron is, as I mentioned, becoming concerned about the delivery schedule. You've slipped twice, Mr. McQuaid. That ain't, er, that's not good."

"It's not a problem, Eduardo. I mean, it's not like I've run into difficulty of some kind. I've simply let myself get distracted. Personal slipup. This project has been far more interesting than I ex— "

"Business is business, Derek." Eduardo leaned forward menacingly. "There are penalties for late delivery, which are not limited to the financial. I would hate for your typing ability to be affected, for instance."

Derek, with a huge effort of will, managed to avoid rolling his eyes. He was scared, of course—these really were the type of people who would burn down your house—but at the same time, the sheer banality and level of cliché left him choking back ironic comments that definitely would affect his typing ability.

"Hold on, let me check the schedule," he said.

He pulled up a window on his phone, a telnet client that allowed no network backdooring—an absolute necessity with the aggy if he wanted to keep it under control. Glancing at Eduardo, he typed in, "We're in trouble. I need some way to put this guy off or deflect him. Suggestions?"

"One moment," the aggy typed back. "Render nonfunctional."

Nonfunctional? What the hell did that mean? Just as Derek was about to speak, Eduardo exclaimed, "Ow!" and slapped the back of his neck. Then he began to make a choking, gargling sound and fell over.

As Derek watched in increasing horror, Eduardo... changed. It was like watching a sped-up video of a fruit being dried under a heat lamp. In moments, he was very, very obviously dead, and now Derek had two problems to deal with. First, Eduardo was deceased, and the Coffee Club wasn't going to be happy about that. There would be more visits, with explanations required, and very probably the actual breaking of fingers, if not worse.

The second problem, and one that perhaps was more immediate, was that his experimental artificial intelligence had just reached into the physical world and killed someone. He'd thought he had the thing thoroughly sandboxed, but apparently not. And if it could kill Eduardo, it could—

Before he could complete the thought, Derek was moving. He closed down the app, dialed the combo on his safe, grabbed his notebooks, and sprinted downstairs. Pausing only to grab a sweater and trench coat, he rushed out the door, almost tripping over himself in his haste. He didn't slow down until he was a block away, standing in the park by a bench, panting.

Once he got his breathing under control, Derek placed his pile of books on the bench, then scrubbed his head and neck to make sure there was nothing foreign on him. What that foreign something might consist of, he had no idea. But Eduardo had acted like he'd been bitten just before he...well, died. Gruesomely.

The aggy was out. There was no question. And as had suddenly become obvious, it wasn't friendly.

CHAPTER FOUR

Deconstruction

Philip pulled his watch phone out of the top left drawer of his desk and wrapped it around his wrist, the magnetic strap automatically adjusting itself to his preference. The holographic display briefly flashed up, saying *No Messages*. He retrieved his jacket and umbrella from the coat-tree in the corner and adjusted his overcoat for maximum coverage. It was autumn in Chicago, and the temps dropped quickly as soon as the streets fell into shadow.

As usual after a long day, he felt bone-weary. A drink, a good soak in the hot tub, and an early bedtime would be just what the doctor ordered.

Outside the building, Philip paused and looked around for his ride. A traxi pulled up, and an androgynous voice said, "Dr. Moray?" The traxi SPI knew it was him, of course. Facial recognition and the signal from his watch combined to identify him. The door opened upward with a soft hiss, and he climbed in.

"Destination, home. Please confirm," the SPI said.

"Confirmed. No interaction today, please. Wake me when we get there."

"Of course, Doctor."

Without another word, the traxi pulled away from the curb and accelerated into traffic, its electric motors emitting barely a whisper. The other cars automatically adjusted their spacing. Philip closed his eyes and slouched in the seat, which reclined to accommodate him.

This whole weirdness with the robot fly was equal parts annoying and perplexing. Was he being spied on? Why? His research wasn't particularly secret or classified. It was potentially valuable, of course, especially to competitors in the asteroid-mining business. Or would be, if he were making more progress. In fact, there were probably a half dozen different companies working on the same problem. He could name three off the top of his head. And it wasn't like he was ahead of the pack.

Could it have been intended for someone else? But who? As far as he knew, no one was head and shoulders ahead of the competition. Celia was working on semi-biological bacteria that would ingest specific metallic ores and excrete them in exchange for food. Useful for mining. Mark was working on small remote worker bots. Philip had seen some of the experimental versions. They reminded him of spiders. But Mark had nothing like that flybot, in terms of miniaturization or independence. The other researchers on the project were working on incremental improvements to even more mundane categories, such as navigation, claim registration, and Earth-return orbital mechanics.

He sighed and rubbed his forehead. Best to hold off speculation until Mark had taken the thing apart. Until then, he'd just get himself into an anxiety spiral. Maybe Mark would find out enough to be able to go talk to the manufacturer. Then they could get some answers.

Unless it was time travelers. Philip snorted at the thought. Mark had been adamant that the flybot was way ahead of current technology, and Philip hadn't seen anything to contradict that. He raised his hand and made the gesture that brought up the watch's hologrammatic interface. "If time travel turns out to be possible, I will send myself a text...now." No text appeared, and Philip dropped his hand with a chuckle. *So much for that.*

***

"We have arrived, Dr. Moray."

Philip jerked awake. Blinking the sleep from his eyes, he muttered, "Thank you," as the door opened for him. The traxi drove off, the artificial low-speed whine fading as it accelerated. Philip watched it go and remembered the Mustang he'd owned as a teenager. Manually controlled vehicles were no longer legal in most urban settings or on highways. Only in rural areas could you still find actual cars with steering wheels, some still even sporting internal combustion engines.

And that was okay. The economics of owning your own car in the city simply didn't make sense—fuel, insurance, maintenance, repairs, parking—not to mention the cost of the vehicle in the first place. Against that, you had the traxi system in virtually every city in the industrialized world, which could deliver you anywhere in your town with no stress and for less than what most people paid for a coffee. Financially, it was a no-brainer.

Still, he'd loved that Mustang.

The front door recognized him and released the lock as he put out his hand to push it open, then hissed softly shut behind him. "Home program," he said into the air. The lights came slowly up, and the sound system began playing his favorite jazz channel. The front window curtains moved slightly as the forced-air heating system began working to bring up the house temperature to the *occupied* setting. "Warm up the hot tub," he added as he headed for the bedroom.

A few minutes later, Philip was in the tub, relaxing against the jets, with a glass of Jameson in his hand. This was a good life. It was a solitary life; Philip had never married and didn't believe that would ever happen. He was simply too driven, too consumed by his work, to be able to give someone else the mindshare they deserved. And this way, he set his own schedule, ate when he wanted, and kept the work hours that he needed to. Still...

The jangle of an incoming call made him jump. He lifted his hand from the hot water and gestured, and the interface popped up. Mark Bernham? He and Mark weren't friends, just colleagues. They'd never exchanged numbers. On the other hand, Mark could have phoned Admin for Philip's number if it was important. Which meant it *was* important.

He twitched his index finger to answer, and Mark's face filled the hologram. "Phil! Glad I caught y—are you not wearing a shirt? Should I turn off video?"

"I'm in the hot tub, Mark," Philip replied with a touch of annoyance and held up his Jameson. "Alone, so don't start any rumors!"

"Uh-huh. A large tub of water just says *electrocution risk* to me. Anyway..." Mark held up a tweezer. In the watch's display, Philip couldn't make out if the tweezer was really holding anything, so it was likely just a dramatic gesture. Mark continued, "I've been deconstructing the flybot, and it's getting very, very interesting."

"You're still at work?"

"I work vampire hours, Phil. Don't interrupt. So, interesting thing, the controller chip for this flybot is labeled *JCN, Inc.* Heard of them?"

Philip rolled his eyes. Juno Computer Neuromatics was possibly the biggest electronics and computer systems firm in the country. The successor to IBM, everything, but *everything* had JCN components in it somewhere. So really, Mark's proclamation was no surprise.

"So yeah, there are some other chips in there from various specialty companies," Mark added, "but interestingly, there's no manufacturer ID."

"None?"

"Nada. I used an electron microscope, bud. I didn't miss it."

Philip's eyebrows slowly went up as he considered this. All electronic items were required to be registered and display the manufacturer ID, by ATLAS edict. Even something as mundane as a toaster. ATLAS—the Authority for the Treaty Limitation of AI Systems—had broad powers of enforcement, and contravening its regulations was a very, very bad thing. Unless you wanted to spend the rest of your life in prison.

"So this is not a legitimate product." Philip paused. "Which means it's probably a dead end."

"Mmm, maybe not. Look, you're obviously entertaining, so I don't want to lay this on you right now. Why don't you come by tomorrow—tomorrow *afternoon*—and we'll talk more. 'Kay?"

Philip nodded and ended the call. All his anxiety bubbled back up as he began to realize that something weird really was happening.

This was going to be a two-drink night.

CHAPTER FIVE

Flybot Guts

Philip was in the middle of configuring his test system when the alarm on his watch buzzed. He canceled the alarm without bothering to look. He knew it was a reminder to visit Mark Bernham. Mark's comments the previous evening had piqued Philip's curiosity to the point where he'd had trouble getting to sleep, with ever-expanding scenarios chasing each other in circles in his imagination.

With characteristic discipline, Philip finished the configs before carefully stowing all his tools. Rushing and cutting corners caused accidents, and an accident when dealing with the energies involved in this project could be catastrophic.

With everything finally in its place, he headed for Mark's lab.

Mark looked up as Philip entered and said, "Ah, welcome back to the land of the fully clothed. Hold on, let me grab the file." Philip was slightly surprised to see Mark haul out a manila folder stuffed with papers. Of course, he himself made extensive use of paper, but that was because of the impossibility of using any kind of electronic notetaker in his lab.

Mark, seeing the direction of his gaze, said, "Old school. Until I can get funding for a virtual desk, this is the only way I can spread things out and look at them."

Mark spent a few moments placing documents on his lab desk, then pointed at one. "This is the backplane for the little beast. Totally nonstandard, and I bet it was designed by an AI. This was created as a one-off, not intended to use standardized or interchangeable components. Interesting thing..." He flipped to a second image. "This is built as a two-piece unit, almost like Lego blocks. The fly 'body' is an add-on to the processing unit. It literally snaps on."

He pointed to several other images. "The whole thing uses components from several companies, hardwired in. You can see the manufacturer labels. Most of them are pretty standard items, which is why they were used. But not this one. It's the JCN chip. I had to deconstruct it to figure it out. It appears to be a single-chip neuromorphic AI module, but with some really weird tweaks."

"But it's a labeled part," Philip said, "so it's a legitimate item."

Mark waggled a finger. "Not so fast. The serial number encoding indicates experimental. This shouldn't be outside of a Level 4 testing lab for any reason."

"So this"—Philip looked again at the series of printed images—"is absolutely, definitely not a legal device. And possibly ATLAS-level illegal."

"Hmm, I'd have to say yes." Mark tapped the JCN image. "Not certain, mind you. I had to make some guesses as to function. But if I had to put money on it, yeah."

"We need to report this."

Mark looked alarmed. "Buddy, where ATLAS regulations are concerned, investigators use more of a napalm approach than precision bombing, if you know what I mean. They'll not only shut down our company, but they'll probably freeze all employee assets as well. And we could easily lose months of work while we wait for them to loosen their grip. Funding could dry up if the investors stampede. The ATLAS investigation standards do not place any limits on how much collateral damage they can do. We need to be sure of what we have here."

"And what *do* we have here?"

Both men turned to see Celia standing in the doorway. She stepped into the room and said, "I caught the tail end of that. Something about ATLAS?"

After Philip gave her a capsule summary, Celia pursed her lips and said, "I agree with Mark on this. Generally speaking, if the cops are investigating an ATLAS breach, they can be a little more *guilty until proven innocent*. And for us to file a complaint is a lot more complicated. I think before we attract that kind of attention, we should verify our concerns."

"And how exactly are we going to do that?" Philip asked.

"Talk to JCN?" Celia pointed to the image of the AI chip. "If they can explain that, this becomes just garden-variety corporate espionage. We report it to Admin, and it's no longer our problem."

Philip did a slow facepalm. "I don't have time for this."

CHAPTER SIX

A New Order

Seth Bradley sighed and paused to take a sip of his coffee. Business wasn't great. Hell, it wasn't even good. Biofabbing had reached that point in the business cycle where the large companies and conglomerates started pushing out the little guys. And as his cash flow shrank, it became harder and harder to keep up with the technology changes. Pretty soon, he'd be a buggy-whip maker in an automotive world.

With a growl, he put down the coffee and opened the next email, doubtless another bill.

Or not.

It was a work order with specs. Bradley scanned the attached document. Standard Venter cell—good. Fully specified synthetic DNA sequence—also good. Some novel cellular automata—difficult but not outside his capabilities. He scanned down to the bottom. Good quantity, short delivery deadline. That meant he could bill more for a rush.

Except...

He frowned as the thought solidified. He was a small biofab and couldn't afford much in the way of marketing. There was really no reason for whoever this was to have picked his company over the bigger, better-advertised competitors. There had to be a reason. There was always a reason. Were they hoping he'd overlook something illegal?

Bradley scrolled back up through the pages he'd skipped. There was no obvious purpose to the project. It took in some unspecified enzymes and pumped out some proteins based on that. This had to be a component of some larger project. Or maybe a test order to see how he'd do. Or maybe the customer just wanted to spread the load so things would get delivered faster. Didn't matter. There was nothing that was, strictly speaking, illegal. They hadn't demanded a competitive quote, they offered cash for quick and uncomplicated delivery, and Bradley was not in a position to ask too many questions. Just as well.

But the delivery address was a mail drop. That was never good.

Concentrate on the money. Don't sweat the other stuff. Bradley repeated the mantra as he set up his fab unit.

CHAPTER SEVEN

Detective Work

Philip took a deep breath and glared at the phone, trying for calm. "Listen, I am not trying to sell you anything. I want to talk to one of your engineers, or managers, or supervisors, or whatever you can give me, about a piece of tech *made by your company* that I found in my lab, and which had no reason *being* in my lab. *I* am trying to do *you* a favor, do you understand?"

Apparently, they did not, since the person on the other end simply repeated an obviously memorized script about proper avenues for contacting JCN regarding business proposals. Or maybe that was a SPI he was talking to. Certainly, it or he or she was both inflexible and uncomprehending.

Philip said goodbye and hung up. He looked over at Celia, who had been standing in his office doorway for part of that conversation. She did that a lot, it seemed. She looked like she was trying to hold back a smile and only barely succeeding.

"I may have a way to do an end run around their first line of defense," Celia said when she'd gotten her face under control. "One of my friends in IT has a cousin who works at JCN. Obviously, we'd have to avoid any hint of industrial espionage, but maybe Lynn can invite her cousin over. We could buy lunch."

Philip nodded. "It sounds like a good plan. More important, it sounds like our *only* plan. Let me know what you get. And we'll want to schedule Mark in. He might have to come to the lab before noon for a change."

"Meanwhile," Celia responded, "we have the other parts that Mark was able to identify. Maybe we can get somewhere with those companies."

"How? We don't have any kind of authority. They won't want to talk to us any more than JCN did."

"JCN is a large multinational, heavily involved with AI-related hardware and software," Celia replied. "They'll be very defensive by default. No one wants the slightest whiff of anything that might look like an ATLAS infraction, especially given Mark's comment about it being a neuromorphic chip. But these other companies are just producing standard support components, the kind of stuff that goes into everything these days. They have no particular reason to be suspicious of someone calling to inquire about their products."

"Sure, to buy them. But—"

"References. Ask for a couple of recent customer names for reference. This is Astro Resources, Philip. High-tech and bleeding-edge. They'll jump at the chance to add us to their customer list."

Philip narrowed his eyes. "Say, you're pretty knowledgeable. You have a second career as an industrial spy or something?"

Celia grinned back. "C'mon, Philip, this is Detective 101."

Philip chuckled dutifully. Celia had an addiction to detective and spy novels that went back to her preteen years. "So are you going to do the dirty deed?"

Celia snorted. "No, why would I? We have a procurement department. I'll submit a request. Or maybe Mark should, since it's more in line with his work. The staff will be completely convincing because it's actually part of their job. The callback number will be legit."

"That'll take a few days. Meanwhile, what?"

"Lynn will phone her cousin and invite her for lunch."

CHAPTER EIGHT

Lunch Meeting

Philip mechanically sipped his coffee, both elbows up on the counter, while the TV played in the background. As usual, he had the news on with his breakfast, and as usual, he was barely paying attention.

But there was one phrase that always captured his attention: "Gen Omega." He looked up as the TV showed a scene of people lined up in a hospital and began to listen.

> *Gen Omega has claimed responsibility for an apparent terrorist attack on the city of Las Vegas. Residents this morning became ill en masse, with widespread reports of uncontrolled vomiting. Officials at first suspected a viral pathogen, but the source was eventually traced to a powerful emetic that had been added to the city water supply.*
>
> *Gen Omega, so named because it styles itself as representing what will be the last generation of humanity unless drastic changes are made, continues to threaten industries and organizations that it characterizes as environmentally destructive.*

Its recent attacks have become bolder and more aggressive. In an attack this week that destroyed the Port Charles electric generation plant, four workers were injured.

Philip shook his head slightly and resumed eating his toast. He understood and could sympathize with the Gen Omega generation. They would be inheriting a planet worn and damaged from several hundred years of uncontrolled exploitation. But the terrorists who had piggybacked on the name were not helping. People had become numb to such antics in the 21st century, and the attacks wouldn't achieve Gen Omega's goals. The destruction of the power plant, for instance, would be barely a blip in annual carbon emissions. Meanwhile, the people who would be going without power for a time would blame Gen Omega, and no one else.

And they knew they weren't making headway, judging from the increasingly strident pronouncements coming out of the group. It sounded to his ear like people winding themselves up to a good old-fashioned conniption. The danger was that the extremists might decide they needed to do something more extreme, something that would cost lives.

Meanwhile, closer to home, Philip had his own problems. Another day of work loomed before him, another day of experimental failures and snide remarks from the CEO, Usiah Bradshaw. With a groan born more of frustration than physical effort, Philip got up and put his dishes in the dishwasher.

***

Philip's watch dinged with a reminder. It was 11:30 a.m., and they were supposed to meet Celia's friend and her cousin. Quickly closing down his files, Philip grabbed his empty mug and headed for the cafeteria, where he found Celia sitting with two other women and Mark.

He immediately recognized Celia's friend Lynn from occasional encounters in the cafeteria, although he didn't know her well enough to talk to her. He knew that Celia and Lynn were close, though.

Lynn introduced her cousin Joyce, an IT specialist with JCN. Joyce looked somewhat nervous. He hoped Lynn had filled her in; otherwise, Joyce might be feeling ambushed right about now. And in any case, she'd be worrying about how this could look to her employer if it blew up. Philip decided that a soft sell was needed.

As he settled himself at their table, he began. "First off, Joyce, we aren't here to ask you to do anything that will jeopardize your job or cause ethical issues. Or to ask you for information or corporate secrets. We've been trying to get JCN to pay attention to us, and we're getting completely stonewalled. But this is something that could be devastating for JCN if I have to take the time to go through normal channels."

Joyce looked relieved and visibly relaxed. Getting a nod from her, Philip opened the file folder that Mark had given him and began laying out images. Joyce examined each, with occasional commentary from Celia and Mark. Lynn was silent throughout the entire presentation, although she displayed interest in the images.

At the end, Joyce said, "So this robotic fly was in your lab? That certainly feels like some kind of industrial espionage."

"Any chance it really is JCN that's responsible?"

Joyce gave him a look of disbelief. "What, they built this, and left off the unit label—a huge contravention of ATLAS regulations—while leaving their label on the incriminating part? That seems like a really comic-book-villain move."

Philip grinned at her. "Fair enough. But then why would the maker have labels at all?"

"Too much trouble to take them off. These are real parts made by legitimate companies. Whoever put this together didn't care if those companies were implicated."

"Okay, fine," Celia interjected. "So why did JCN stonewall us?"

"No idea," Joyce replied. "Probably reflex. But I'll tell you what. Email me the images and I'll talk to my boss."

CHAPTER NINE

AirTagging

Philip looked up at a knock. Celia stood in the open door to his office, smiling and waving her pad. "Got some results," she said.

"On?"

Celia gave him an eye roll. "The inquiries to the companies that make the support components. As expected, they were quite cooperative."

"Well, okay, then." Philip sat back and gestured to a chair. "Let's have a look."

Celia poked at her pad for a few seconds, and Philip's pad dinged as it received a document.

"I did a comparison," Celia said, not waiting for him to finish reading. "There are three companies that appear on more than half the suppliers' lists. Two of them are legitimate companies that have been around forever. The third..." Celia hesitated and shrugged. "Spectre Enterprises. I've never heard of them. And a web search turned up nothing except the incorporation notice."

"And that's not suspicious, no siree."

"And that's where the good news ends," Celia said. "There's one corporate officer, a Derek McQuaid, and his contact info is care of the company's Registered and Records Office. Which is a law firm, so we won't be bluffing them out."

"Can we look up the contact by name?"

"Sure. Forty-seven hits nationally, and no guarantee that our boy is even one of them. Although we can be confident it's not an alias, given the regulatory requirements."

"Damn." Philip leaned back and put his hands behind his head. "Do your detective novels suggest any solution?"

"One. Already talked to Mark, and he's on it."

Philip stood. "Well, then, after you."

***

A few minutes later, Philip was looking at the electronic parts spread out on Mark's workbench. "This is an AirTag?"

"Uh-huh." Mark nodded and began poking at the components. "Took it apart, got rid of the speaker, soldered the leads directly to the button battery. Laid out like this, it's thin enough to go between two pieces of card stock and into an envelope. Much less suspicious than a package."

"Great," Philip said. "And we're mailing it to...?"

"Spectre Enterprises," Celia replied. "Care of Dicker, Bicker, and Hyde."

"Huh?"

"The law firm."

Philip's eyes goggled. "That's their name?"

Celia laughed. "No, it's something boring. But I like mine better."

Philip shook his head, then pointed to the gutted AirTag. "So we just hope the lawyers will forward this thing to their client, and we track it until it arrives wherever?"

"Yup. Courtesy of *The Black Banner* by Hanson Gretting. The protagonist mails one of these to a suspect and—"

Philip held up a hand. "Do not start. In every movie I've ever seen, someone always gets killed before the scenario plays out. I don't need to know." He paused. "And we're still not ready to just hand this over to the cops?"

"Can't speak for anyone else, but I'm kind of having fun," Celia replied.

Mark grinned. "Me too. Don't be a downer, Philip."

"Fine," Philip replied. "But at the first sign of a gun, I'm out."

CHAPTER TEN

Meeting with the COO

It took less than two days to get a response from JCN. Philip found a meeting proposal in his inbox when he checked his email in the morning. An *in-person* meeting, which Philip found surprising. A quick check with Celia confirmed that she had received one as well. The meeting was for that afternoon, which certainly indicated they were being taken seriously.

Philip spent the morning working in his lab, trying to keep his mind off the impending meeting. But he found himself unable to concentrate and finally gave up on getting anything original done. Instead, he took the time to take care of the administrivia that had been building up.

Finally, the appointed hour arrived. Philip wrapped up his work, grabbed his stuff from the coat-tree, and rushed to the lobby to meet Celia. A traxi was waiting at the curb for them, and in moments, they were on their way.

The trip took about forty minutes, as JCN's HQ was on the opposite side of Chicago, and a Gen Omega protest on the ring road had backed up traffic significantly. Fortunately, the SPI in charge of trip scheduling had allowed for the delay.

Once they arrived, they checked in with the security desk in the lobby and were directed to a specific elevator, which took them to the 18th floor. The elevator opened directly into a reception area, where a young man in a business suit was standing, waiting for them. "Doctors Hunt and Moray?" he said. "I'm Donald Gleason. I'll take you to see Ms. Buto now." He made a gesture and began to lead them down the hall.

Philip eyed the suit as they proceeded. He had no interest in expensive clothing, but he could recognize it when he saw it. Their guide's outfit was worth more than Philip's entire wardrobe. Either JCN paid their junior staff an insane salary, or they provided an equally insane clothing allowance.

Donald stopped in front of an office that had *MATILDA BUTO, COO* emblazoned on the door. He knocked, then opened the door and gestured them in. Philip looked around as they entered. The office, in keeping with the company's tendency toward ostentation, was huge. Unreasonably so, even for a COO, in Philip's opinion.

Matilda Buto didn't bother to stand or even invite them to sit, simply waited for them to take chairs. Philip saw the images he'd sent to Joyce on Buto's virtual desktop.

"These are interesting," she said without preamble after they'd settled in. She tapped one of the images, spun it 180 degrees with two fingers, and pushed it toward Philip and Celia. It was the image of the JCN chip. "How did you get this?"

"Mark Bernham deconstructed the flybot," Philip replied. "He took the images as he—"

"I meant, how did you get the chip?" Buto said, cutting him off.

Philip frowned. "It was in the flybot. Was that not—"

"I find your explanation puerile and totally noncredible. I want to know how you got the components for this obvious bit of industrial espionage."

Philip felt his face go red. Celia's eyebrows went up, and she spoke for the first time. "So who do you think you are, exactly?"

Buto jerked her head back and glared at Celia. "Excuse me?" she said in a haughty tone, specifically designed to chill subordinates.

Celia was unaffected. She leaned forward in her seat as she replied. "We don't work for you, Ms. Buto, so don't treat us like underlings. The summary we gave your employee is what happened, and you're not going to get anything different now. If you don't like it, then we'll be on our way."

The two women glared at each other across the desk surface as Philip tried to suppress a smile. He knew from personal experience that he became flustered in confrontational situations, and Buto's verbal assault would have had him stammering and trying to offer excuses. Which was likely the purpose. Celia, on the other hand, seemed to be happy to meet fire with fire. He decided he'd let her take point.

"I don't like your attitude, Ms. Hunt," Buto said.

"It's *Doctor* Hunt, and again, so what? We're here in a spirit of cooperation to try to resolve a mutual mystery. But you don't seem to have the same goals. So if you can't—"

"You have possession of our experimental technology, Ms. Hunt. If you'd prefer, I can unleash our legal department on you. You'll spend the rest of your life in court—"

"Technology that we contacted you about, Matilda—"

"It's *Ms. Buto.*"

"And it's *Doctor Hunt.* And since we're lobbing threats, your technology, which appears to be an experimental AI module, was discovered in an *unregistered* autonomous unit. Tell you what, why don't we just file an ATLAS report with the police and let them decide who to arrest?"

More glaring followed. Philip could swear the air in the room was heating up. Then Buto, apparently deciding that a new tack was called for, relaxed and sat back. "All right, *Doctor*, let's start again. The component in question is, in fact, an experimental chip code-named Q-32 and should only be in a Level 4 isolation facility. I've checked with our people, and there is no reason for it to be out of the lab. Particularly installed in something like..." Buto gestured to the image of the flybot. "So whether or not you are directly involved in the creation of that thing, you are currently in possession of stolen property. *And* restricted technology, under the ATLAS statutes. That *is* a crime, at least potentially."

Celia replied, unfazed, "On the other hand, we have a device that was clearly being used for industrial espionage, given how we came into possession of it. Which makes us the victim. It seems to me that the item should be delivered to the police for their investigation." She ended with a thin smile.

Philip decided he'd had enough. He interjected just as Buto was drawing a breath for the next salvo. "As entertaining as it is watching the two of you spit at each other, I think the best solution would be one that serves us both. You want your Q-32 chip back, and we want to know who's been trying to spy on us. If you can help us with the latter, we can certainly help you with the former."

Buto considered him silently for a moment before replying. "A reasonable proposal, *Doctor* Moray. I will have my people do some quick inquiries. I can't promise definitive results, though. We have even less information than you do at this point. Meanwhile, our component...?"

"We can arrange an exchange once you've done those inquiries." Philip stood and gave Celia a significant glance. She smiled back and stood as well. There were terse nods all around, and then Philip and Celia showed themselves out. On the way down in the elevator, Celia said, "They won't do diddly."

"They'll do something, just so they can give us a list of things that failed to turn up any information. Anything we can think of that's not on that list was probably successful."

Celia did a double take. "Whoa. Nice analysis, Secret Agent Man. Let's see what we get."

***

Matilda Buto pressed the button on her desk after the two visitors had left. The image of Carl Wright, the chief of security, popped up immediately.

"You heard all that?" she said to him.

"Yes, and I was running facial and tonal analysis during the whole interview. They did seem to be hiding something. Although"—he held up a finger as Buto started to speak—"not around the parts having to do with the technology item, so it isn't necessarily what you're thinking. They may have something else on their minds."

"That's just a different shit pile, Carl. If they're hiding something, it's because they don't want me to know. If they don't want me to know, it's bad for JCN. See where I'm going?"

"Yes, ma'am," Carl said, a trace of sarcasm in his voice.

Buto was careful not to react. She and Wright did not like each other, to put it mildly. He liked to bait her but always stayed just this side of insubordination. She wasn't going to give him the satisfaction of thinking he'd scored a hit. "Keep an eye on them, Carl. If this is some kind of shakedown, or if they're up to something else, I need to know immediately."

CHAPTER ELEVEN

Poosday

Seattle, Washington, had one of the oldest nonpassive sewage systems in the US, made an early priority because of the tides. There were any number of old pictures (often on the walls of pubs) of outhouses perched at the top of ten feet of scaffolding to avoid backflow during high tide. It was said that in those days, being on the crapper at the wrong time of day could result in you being launched through the roof.

The sewage system had, of course, been modernized over the last hundred and fifty years, with backflow controls and treatment facilities. There were far too many interlocking safety systems now for backflow from tidal pressure to be possible.

In theory.

It was a cold, rainy winter Tuesday in December, with a combination of warm temps melting the recent snowfall and a Pineapple Express from the direction of the Hawaiian Islands bringing levels of rainfall that even Seattleites found daunting. Without warning, every ground-level toilet in downtown Seattle abruptly and explosively backed up. Many of the events were powerful enough to knock out windows, break open bathroom doors, and in one case, blow a hole in the bathroom ceiling.

The 9-1-1 system was immediately overwhelmed as frantic home- and business owners looked to the authorities for answers and assistance.

The authorities, unfortunately, had problems of their own.

The backflow, which should have been impossible in the first place, jumped into the combined sewer system (another impossibility) and, within minutes, was also flowing out of streetside drainage gratings.

A city the size of Seattle generates a lot of effluent. The city also has many high-rises. In these buildings, the effluent forced its way up the drainage pipes for several floors, creating a vertical column of waste with nowhere to go but down. As the backflow ebbed and gravity won the battle, it produced a second surge at ground level. People who had just been examining the mess from the first surge found themselves with a face full of more of the same.

Within an hour, the governor had declared a disaster.

Over the next several days, systems were examined with microscopic detail, and multiple software audits were done by independent companies. The conclusions were, well, inconclusive. Nothing so blatant as a virus or sabotage of equipment was found. But the series of cascading failures that would be required, one after the other, to result in what came to be known as Poosday stretched the limits of believability. Officials would not publicly commit to a diagnosis of sabotage, but behind closed doors, it was acknowledged that there was no other reasonable explanation.

No person or group ever claimed credit.

CHAPTER TWELVE

No One's Home

Philip looked up at the knock, already fairly sure who it would be. Sure enough, Celia stood there, leaning against the jamb and grinning at him.

"What?" he said.

"The AirTag has been delivered. Or at least it left the lawyer's office and arrived somewhere else. I have an address."

"So what do you think the recipient is going to say when they open up the letter and find a disassembled AirTag?"

"Oh, shit."

"Hah. Very funny."

"No, seriously. Oh, shit. I hadn't thought of that." She frowned. "Come to think of it, Gretting never dealt with that little detail either. It's almost like detective novels aren't real life."

Philip grunted, then closed the file he'd been working on and tossed his pad onto the desk. "Of course, we aren't actually going to just walk up and knock on the door, right?" He glared at her as she examined the ceiling. "*Right*?"

"Let's just see what we're faced with when we get there."

"And let's leave a note about where we're going so they can recover our corpses. What's at the address, anyway?"

"A house. Just a small, old, suburban nothingburger of a house. Registered owner is, indeed, Derek McQuaid. The Spectre Enterprises guy."

"I'm impressed. You really have been doing your homework." Philip got up. "I'm still going to run like hell at the first sign of trouble."

***

They ordered the traxi to circle the block a few times, passing by the house without slowing down. It was impossible to tell anything specific from the outside. There was no activity, no sign of life, but the house wasn't run-down. It also wasn't well kept. There was no garden, shrubs were sparse and hadn't received any love, and there was nothing like planters or other decorative touches. It looked like, as Celia commented, a bachelor pad. Private, though. The trees and border shrubs meant there was very little line of sight for the neighbors. Philip wondered if McQuaid had picked it for that reason.

Finally, no robot dogs having run out to attack the traxi, they decided to risk more direct contact. Philip ordered the car to let them out in front of the property, and they walked up the concrete path, trying to look like they belonged there.

At the front door, Celia took out her phone and checked it. "The AirTag is right there," she said, pointing down at the front door. Philip noted the antiquated mail slot in the middle of the door and felt relieved that the owner didn't seem to have checked his mail yet.

Celia pressed the doorbell, then knocked. They waited thirty seconds or so, and then she repeated her actions.

With no response, she said, "Let me just try something." She poked at her phone, then pushed open the mail slot with a finger and stuck the phone in partway.

"What are you doing?" Philip asked.

"Getting video. I want to see how much mail there is, and maybe I can learn something." She pulled the phone back out and checked the video. "Wow, that's at least a week or two worth of mail. Actually, I'm kind of amazed anyone still uses snail mail, but there it is. Let me just check upward. Maybe there's something—oh, *shit*!"

Philip leaned past her to look and realized she'd dropped her phone through the slot. She looked at him, stricken. "I... I... I can't just leave it there. My whole life is in that thing."

"Not to mention that accidentally dropping your phone through the mail slot could be hard to explain."

Celia's expression became even more panicked, and Philip sighed. "Okay. Let's look around."

They set off counterclockwise around the house. In several spots, the windows were close enough to ground level to peek into, although most had some kind of blinds or curtains that limited the view. The back of the house was a mess as well. Items had been haphazardly placed in the backyard, giving it a distinctly "junkyard" vibe. There was even an old sink, rubber stopper still over the drain, allowing it to collect rainwater and act as a mosquito breeding ground.

Celia came out of her funk enough to look around and comment, "Ugh. Definitely bachelor."

They continued around until they had circumnavigated the house, without discovering anything significant. Or helpful. All the windows were closed and latched; all the doors were locked. Nothing shouted, *There's a key under me.*

"I need my phone back," Celia said into the air. "I can't believe I was so stupid."

Philip noted that she was looking outright ill. Feeling sorry for her, he cast around for a solution. Then an *aha* moment. "We're taking a huge chance here," he said, tapping on a window, "but these are really old windows, and the panes are individual pieces of glass, glazed in with putty."

"Uh-huh?" Celia said, puzzled but interested.

"Bachelor pad, like you said. Not being kept up. I bet at least one of these panes will be loose." He began pushing experimentally. "Go get me the plug from that sink in the backyard, would you?"

Celia looked perplexed but did as asked. She was back in a few moments with the required item, just as Philip found an especially loose pane. He took the plug from her outstretched hand and pushed it against the glass with a squeeze. The item stuck to the glass, and he grinned. "Suction cup."

Celia laughed out loud. "You're better at this than I am."

In a few more moments, the putty on the inside had given up the fight, and the pane came loose. Philip maneuvered it sideways through the gap, then stuck his arm in and reached up to undo the latch.

The window wasn't ready to give up yet, though. Either because it had been painted in place, hadn't been opened in centuries, or the frame was simply swollen into immobility, the window wouldn't budge. "Give me a hand here," said Philip. Celia came over, placed her hands on the frame, and with simultaneous grunts, they pushed upward.

The window finally yielded with a squeal, and Philip instinctively cringed, worried about nosy neighbors. But a glance around confirmed that there was no line of sight with any other residences.

"Here's hoping there's no motion alarm," he said and levered himself into the house. He turned to instruct Celia to wait but found her already halfway in.

"In for a penny..." she said.

They were in the living room. Philip looked around, completely nonplussed. "Are you *absolutely sure* this is Derek McQuaid's home?"

"Maybe his grandma does the decorating."

That was a valid hypothesis. The living room was filled with old, somewhat musty but ornate furniture, complete with patterned fabric, and featured stained-glass lamps on the decidedly French provincial side tables. Completing the look was a glass display case featuring china teacups in various patterns.

"This..." Philip shook his head. "Even money says he never used this room."

"Maybe Grandma forbade him," Celia replied with a giggle.

"Okay, let's get your phone."

As they made for the front door, they passed several pictures on the hallway wall that were decidedly out of character for a twenty-first-century bachelor. Or anyone from the twenty-first century, really. "Did he even live here?" Celia muttered.

When they arrived at the front door, they found Celia's phone sitting in a pile of mail. A large pile. Mostly bulk mail and flyers, of course. Somehow, even halfway through the twenty-first century, snail-mail spam was still a marketing force.

"I get the feeling Mr. McQuaid doesn't come home a lot," Philip said. He pushed the pile around until he found the AirTag letter, which he pocketed. A little more inspection, and he said, "It's mostly from his lawyers and addressed to Spectre Enterprises. I don't know why he didn't just register a PO box if he didn't want to use his home address."

"You can't do that for a records office," Celia replied. "It's right in the Company Act. The public has to be able to come and inspect the company registry and records. At least in principle." She looked around for a moment. "I'm beginning to get the feeling that this is all a bunch of props. The house, everything. Just staging, made to look as boring and uninteresting as possible."

"Uh-huh. I can't really... Hello!" Philip stood up with two letters in his hand, both clearly labeled *Property Tax Notice*. "Why two? And—oh. This one's addressed to a corporation. Interesting."

"Take it," Celia said.

"Are you kidding? This is—"

"Philip, we are already way over the line. After all this, I don't want to hit a dead end. I want to get the address of the other property, and I have a funny feeling that we're going to come up with diddly-squat here."

Philip grunted and pocketed the letter.

They proceeded to search the rest of the house quickly, being careful not to move anything. The main floor was as unimpressive as the living room had been. The kitchen had no food other than items with a long shelf life, such as pasta and canned goods.

The basement was considerably more interesting, though. It had been fixed up as a large studio space. There they found a very high-tech and very expensive suite of computers, video-editing equipment, and monitors, arrayed in an efficient, professional layout.

"Wow," Philip said. "This is hundreds of thousands of dollars' worth of gear. Really, really high-end stuff. My home setup would melt away with shame. He must have been in the video-production business."

"Can you tell if the stuff has been used recently?" Celia asked.

"It *does* look a little dusty." Philip idly glanced at one of the video-processing units, then pushed the power button.

"What are you doing? Are you crazy?"

Philip made a *calm-down* motion. "It's just a PC, not a missile launch system. It's not like—what the frig?" Philip frowned at the monitor attached to the unit. "The boot banner doesn't match." He looked at the front of the unit, then back at the monitor. "That is so weird. The bootup thinks this is a much older model."

Shaking his head, he powered down the unit.

"Explanations?" Celia said.

"Let me think about it," he replied. "Meanwhile, let's look around and see if there are any log books or notes."

Further searching turned up nothing, however. There was a set of keys in a drawer, but it was the usual miscellaneous mass that most people have somewhere.

Philip held it up and examined it, but it was extremely unlikely that he'd be able to do anything with it without more information.

Celia shook her head. "Like I said. It just feels staged."

"I don't disagree. We should leave, though. We have your phone, we have the property tax notice, and we have several felonies under our belts if we're caught here."

"Roger that. Time to retreat and regroup."

CHAPTER THIRTEEN

Second Site

Philip and Celia took a traxi back to Philip's home rather than returning to the office and potentially getting their employer entangled in what they were doing. Philip could tell that Celia was beginning to realize that she wasn't just acting out another of her mystery novels. They had broken real laws today, and if caught, they could lose not only their jobs but their freedom. She still had a slight sheen of sweat on her forehead.

He held the door for her, then said, "Guest program," into the air. Celia parked herself at the kitchen island on one of the barstools, and Philip grabbed a bottle of wine from the rack. He poured for both of them in silence. Celia grabbed the glass, took a substantial mouthful, then finally broke the silence. "The way I see it, we have two choices."

"Pray elucidate," Philip replied.

"We can stop right now, drop everything, shred the tax notice, plead ignorance if asked, and hope no one connects us to anything. We haven't stolen anything, killed anyone, or anything else that would cause law enforcement to get involved."

"True, I suppose. Unless McQuaid has video cameras in his house. He might be interested in why two strangers were wandering around inside. And these days, identifying individuals is dead easy."

"Hmm. But I still think I'm right, Philip, about the house being a staged location. And have you wondered why, with all that expensive equipment downstairs, he *doesn't* have an alarm system? I didn't see any motion detectors or webcams."

"A good question. The only thing I can think of is that he'd rather lose the equipment than have the cops show up." Philip's face lit up as he got a thought. "Oh."

"What?"

"Maybe the equipment is an insurance scam. Old, cheap computers with a bogus faceplate."

"Interesting. Could be. So, second option." She paused, sipped some wine. "If we continue to play amateur detective and discover something significant, we become the good guys."

"Uh, I don't think that's how it works."

"It kinda does. Extenuating circumstances, blah blah."

"What you really mean," Philip said, waving his glass in her direction, "is that you want to keep working on this."

"Well, yeah, that too." Celia smiled at him. "C'mon, Philip, no one's pulled a gun yet. And something is definitely weird." She waved the tax-notice envelope.

"Look, this is basically our only lead. Let's follow it up, and if nothing comes of it, we're done. Okay?"

Philip rolled his eyes. "Fine. So what're you going to do?"

"Steam it open, of course. Where's your kettle?"

The operation took longer than expected, since neither of them had ever actually steamed open an envelope. The trick was to provide enough steam to loosen the glue without turning the paper into a wet mush. But finally, they had the envelope open.

"Interesting," Celia said. "Registered owner is a numbered company. Hmm..." she scanned the tax notice. "This tax form is for foreign owners. So offshore?"

"Wow. Owned by McQuaid. Or was he just doing the paperwork for someone?"

Celia ignored the question and pointed to the address. "It has a unit number, so maybe an apartment or townhouse? Want to go for another traxi ride?"

Philip groaned. "Deeper and deeper. But no break-ins this time."

***

The drive didn't take long, as the address was just a few miles away. Dusk was setting in, and streetlights had just come on automatically. The destination did turn out to be a townhouse complex. They had the traxi drop them off in front, and they ambled casually along the private road, barely glancing at McQuaid's unit as they walked past.

"Someone's home," Philip commented, indicating the light coming through the upstairs window.

"Hmm. Let's circle before we try a frontal assault."

They continued to stroll, taking the walking path around the back, which separated the townhouse complex from a public green space.

"Nothing of note," Celia said. "Shall we knock?"

"Sure. Hi, we're from Astro Resources, and you've been spying on us. We'd like to talk to you about your motives and methods."

"I know you're being sarcastic, but why not?"

"He might shoot us?"

"The same guy who didn't put in an alarm system to protect a buttload of expensive gear?"

"At a staged residence."

"Fine. We'll tell him we've taken steps in case we disappear."

"Maybe we should actually do that?"

Celia glared at him, then pulled out her phone and typed madly. "There. I've sent a text to Mark. Happy?"

"*Happy* might be overstating it, but I'm satisfied. Let's go."

A minute later, they were back at the front of the townhouse. They walked up like they had a right to be there, and Philip pressed the doorbell. He casually noted that it had a built-in webcam. Perfect for vetting visitors, and even for conversing with them when the owner wasn't home.

Inside, a bird started a loud squawking. It sounded like a budgie to Philip, but he couldn't be sure through the door.

After a minute, when there was no answer, Philip pressed the buzzer again. Again, the bird started complaining, but again, no human being responded.

Celia stepped back and looked around the porch. "No other cameras," she said. "Just the doorbell."

"So?"

"Nothing, I guess. I'm out of ideas, Philip." She tried the door handle. "No luck. It looks like it's one of those systems that is always locked."

Philip bent forward and looked closely at the door-latch system. There was a combination keypad just above the latch handle and a key slot just below. He squinted at the key slot. "I think the key for this is back at the house."

"Really?"

"Yeah, it was one of those really thick keys that are always stamped *Do Not Duplicate*. Kinda stood out from the rest."

"But you're sure?"

"No, but it looks about right."

"So you want to..." Celia said in an inquiring tone.

Philip rubbed his forehead. "I can't believe I'm about to do this. Let's go get the key. We can drop off the tax notice while we're there."

***

It took a solid hour to make the round trip, and it was well after dark by the time they were back at the front door of the townhouse. "If this doesn't pan out," Philip commented, "I'm never getting that hour back."

"Key goes there," Celia said, ignoring his complaint and pointing.

He gave her an arch look and fished the key out of his pocket. The key slid into the slot with a gratifyingly greased feel. "Right kind, at least," Philip said. "Now, if we turn this and there's an alarm system..."

"Then we have thirty seconds to run like hell before it goes off," Celia replied. "Turn it."

"You'll look great in stripes," he muttered, then twisted the key. It turned easily in the lock, and Philip pushed the door open. They waited, one second, two, but there was no beep-beep of a cycling entry alarm. However, the same bird sent up a frenzied cacophony of chirps and squawks.

"This guy doesn't believe in alarm systems, does he?" Celia said.

"Yeah, he actually does," Philip replied. He pointed to the keypad just inside the door. "But it's disarmed. Maybe he's home?"

"And not answering the door. It's a little late for cold feet, Philip."

"You're unbelievable."

The townhouse was a two-story unit, and the lone lighted window had been on the second floor. They quickly found the stairs beside the kitchen. They also found a birdcage on a floor stand in the kitchen, with a lone budgie inside. Philip pushed his face up to the cage and said, "Hi there, fella. Lonely?" The bird, a blue male, jumped onto the side of the cage closest to Philip and proceeded to berate him in budgie.

Philip frowned and looked closely into the cage. "This guy hasn't been tended to in a while. His feeder is empty, and there are husks all over the bottom of the cage."

"I'm sorry," Celia replied. "I don't speak bird. What are you on about?"

Philip gave her a look. "He's got an auto-feeder. And water supply. I guess McQuaid doesn't want to have to tend to him every day. But they're empty. They're good for about a week for one bird—"

"Wait, how do you know all this?"

"I used to raise budgies for a while when we were in middle school, remember? This one's very tame but doesn't talk, so I don't think McQuaid is really a bird guy. Anyway, the bird hasn't been tended in a week—"

"Or more."

"Not much more. They don't have a lot of reserves. Couple of days without food is all he'd be good for." Philip looked around, then opened a few cupboards. He quickly located a box of budgie seed and poured some into the hopper of the auto-feeder. The budgie leaped to the feeder and began grabbing seeds hungrily. "Uh-huh," Philip said. "I think we got here just in time." He took a few more seconds to refill the water dispenser.

Celia frowned. "So no one's home? Why is the alarm off?"

"Well, there's the million-dollar question. Let's check upstairs."

They climbed to the second floor, not particularly trying to be quiet. There was an unspoken agreement that sneaking up on someone might be a bad strategy.

The first room was the master bedroom, and unlike the previous house, this one looked lived in. The bed, in typical bachelor style, had been straightened out but not made.

The second bedroom was the payoff. It had been converted into a workshop, in very similar fashion to the basement studio of the house. In one corner was an industrial-grade 3D printer, definitely not the kind of thing you'd normally find in a private residence. However, Philip couldn't help noticing that the computer equipment was considerably lower tier, both older and less powerful models of the same brands of equipment they'd found in the house.

"Why would he keep this dreck?" he muttered as he examined the setup.

He was interrupted by a scream from Celia. He looked over to see her staring at something on the ground behind the desk. He hurried over, then stopped dead in shock.

Behind the desk, laid out full length, was a mummified body. Or perhaps freeze-dried. The body displayed none of the putrefaction or bloating that you'd expect from a corpse, and in fact, there was very little odor, perhaps a slight mustiness, but no more. The corpse was also, for better or worse, *deflated.* In every movie Philip had ever seen where someone had the life force sucked out of them, the result was pretty much identical to this.

And it was wearing an expensive-looking suit and a Rolex watch. The suit seemed much too large for the corpse, but that could be a result of the method of passing.

Celia, finally getting control of her vocal cords, said, "Derek McQuaid, perhaps?"

"As good a guess as any." Philip hesitated. "Honestly, I'm not sure you'd be able to identify him for sure even if we knew what he looked like. That's...nasty."

"No kidding." Celia took a deep breath and turned to him. "Philip, even I'll admit we are in way too deep now. Two break-ins, and now we've discovered a murder. Not to mention, if we attract the attention of the cops, we'll end our days in a dark basement cell."

"Dark basement cell is probably an exaggeration," Philip replied. "And why do you think it's murder? He doesn't have any obvious wounds."

"People don't mummify, Philip. This is not a normal death. And I don't see any mad scientist equipment around that he could use to self-inflict this condition."

"You have a point. But how are they going to associate us with any of this?"

"Cripes, Philip, our fingerprints are all over the place. It's not like we had the sense to bring surgical gloves. And our phones' geo-tracking will show we've been here."

"I have McAfee Privacy installed on my watch," he said. "All they—whoever *they* are—will be able to tell is what cell towers I've been near."

Celia took a deep breath and looked somewhat relieved. "Oh, well, so do I. So that's a good thing. But the fingerprints—"

"We can wipe everything here before we leave. We can go back to the house and do the same. And maybe we'll start carrying around surgical gloves, if we're going to keep doing this."

"Which"—Celia looked around the room—"probably won't happen. I think we may have dead-ended again."

Philip looked around with her, hoping for inspiration. Or rationalization. Either would do. He casually jiggled the mouse on the workstation and watched the screen come to life.

"What the frig?" Philip said, then had a brief flashback to the last time he'd said those words. He turned to Celia and pointed at the screen's contents.

"Remember how the bootup on the house system indicated a much older model? Well, this one indicates a much newer model than the badge on the case shows. McQuaid swapped the guts."

"What?"

Philip pointed to all the various PCs and support hardware. "All of these look like lower-tier versions of the hardware in the house. Same brands, same product lines, but older and cheaper. But I'll bet if I open them up, the guts have been swapped."

"Why?"

"Staging. Like you said. All computer equipment purchases have to be registered these days, like firearms. Buy a bunch of high-powered stuff without a good reason, and ATLAS auditors will come sniffing around. But if you have a valid business reason..."

Celia's eyebrows went up, and she became animated. "And video processing and production would fill that bill."

"Yes, it requires a whole lot of horsepower, especially if you're doing CGI animation. But if he really needed the equipment for something else—"

"He swaps the guts," Celia finished for him. "And if anyone comes a'calling, they see the expensive equipment in his home office—"

"And meanwhile," Philip said, taking up the narrative again, "the real hardware is here, being used for—"

Philip and Celia looked at each other, dead silent. After several seconds, Celia said, "Being used for what?"

"Well, that is yet another million-dollar question. The facile answer is 'being used to create and control flybots,' but that doesn't really make sense."

"And we don't even know why he was creating flybots or why he was spying on you."

"Frig."

"Okay, let's search around a little more. But"—Celia held up a finger..."maybe without leaving fingerprints?"

"Um." Philip looked around, then pulled a pack of Kleenex out of his pocket. He extracted one for Celia and one for himself. "Just pretend you're a germophobe. Also, wipe anything you've already touched."

They spent a few minutes looking around the room. Celia quickly found a small safe, its door slightly ajar, but it was empty.

"Not forced open," Philip said. "Or the frame would be askew. They knew the combo. Didn't leave anything behind, either."

"So we're still SOL," Celia said dejectedly.

Philip spotted something poking out from under the desk near the safe. "Or not." He bent down and pulled out a notebook, the kind you'd buy at any stationery store. It was labeled *Hi Q, August 2336 to—*, with no end date.

"I guess whoever killed him was in a hurry," Philip commented. "I'm guessing there are some number of notebooks for three-month periods or whatever."

"Great. Let's take that, go erase our tracks at the house, and then we can examine the contents."

"We'll have to swing by my place first."

***

As they waited for a traxi, Celia glared at the cage in Philip's hand. "Why would you take that?"

"We can't just leave the little guy to die of starvation. And we can't let him loose; that'd be a death sentence in this climate. Budgies are subtropical."

Celia made a growling sound but didn't comment further as the traxi was just pulling up to the curb.

In short order, they arrived at Philip's place. Leaving Celia in the vehicle, Philip carried the cage with his new guest to the house. He ordered the house system to buy budgie seed and some accessories for the next grocery delivery.

Back in the traxi, he ordered the vehicle to head back to McQuaid's house.

But things at the house were not the way they'd left them. When the traxi arrived, they found police cars, ambulances, and fire trucks saturating the scene.

The McQuaid house was a charred wreck, still smoldering.

"Don't stop," Philip said quickly to the traxi. "Drive slowly past so we can get a look."

"Yes, sir," said the traxi and slowed obediently.

The fire had been thorough. There was very little left except the framing and the foundation. Firefighters were still hosing down sections, and steam mixed with smoke as it rose from the wreckage. The smoke from charred wood and burned tar pervaded the area, and the odor even seeped into the air-conditioned cabin of the traxi.

"Did we do this?" Philip said, a mix of awe and terror plain in his tone.

"How?" Celia replied. "The only thing we touched was that computer you turned on. And you turned it off."

They pulled over and got out. Walking up to a cop, Philip said, "What happened here?"

"Do you have business here, sir?"

"Well, uh..." Philip thought fast. "We were trying to connect with the occupant, a Mr. McQuaid. He wasn't home earlier, and we were coming back to try again."

"You couldn't call him?"

"We've never met, and we only have his address."

The cop frowned slightly and leaned to look into the traxi. "Hmm. And why is that?"

Celia jumped in. "He's the owner of a company we wanted to talk to, and this is the registered business address. That's all we have. There's no social media presence, and his web page only has an email contact page." She fished out a business card and handed it to the man. "We were interested in some technology he produced."

The cop looked at the card, and his expression softened. Astro Resources was well known and had a good reputation. "Understood, Doctor Hunt. To answer your question, we're still investigating. A couple of neighbors reported suspicious activity around the house earlier, but we've got nothing definite yet. Hopefully, your Mr. McQuaid hadn't returned home."

Celia and Philip thanked the officer, then climbed back into the traxi.

"Omigod, Celia, why did you give him your card?"

"He could have identified us just by subpoenaing the traxi logs for the area. Being forthcoming looks less suspicious. Why did *you* tell him we were here earlier?"

"Because we were, and cell-phone-tower logs would place us in the area. And having legitimate business here made him more inclined to answer my question."

Celia thought for a moment, then nodded. "Okay, so we're both right. But we'd better make sure we have our stories straight. I didn't like that bit about the neighbors."

"Yeah, I wish I'd asked about when that might have been, but that *would* have been suspicious."

"Let's head back to your place. You can check on your new pet, and I need a drink. Or two."

***

The budgie chortled away at his mirror, his cage sitting on the dining room table. Philip would have to get a stand for it—budgies were notorious for scattering seed husks and less healthy by-products with their frenetic wing-flapping.

Celia sat at the island, wineglass in one hand and her head propped up with the other. She appeared distinctly green as the day's events caught up with her.

"We're felons. *Felons!* Jesus, what was I thinking?"

"You were thinking, 'Gee, it'd be fun to drop my phone through the mail slot.'"

Celia glared at him over her glass, and he continued, "Seriously, everything descended from that. We wouldn't have had to break in, we wouldn't have discovered the tax notice, we wouldn't have visited the second site, and so on. Maybe it's time for you to get a wrist phone."

"Still don't like 'em. And I'd like to see you take pictures through a mail slot with yours."

"I think, in retrospect, that's not a desirable feature."

Celia sighed and closed her eyes for a moment. "Philip, I don't think they can connect us with the fire, unless it started immediately after we left. And it certainly took care of any issues with fingerprints or security cameras. We got lucky. But the townhouse—"

Celia's phone rang, and she jumped. She picked up the phone and answered, and Philip got to listen to half a conversation.

"Hello?"

"This is she."

"Yes, that's correct."

"I—all right, tomorrow morning would be fine."

"Doctor Philip Moray. He works there as well."

"Thank you. Goodbye."

Celia glanced at the phone to make sure it had ended the call, then gave Philip a bilious glare. "That was one Detective Shankar. He will come to our office tomorrow morning to interview us about the fire at McQuaid's house." She rubbed her forehead. "We are so screwed."

***

The figure in the trench coat stood silently, staring in the direction of the townhouse. He'd been there for hours, almost invisible as he blended into the night, ever since the man and woman had entered the unit. He still wasn't entirely sure how they'd gotten in, but it looked like they had used a key. That should not have been possible.

Even more incredible, they had walked out of the unit a short time later, still alive! Something wasn't adding up. They clearly weren't cops or FBI or ATLAS, and he'd never seen them before. But they came out with the notebook. And...the birdcage?

Derek shook his head. This made no sense. They'd have to be followed and identified. And if necessary, neutralized.

CHAPTER FOURTEEN

Inventory Error

Erik McKendrick read the directive again. What was it with management anyway? Check inventory of Q-32 chip? There *was* no inventory. They were made to order. Account for all production? What production?

Grumbling about make-work and high-paid idiots, Erik got to his feet and headed for JCN's fab lab.

The clean room contained exactly the number of Q-32 chips that he expected—zero. The log showed four manufactured, four signed out. As expected. Switching to his next-level cursing, Erik moved to the printer responsible for the Q-32, waved his card at the reader, and checked the sequence number. Four. Uh-huh. Stupid management.

As a last step, and simply because he prided himself on being thorough, Erik checked the raw material hopper levels. As a ten-plus-year fab-lab employee, he could estimate production just by eyeballing the reservoir. And of course, it showed—wait, *what*?

Erik did a double take, then tapped the reservoir indicator twice with his index finger. Well, that just could not be right. The Q-32 chip used a synthetic biomaterial to print the neurosimulant memory cells. It was, at the moment, the *only* chip being manufactured with this component, so there was no reason for the hopper to be low.

Erik pulled out his phone and did a quick calculation. Oh, that wasn't good. To double-check, he read the usage minutes on the printer and compared it to the log. Not good at all.

Hands now shaking and his cursing totally forgotten, Erik composed an email to Matilda Buto:

In response to your query, evidence indicates several hundred chips have been printed. Log appears to have been modified to hide the operation. No way to retrieve exact number, but material usage indicates 200 to 250 units.

Erik pressed *send*, then drew a shuddering breath. The shit was about to hit the fan. Big time.

CHAPTER FIFTEEN

Break-In

Philip was slouched down on his couch at home, listening to his favorite music playlist, when his watch vibrated. "Music pause," he said and gestured to answer the phone. The image that came up was of one of the night security guards at Astro Resources.

"Doctor Moray?" the man said, then continued before Philip could confirm. "There's been a break-in. Your office and lab were among the areas that were hit."

"Break-in? What in hell could they want with—" Philip cut off the sentence as the obvious answer popped into his head. "Were Hunt's and Bernham's offices hit as well?"

"Just Doctor Hunt's. How did you know?"

"Never mind. I'll be there in a half hour."

"Thanks, Doc. Bye."

Philip levered himself off the couch. It was a good thing he hadn't gotten changed for the night. "House, call a traxi," he said as he began getting ready.

***

Philip arrived at the lab admin area, where all the researchers' offices were located, to find both Celia and Mark already there and in discussions with security.

"I thought they said you weren't affected," Philip said to Mark.

"I wasn't, but Celia called me anyway."

Celia turned at the mention of her name and gave Philip a nod, then went back to her discussion.

One of the security guards came up to Philip. "Doctor Moray, have you checked your area yet?"

"No, I'll take a look now."

Philip checked around his office, then his lab. Items were strewn around haphazardly. The searchers had not been careful, but they had been methodical. Everything had been opened and emptied. And as he'd expected, there was only one item that he could confirm was missing.

The flybot.

"My office and lab were completely trashed, too," Celia said, now standing at the doorway.

"And that's interesting," Philip said, "because if they were searching specifically for the flybot—it's gone, by the way—they would have stopped once they found it. Instead, they continued digging. So they were looking for something else as well."

"The notebook."

"Uh-huh. And see, if it was JCN trying to get their tech back, well, they don't know about the notebook."

"So it might be whoever built the flybot?"

"That seems reasonable," Philip said. "Whoever was responsible for the flybot probably wants it back at least as much as JCN does, if only to prevent us from getting any clues from it."

"Well, that's just peachy," Celia grumbled. "So where *is* the notebook?"

"At my place," Philip replied. "I should move it before we lose it, too. Maybe I'll scan it, then put it in a safe deposit box."

"We haven't lost as much as you seem to think." Mark slapped a folder that he'd been holding onto Philip's desk and opened it to reveal all his notes and images. "We still have all the information on the flybot."

"And the name of the person who made it," Celia added.

"Assuming," Mark pointed out, "that he isn't just a figurehead or patsy."

Celia shook her head. "You guys are real downers, you know that?"

***

The trio retreated to the cafeteria. The facility was open 24/7, in keeping with the odd work habits of scientists and engineers, but at three in the morning, fare was limited to coffee and yesterday's donuts. Still, a few seconds of nuking could bring a donut back from rigor mortis.

Philip sat nursing a coffee while Celia updated them.

"Security has no idea how the intruders pulled it off. There's literally nothing on the security footage, no broken windows or doors, nothing. It's like they teleported directly into the rooms. Perimeter surveillance is supposed to catch anyone breaking in, at least in a three-dimensional universe."

"No needless vandalism or petty theft," Philip added. "They took exactly what they wanted, and nothing more."

"I think that's strategic," Mark replied. "They want us to be thankful it wasn't worse—which we are—and simply move on with our lives."

"Which we aren't," Celia growled.

"Really, are you sure about that?" Philip said. "I mean, despite all your mystery novels, we are not detectives or cops or anything. We're scientists and researchers, and we have projects we're supposed to be concentrating on."

"Which we can't do right now until Admin cleans up the mess left by the break-in."

"Speak for yourself," Mark interjected. "I'm fine."

Celia gave him a dark look but didn't comment.

"We should get the cops involved," Philip continued.

"Once we've finished with JCN," Celia retorted. "C'mon, Philip. Think of it as an intellectual exercise. Don't you want to know what's going on?"

"Um, maybe. But my earlier comment about guns still applies."

"Chicken."

"Uh-huh. That's not the insult you think it is."

CHAPTER SIXTEEN

Witness Statement

Philip, still bleary-eyed from lack of sleep, spent the morning at work doing final cleanup and reorganizing in his office. The recovery crew had done everything they could, but it was one thing to reorganize furniture and reinsert drawers and quite another to re-sort and file notes. Philip found himself quite amazed at how much paper he still generated in a century that was originally supposed to be paperless. Sure, and everyone should have jetpacks and flying cars by now as well.

He'd looked in on Celia once, but she was not in the mood for company. She swore she'd get it together for the police interview, but at the moment, she looked like an overcaffeinated cat that had just been startled.

Finally, 10:00 a.m. arrived. Philip stacked the file he was currently working on and headed for Celia's office to meet with the detective. Instead, he found her talking to her tablet. As he hesitated at the door, Celia motioned him to a seat and turned the tablet to face Philip.

"Detective Shankar is meeting us over Zoom," she said. "Scheduling issues."

"Unfortunately true, Doctor Hunt. A detective's work is never done. I have had to travel to Seattle in regard to some evidence that pointed our way. You heard about Poosday, as they are calling it? And anyway, your case seems to be more about cleaning up some details."

Celia turned the tablet back to face her, and Philip wheeled his chair around the desk so that he was in view.

Shankar continued, "Cell-tower records clearly show that you two came and went well before the fire broke out at Derek McQuaid's home. Nor were you there long enough to set an incendiary device, even if you had a motive."

Philip tried to keep his face neutral. "That seems very un-detective-like, Detective. Aren't we your primary suspects by default?"

"You would be, Doctor Moray, except we have several eyewitness accounts of a group of people essentially assaulting the house after you left."

"What?" said Philip and Celia at the same time.

"The description sounds very much like a SWAT raid, except I've checked, and there was no police action at that location. And shortly after that, the first smoke appeared, and someone called the fire department. I'm hoping you might have some information to add, maybe something about the type of business Mr. McQuaid was engaged in."

"Well, Spectre Enterprises seems to be a video-production company," Philip replied, "which doesn't interest us in the slightest. But Mr. McQuaid also does some robotics work on the side, and we've seen one of his experimental products. We wanted to ask him about it and see if he did freelance work." Technically, all of that was true, but Philip had been very careful to phrase it as casually as possible.

"But you've never met him?"

"Nor talked to him," Celia replied. "We don't even know what he looks like."

"He's kind of a cipher," Philip added. "No internet presence at all. Probably an offliner."

"Yes, I admit I've noticed that," Shankar said. "We've not found a body, so presumably, he's still alive. But he hasn't contacted the authorities to inquire about his burned-down residence, which seems odd."

"Vacation?" Celia suggested.

"Maybe. But no passport, no car, credit cards are sparsely used and mostly for routine things like food and clothing. Bank accounts are similarly unimpressive. Almost too much so."

"Weird," Philip said.

"It certainly is. As you say, probably an offliner. Well, thank you for your time, Doctors. If I have more questions, I'll contact you. And if you think of anything else, or find out more about our mutual interest, please contact me." Shankar signed off with minimal pleasantries, leaving Philip and Celia staring at each other.

"What did he mean, we weren't there long enough?" Celia said.

"Yeah, I caught that, too. We were there more than long enough. I think he was trying to trap us. It's a little odd that he didn't probe that issue more, but I expect he'll be back."

***

Philip was back in his office, putting the last few items back in their proper place, when he got a phone call, which the caller ID identified only as coming from JCN. That was enough of a surprise for him to hesitate, but curiosity got the better of him.

"Good morning, Doctor Moray." Matilda Buto's face peered at him from the hologrammatic screen. She seemed uncomfortable.

Philip's eyebrows rose almost to his hairline. "This is a surprise. What can I do for you, Ms. Buto?"

"I would like to arrange another meeting with you and Ms. Hunt, at your convenience."

"At your office? And it's *Doctor* Hunt. I really don't want to have to sit through that discussion again."

"Understood. And yes, at my office. There are good reasons."

"I'm game. I'll have to coordinate with Celia. Why don't you send us an invite and we'll respond or reschedule?"

"I'd prefer not. As an alternative, get back to me with a suitable time. I'll make myself available."

She signed off, and Philip was left staring at his wrist, bemused. Rather than wasting time analyzing the woman, he called Celia and explained the situation.

"Honestly, it sounds like she doesn't want things on the record," she replied. "And having us at her office means she can ensure there's no recording going on."

"We could be carrying a recording device..."

"Betcha anything we'll be scanned."

Philip shrugged. Either way, maybe they'd get some answers.

CHAPTER SEVENTEEN

Cards on the Table

Celia had been right. As soon as they stepped off the elevator at JCN, she and Philip were subjected to the attention of a crew of wand-waving security guards. Once the scanning was over, Donald Gleason stepped forward and motioned them to follow him.

"This isn't the floor your boss's office is on," Celia commented. "So where are we going?"

"Meeting room," Gleason replied. "It's more appropriate for the discussion."

That was certainly cryptic, and Philip felt himself tensing up as if for physical combat. Silly, of course, but the human psyche had certain hardwired flight-or-fight reflexes that wouldn't be denied.

Matilda Buto was waiting in the room, seated at one end of a conference table—the power seat, according to any book on business psychology. At a gesture from her, Philip and Celia took seats at the near side.

Buto started in without preamble. "I would like to have this discussion in a spirit of candor—putting all our cards on the table. We have a problem, as you are no doubt aware, and I believe we can accomplish more by working together than at cross-purposes."

What the bleep is she talking about? Philip thought. Carefully keeping his face neutral and deliberately not glancing at Celia, he replied, "I'm amenable in principle. Let's start with whether or not you were responsible for the break-in at our lab."

Buto gave him a thin smile, acknowledging that he wasn't about to give anything away without a show of good faith. "We were not. The images and scans you provided at our last meeting were enough for us to form some conclusions. Those conclusions are alarming, though, and make the break-in and theft of what you call a flybot a matter of deep concern."

"Why?"

"Because someone else is involved. And it isn't the police."

"Of course not," Celia interjected. "They wouldn't sneak in through a window. They'd break down the front door and march in."

"Indeed. Although that eventuality is becoming a distinct possibility."

"Oh?" Philip sat up straight.

"As much as it pains me to confide in outsiders, I feel it necessary to come clean with you two. For some reason, you are in this up to your necks, and it's not clear that it's by choice. So I'm going to tell you some things, and I hope you'll be forthcoming with anything you might still be withholding. At this point, if ATLAS were to get involved, the fallout would be considerable. For all of us. So, like it or not, we are allies."

Buto paused, took a deep breath, and continued, "The chip we've discussed in previous meetings, the Q-32, is a neurosimulant chip that is designed to mimic in hardware the neural net software used to create an AI."

Celia interrupted. "Correct me if I'm wrong, but aren't neural nets used to mimic in *software* the neurons in the brain? So you've invented hardware to emulate software that emulates hardware?"

Buto gave one of her rare smiles. "Exactly right, and that's been the basic issue all along with trying to get true artificial intelligence working. Software emulations are slow at best, and the nonlinear and recursive nature of neuronal activity makes them even slower, even with quantum computing. As you know, quantum computers work best on linear problems."

"I don't, but I'll take your word for it," Celia replied.

Buto nodded. "So the big problem with AIs is that the more complex and intelligent you make them, the more virtual neurons you add, the slower the emulation runs, and the more power it requires. Aggies are notorious for taking forever to process complex questions. Some of my staff compare them to Ents. I confess I don't know what that means."

Philip suppressed a smile. The tree shepherds from the Lord of the Rings books could take days just to say *Good morning.*

"So," Buto continued, "we've created a chip that emulates neurons in hardware, skipping the whole software layer. It's based on the old IBM NorthPole chip, which, of course, we acquired the rights to when we bought the company."

"Uh-huh?" Celia phrased the prompt with a rising inflection to try to get Buto back on track, as she seemed to be meandering.

Buto gave her a sharp look. "This *is* relevant, Dr. Hunt. The twist is that we added self-modification capability to emulate the pruning and new growth that happens in the immature biological brain as it rewires itself, turning the chip into a neurosimulant variety. Which means no large external memory and no need to freeze the training dataset. Essentially, the Q-32 is a brain on a chip. And one that matures and develops as it learns. It modifies itself in hardware, not in some software emulation layer."

"A small brain," Celia said. "Equivalent to what?"

"Somewhere around mouse level," Buto replied. "But they can be networked together. And the effect is more multiplicative than additive. Or maybe exponential, like powers of two. We can't calculate it exactly, but ten chips networked together are far, far more than ten times smarter."

"Not meaning to derail you," Celia said, "but you said this is relevant, and it still sounds like you are going off on a tangent. What is the point you're building up to?"

Buto leaned forward and put her elbows on the desk, entwining her fingers. "We are missing more than two hundred chips."

"Oh," said Philip. "Oh, frig."

"That'll do it," Celia added. "How exactly are you *missing* these chips? Missing inventory?"

"There shouldn't *be* any inventory," Buto replied. "Officially, we've manufactured exactly four chips. But evidence indicates several hundred chips were produced. This was clearly an inside job, and we're investigating internally. But several hundred chips..."

"It may not be as bad as you think," Philip said. "I get the impression from what I've read in Derek McQuaid's notebook that he was building—or planning to build—multiple aggies. So if he used ten to twenty chips per unit, he'd have a dozen or more aggies."

Buto nodded. "That makes sense. But the bottom line for us is we have to get them back. If ATLAS investigators get hold of even one of those chips—"

"Why the hell did you label them?" Celia interjected.

"We're required to, by law," Buto replied. "And the printers are designed to do that automatically. It's not like we *planned* to have all this inventory out in the wild. Please keep this straight in your head, Doctor. We are victims here, not perpetrators."

Celia opened and closed her mouth a couple of times, then nodded. "Noted. And something that's hard to keep in mind. Normally, the big corporation *is* the bad guy."

Philip tilted his head in Celia's direction and said to Buto, "Spy novels. She's addicted."

Rather than replying, Buto said, "First slide" into the air. A monitor lit up opposite Philip, showing a close-up of the flybot. He recognized it as one of the images that Mark had taken.

"Second slide," Buto said, and the image switched to a schematic. This was new. Philip squinted and turned his head slightly. The schematic was...off, somehow.

"I see that you've already noticed the oddness of the diagram," Buto said. "This is an AI-generated plan. They're easy for an engineer to spot because they tend to be organic and minimalist. They are also generally quite hard to produce in quantity, as they treat manufacturing standards with contempt." She paused. "We do, of course, have SPIs design our products—as you'd expect—but they've been trained to adhere to engineering standards, *and* the results are vetted by human engineers. This"—she waved a hand at the image—"is freelanced."

"So generated by an AI?" Philip wasn't sure why that was a problem.

"And printed by an AI," Buto replied. "Whoever was in charge either didn't care or didn't know better."

"Okay, so someone needs their hand slapped. I still don't understand why you're so concerned."

Buto gave him an arch look. "It's not just the physical design, Dr. Moray. It's the circuitry. This bot is using our experimental neurosimulant chip, the Q-32, *without* any of the constraints that ATLAS regulations would mandate, even for a lab-isolated experimental unit. Having one out in the wild...well, to expand on your facetious comment, Dr. Hunt, the police would not only break down the front door but most of the wall it sits in, along with possibly some ceiling and roof, if they were made aware of this."

"Uh..." Philip paused. She was right. Where matters of aggie regulation were concerned, ATLAS policies gave the police increased powers and broad discretion, beyond what most law enforcement agencies were normally authorized to do. People could and did disappear for long periods of time, based only on suspicions. Even a corporation as large as JCN wasn't immune.

On the other hand, what Buto had just revealed was potentially hugely damaging to the corporation, which made this meeting all the more odd. Why would she confide in a couple of random midlevel scientists?

Seeming to read his mind, Buto looked directly at him. "The flybot was interested in you specifically, Doctor Moray. Or your research. We need to find out why, as a first step to finding out who."

"Derek McQuaid," Celia said, speaking for the first time in several minutes. She looked at Philip and shrugged. "We tracked him down as having bought several of the other components that make up the flybot."

"Have you contacted him?" Buto asked.

"We visited his house. No one was home. A short time later, the house burned down under mysterious circumstances, right after being assaulted by something that looked like a SWAT team."

Buto sat back, looking poleaxed. "Interesting. Doctors, I will make you a deal. Of course, we are not going to share all of our secrets and internal development strategies with you, and you would not believe me if I promised to do so anyway. But I believe what you are really interested in is why someone would be spying on you and whether it creates safety concerns for you in the future. I *will* promise to share information relating to that with you, in return for any other information you can give us on this McQuaid person. Agreed?"

"Agreed," said Philip and Celia together. Philip noted, though, that Celia had *not* mentioned the townhouse, nor did she seem intent on bringing it up.

Celia gave Buto a carefully sanitized version of their research that resulted in the discovery of McQuaid's home address. She did mention the interview with Detective Shankar but didn't elaborate beyond the information about the fire and SWAT team.

After Celia finished, Buto said to them, "It is possible that whoever is responsible has more than one Q-32 chip, so please be on the lookout for more flybots." She stood, a sure sign that the interview was over.

On the way out, Philip started to say, "So I don't—"

Celia cut him off with a chopping motion. "Later."

Once they were seated in a traxi, Philip said, "Celia, I think we're about at the end of this. Honestly. My job is creating a method of scanning asteroids at a distance for metal. Yours is making synthetic biological nanobots to extract that metal. Can't we just hand this over to the professionals and get back to our lives?"

Celia appraised him silently for several seconds. "Tell you what, Philip. We still have that notebook that we found in McQuaid's townhouse. Let's get everything we can out of it first. Then, if we don't have anything new, you can hand it all over to Buto." She hesitated. "I think she'll soft-pedal anything we give her to investigators if they get involved, just out of self-preservation. But it's probably worth bringing up mutually assured destruction."

Philip nodded and tried not to think too much about that last phrase, especially as it might apply to his life.

***

Buto buzzed Carl Wright again once the doctors had left. His image came up on her tablet, but Buto noticed right away that he appeared agitated. Normally, Wright was very good at controlling his body language and expressions; you had to be, in order to rise this high in the cage match that was corporate politics. So something must have spooked him. "Carl?" she said noncommittally.

"Oh, er, nothing really significant about their reactions. Even with what they gave you today, I think they're still hiding something. But it's a peripheral item. I'll...keep monitoring." With that, he ended the call.

Peripheral item, my ass, Buto thought. Wright wasn't the only person with facial-analysis software. And hers had registered his last statement as a big ol' whopper.

What was it about these two doctors that was spooking the chief of security? It bore looking into.

CHAPTER EIGHTEEN

The Notebook

Philip and Celia returned to the lab and retired to his office. Philip paged slowly through the scans he had taken from Derek's notebook, his feet up on his desk, occasionally jotting notes in a notebook of his own.

Celia had become increasingly fidgety, annoyed by Philip's silence and deliberate actions. Finally, she blew up. "God's sake, Philip. What're you, reading a novel? Mind filling me in? And by the way, why are you making paper notes?"

Philip tapped the screen of his tablet. "Derek put his notes on paper for a reason. And wrote most of it using a lot of personal acronyms and abbreviations, by the way. It's worse than trying to decipher a teenager's texting. And anyway, anything online is potentially hackable. Or can be searched with an e-warrant. Physical notes are as secure as you can get these days. You have to know where they are and physically apprehend them. Maybe that's why he had the decoy house."

"Okay, provisionally accepted. But have you found anything?"

Philip felt his face fall as he truly considered what he'd been reading. "Celia, this guy was working on creating an Artificial General Intelligence. I'm sure of it. The cops wouldn't have even bothered with a trial if they caught him making an aggy."

"But why?"

Philip shrugged. "Why does anyone do anything illegal? He might have been railing against the Man or taking a stand against regulating intellectual pursuits, or maybe it's just the oldest of reasons."

"Drinking?"

Philip rolled his eyes before continuing. "Profit. This guy could be the computer-geek version of a gun smuggler. Highest bidder, yadda."

"Building illegal aggies for sale?" Celia looked horrified.

"Sure. His customers could be anything from terrorists to day traders to people who bet on sports. The value of an unregulated aggy can't be overstated."

"And he thought it would be a good idea to document all this," Celia retorted. "For his memoir, maybe?"

"Well, no, I'm doing a lot of reading between the lines. This is mostly technical notes and reminders to self. This isn't the only notebook, as it seems to start midproject. So I'm sure there were notebooks right back to the beginning of things."

"Stolen in the break-in."

"Uh-huh. If it *was* a break-in. Safe wasn't forced, remember? But whoever they were dropped this one. I wonder if it'll make a difference."

"Will it make a difference to us?"

Philip sighed and tossed the tablet onto his desk. "Good question. Probably not. Unless he drew a treasure map or something, I think we've about reached the end of this adventure."

"So..."

"Let's hand the thing over to JCN and call it a day. Honestly, I'd like to get back to my sensor research."

Celia replied with a small smile, "Yeah, I get it. And I have a batch of artificial bacteria currently being paid to just sit around."

"You pay them?"

"Don't get cute, physics boy."

At that moment, Philip's watch sounded an alert. He jerked upright and gestured *pick up*. The hologram that popped up was from his house SPI. "Intruders are attempting to break in. Police have been called. Any further instructions?" it said.

"No. Standard response," Philip replied and hung up. He glanced at Celia, who wore an alarmed expression.

"I don't understand," she said. "They have the flybot. Whoever *they* are. What else do they—" Her phone rang in midsentence. "Oh hell," she said and glanced at the screen. "It's a text from my home SPI. I'm being broken into as well."

They both leaped to their feet and made for the door, almost jamming themselves in the doorway in their haste. "Call a traxi. Urgent," Philip said to his watch as he half jogged down the hall. He heard Celia make a similar request.

***

A half hour later, Philip was looking around his living room while a cop took a video. "This wasn't a smash-and-grab," she said. "You have some nice equipment here, and they ignored it. Any idea what this was about?"

Philip decided to play dumb. "I got broken into at work recently as well. Actually, several of us did. And my colleague got an alert at the same time as I did. So this is probably company related. But I have no idea why."

A lie, of course. This had to be related to McQuaid and the flybot. Had Buto been lying to them? Was this her work as well? But to what end? Maybe a direct challenge was the best response. Philip exchanged some more info with the cop, accepted an e-card with the case number, and thanked the woman. She nodded and turned for the door, then stopped. "I'll be honest, it's unlikely you'll hear from us on this matter unless something else connects to it. Minor damage, nothing stolen, no injuries…it'll go to the bottom of the pile. No offense."

"Got it." Philip watched as the cop showed herself out, then lifted his left arm and gestured. "Call Matilda Buto," he said to the watch.

There was a short pause, and then Donald Gleason's voice said, "Ms. Buto's office."

Skipping any niceties, Philip launched right in. "This is Philip Moray. Both Dr. Hunt and I have had our homes broken into. I'd like to know if Ms. Buto has some insight into this."

"What? That's terrible! Mr. Moray, er, Dr. Moray, I'll forward this to her immediately. She's in a meeting right now—"

"Isn't she always?"

There was a brief hesitation, then Gleason replied, "Well, yes, pretty much. It *is* her job."

"That's fair. Sorry, I shouldn't be snapping at you, but I'm a little on edge right now. Please have her call me when she can."

"Understood and understandable, Dr. Moray. I'm sure she'll be in touch."

Philip ended the call and was just starting to pick up some of the mess when his phone rang. He lifted his arm to see that it was from Buto, and she was requesting a conference call with himself and Celia. He gestured to answer. "Hello, Ms. Buto. Thank you for responding so quickly."

"Dr. Moray, I—" Buto got only the three words out before Celia connected.

"Celia here."

"Dr. Hunt, Dr. Moray, I'm sorry to hear about the break-ins. I called as soon as Donald gave me the message. I'm sure there's an unspoken subtext where you suspect JCN of having a hand in this, but I assure you, we were not involved in this or the matter of the flybot."

"Thanks for that, Ms. Buto," Philip said. "But if it's not you, then someone else is still interested in us."

"Which makes no sense. You no longer have the flybot, as I understand it," Buto replied. "I will do some investigations from this end, but I can't hold out a lot of hope." She said goodbye and ended the call.

"I'll call you back," Celia said to him, then hung up. Of course, Philip thought, Buto had arranged the conference call and could still be monitoring it even if she'd hung up. He quickly ended the call, and a moment later, his phone rang with Celia's image.

"Are we going to give her the notebook?" Celia said without preamble. "I'd bet any money that's what the intruders were looking for."

"You'd win that bet," Philip replied. "The notebook is missing."

"Aw, crap. You're sure?"

"Uh-huh. I used 'The Purloined Letter' technique. Hid it in plain sight on my bookshelf. Turns out that doesn't work so well in real life." Philip sighed. "Never got around to the safe deposit. Too busy. Or too lazy."

Celia rolled her eyes. "Jeez, Philip." Then, apparently thinking better of it, she continued, "On the other hand, you still have the scans, so we haven't lost the information.

And since the physical notebook is gone, as is the flybot, maybe people will leave us alone now. I know this is usually your line, but I do want my life back."

"It's all fun and games," Philip replied, "until someone gets broken into."

***

Carl Wright held the notebook in his hands, flipping it over and over as if overcome by some nervous tic.

Derek McQuaid. He hadn't heard that name in years. He would have been just as happy to never have heard it again. But in this context, it was a particular disaster. If McQuaid was involved, if McQuaid was making illegal aggies using the Q-32 chip, then it was almost certain that McQuaid was the anonymous contact he'd been selling the chips to.

And that couldn't be a coincidence.

Carl stopped flipping the notebook and instead began slapping it into his other hand. It was pure luck that the idiot doctor had mentioned McQuaid and the notebook during the discussion with Buto. Then the two scientists had discussed it in the traxi. He'd been smart to have a bug attached to one of them during the pat-down. And smarter not to have mentioned it to Buto. And he'd been right. The team had been in and out of the doctor's house in less than five minutes, prize in hand.

***

A short while later, Carl slammed his hand down on his desk, loud enough to cause people in the cubicle farm to look up. He glared through his office window, and they quickly found other things to do.

He'd been reading through the notebook as best he could. Most of the TLAs and jargon were standard college computer science geekery, but Derek had invented a few new ones over the years, and only some of it could be inferred from context.

The problem was the section talking about "CW." There could be no question who CW referred to, given some of the other language Derek was using. It put to rest any question about Derek's motivations.

Unfortunately, it also incriminated Carl. In fact, it looked like the whole point was to engage Carl in a criminal enterprise, then expose him.

Well, it would have been ironically appropriate payback.

It was time to clean up his tracks.

CHAPTER NINETEEN

The Cleaners

"It's easy money, Ned." Buzz slapped the tablet screen with the back of his hand. "Half up front, half on completion. And they didn't haggle on the amount."

"That's what bothers me." Ned looked to his left, where Andy was steadily chugging a beer. No help there. "We've got no connection to this group, no references. And they're just agreeing to everything like they don't care."

"Or like they're desperate. This sounds like someone who's new to this. Look, this is our job. We're cleaners. We clean up. Jeez, I'll do it by myself if I have to. And I'll keep the dough."

Ned sighed. "Fine. But if this goes south, it's on you."

***

The job was simple. Visit a townhouse (door code supplied), dispose of one corpse, collect some computer equipment and a 3D printer, wipe, and dispose. The equipment was a bonus. They'd get some money for shifting it.

Everything seemed routine until they entered the townhouse and got a look at the corpse.

"Holy fuck!" Ned exclaimed, backing away. "I'm not touching that!"

Buzz admitted to himself it was freaky, but a job was a job. In their line of work, you didn't back out of a job once you accepted it. If you screwed people around, you didn't get sued or get a bad rating on the Better Business Bureau—you got your hands broken, or worse.

"Dude, we have to do this," he said. "Look, we can wrap it up without touching it." Buzz proceeded to move furniture and lay out the tarp.

Ned and Andy glanced at each other, then moved to help. But Ned was still agitated and kept muttering imprecations and complaints. Buzz was sure he even heard part of an *Our Father*.

They managed to bundle the corpse into the van, then went back for the computer equipment. But the van wasn't big enough, as it turned out, for everything. And Ned was adamant that he wasn't going to cozy up to that desiccated mummy, even to stack computers.

After twenty minutes of arguing back and forth, the men decided to dump the corpse in a nearby park. If they could get it under the bushes and out of sight, natural processes should break it down to the point where it would just be another dead body. At least that was Ned's argument. By this point, Buzz was getting nervous about the amount of time they'd spent there.

One of the basic rules of their profession was get in, get it done, get out. Every minute was an opportunity for some passerby to notice them and remember something.

The corpse having been dumped, they came back and loaded the computers, then cleaned every single surface of prints or DNA.

Finally, the job was complete.

Back in the van, with Andy driving, Buzz pulled up the contact and uploaded the required photos of the completed job. A moment later, there was a notification as a large sum of money was deposited into their account.

"Woo! Guys, we are flush!" Buzz exclaimed. "I feel like a steak. Who else?"

"Works for me," Ned replied. Andy drained the last swallow of the beer he'd just opened and belched loudly.

A manually driven van being illegal in the city, the men dropped it off at their place and called for a traxi. Apparently, things were going their way, as one arrived within moments. They piled in and gave their destination to the controller. But as the traxi pulled away, all three men simultaneously cursed and slapped the backs of their necks.

CHAPTER TWENTY

Tanker Attack

Private Mills released the rappelling rope as he touched down on the tanker deck. Around him, other members of the squad were doing the same. The squad leader made a gesture, and they fanned out, AKs at the ready.

The tanker, a Panamax crude container delivering product from Kuwait, had abruptly gone radio silent, then started drifting. The navy had been called, and Mills and his crew were tasked to investigate. It could be anything from mass food poisoning to terrorism to alien abduction. There was simply no information. Orders were to proceed with utmost caution, don't shoot tanker crew, but be prepared to defend themselves.

Mills and two others, Harrison and Benson, had been directed in the briefing to head for the bridge. Other groups would be checking the mess, crew quarters, and engineering sections.

Slowly, they crept up the stairway, weapons at the ready. One soldier grabbed the hatch handle, twisted it slowly, then pulled the door open. Mills and the other soldier jumped in, heading in opposite directions in a crouch.

There was no reaction. The bridge was still and silent. But not empty. Several members of the bridge crew were sprawled on the floor or slumped in their seats. Mills counted four bodies. As he swept the bridge for any threats or oddities, one of his squad mates said, "They're not dead."

Mills looked over. Harrison had his hand to the neck of one of the bodies. "Strong pulse," the man said.

"Same here," Benson said a moment later.

It took only moments to check the remaining two bodies. Also alive. Mills bent over to look in the face of one of the crew. The man's eyes were open, but fixed and staring straight ahead. But as Mills watched, the eyes blinked. So, blinking and breathing, but not conscious. Then Mills drew a shocked breath as the man's eyes welled up with tears.

"Shit, he's crying," Mills exclaimed. "I think he's awake."

Benson and Harrison checked other victims. "Same here," both said.

At that moment, the radio crackled, and the squad leader, Salazar, said, "We've got crew here. Unconscious but alive. No one's moving."

Mills pressed his transmit button. "I'm not sure they're unconscious, sir. See if they're tearing up. I think they're just paralyzed."

***

Mills stood with the other men as the tanker crew members were hoisted, one at a time, into the medivac chopper. "Isn't this just creepy as fuck," he said.

"They're all the same," Benson replied. "They can vary their blinking, at least some of them, but nothing else. They're going to have to learn Morse code."

"Well, they've got nothing else to do," Harrison said. Then, at the shocked looks, he grinned and added, "Too soon?"

Mills shook his head. "Jesus, you're an asshole, Tom."

CHAPTER TWENTY-ONE

Police Interview

Philip looked up from his notes as his watch buzzed with an incoming text. He gestured and saw that it was from Celia. She was fifty feet down the hall, ferchrissake. Then he had a sudden flashback to himself as a teen, phoning his mother from the basement rec room to ask when dinner would be ready, and he flushed with embarrassment.

Philip tapped the message and began to read:

Shankar called. Wants to ask us more questions. At the cop shop. This afternoon at 2. He didn't come out and say "or else," but you could hear it.

Well, crap. There might be other reasons for the interview, but the most likely was, of course, new evidence or perceived inconsistencies in their statements. Philip felt his stomach drop, a sensation that he was getting thoroughly sick of.

He texted back: *Fine. We'll go together.*

Within moments, he received a reply: *No shit, Sherlock. See you at 1:30 out front.*

Philip glanced at the time. Midmorning. He probably wouldn't be able to eat with this hanging over his head, but hopefully he could get a few hours of work done.

***

Precisely at 1:29, Philip's watch beeped to remind him of his appointment. He wrapped up what he was doing and headed for the front of the building, where he found Celia already waiting. "Bit of an eager beaver, aren't you?" he said.

"More like anxious," she replied. Philip nodded, and they waited quietly until the traxi arrived.

The ride to the police station was spent in silence, broken only by the occasional monosyllabic comment. Neither person wanted to start a conversation. They'd already long since established their story, and too much rehashing would result in individual statements that were too similar and seemed to have a single point of view. As Celia had pointed out, this was a red flag for the cops.

At the front desk, Philip let Celia take point. She explained to the receptionist why they were there. The woman tapped away at her keyboard for a few moments, then replied, "According to the log, Detective Shankar was supposed to meet you here for the interviews, but he's left a message that he's still stuck in Seattle. However, he did arrange for someone else." She pressed a finger to her earpiece and mumbled for a moment, then looked up. "Officer Han will be out in a moment."

Philip and Celia exchanged a glance; then Philip shrugged. If he was being honest, dealing with someone who had no stake in the case seemed like it would be less stressful.

Officer Han showed up within seconds and ushered them into separate interview rooms. He provided Philip with a police-issue tablet, then offered him a choice of a stylus or keyboard. "I have instructions from Detective Shankar to solicit as much detail from you as possible on the events surrounding the fire at the residence of one Derek McQuaid. In particular, he's interested in the timing of events. Anything you can add to your original statement would be appreciated."

Philip looked at the officer askance. This didn't feel like much of a grilling. Han noticed his look and smiled. "It's just a witness statement, Mr. Moray. If the detective feels, at some point, the need to interrogate you, I'm sure the atmosphere will be more in line with your expectations."

Philip snickered and pulled the tablet around to get comfortable. He had chosen a stylus and used the tablet in pad mode to write out his statement longhand. Months of using pen and actual paper at work had made him accustomed to the all-but-obsolete practice.

When he was done, Officer Han examined his own tablet, probably reviewing Philip's statement. After several minutes of silence, a duration that was far longer than necessary to read the entire statement, Han looked up. "So after leaving the residence in question the first time, you went to the area of..." Han glanced down. "Forty-Fifth and Queens. Why there in particular?"

Philip was ready for this question. He and Celia had discussed the necessity of coming up with a reason for their travels that day. "Celia wanted to look at a townhouse that's for sale in the area. We got out and walked the neighborhood."

"Seems like an odd side quest, Mr. Moray."

"It's *doctor*, not that it matters a lot. But we were just trying to use up some time before checking back. It was either that or hit a McDonald's."

"And what was the address of the townhouse?"

Philip shrugged. "You'd have to ask Celia. It was her side quest." He smiled as he said this. Officer Han was apparently a gamer. And Philip knew that Celia had picked out the address of a legitimately listed townhome in the area.

"The reason I ask, *Doctor* Moray, is because we recently found a dead body in that area."

Philip kept his face still. Had they discovered McQuaid's townhouse and the mummified body? He wasn't sure if this increased his jeopardy, but worst case, if they'd missed wiping off a fingerprint...

With a massive effort of will, Philip frowned. "I'm not sure why that would connect to us. Unless it was found in the listed home."

Han smiled. "No, it was found in the park. But the state of the corpse was...interesting."

"Okay. You're just going to leave me hanging?" Philip sat back and crossed his arms. "Is it 'interesting' in a way that only a physicist could pull off? Is that the connection?"

"Perhaps more along Dr. Hunt's line of work." Han dropped his tablet flat and scooped up Philip's unit. "Thanks for your time, Doctor. If you can wait in the reception area, I don't imagine Dr. Hunt will be very long." Philip's watch dinged, and Han continued, "I've given you my contact info in case you think of anything else."

Philip made his way to reception and plunked down on a chair, still frowning. Of course, you never knew how honest the cops were being. The comment could be misdirection to see Philip's reaction. But *outside*? In a park? Had someone gone in and moved the corpse?

Philip crossed his arms and sat back, trying to work out all the ramifications.

***

Celia quickly typed up her statement for Officer Han. She felt bad at some level about lying to the cops; after all, honest citizens didn't need to do that. It created a bit of a dissonance in her thinking. Was she dishonest? A crook? A criminal? No, she didn't believe that. But she couldn't put her finger on exactly when she'd crossed over the line into something that she couldn't put on a police report.

Other than the obvious breaking and entering, of course.

She finished the statement, careful to put neither too much nor too little detail, and aware that it had to not appear rehearsed.

Han read the statement on his laptop, then said, "What was the address that you were going to look at?"

"The house for sale?"

"Yes."

She dug out her phone, found the real estate ad, then flipped it around for Han to see. He glanced at it, made a notation, then nodded and managed to look uncomfortable. "To be honest, Dr. Hunt, the only reason you and Dr. Moray are even showing up on our radar is because of several odd occurrences that have us on alert. And two of them happened in your vicinity."

"Two? The fire and...?"

"I already mentioned to the other doctor that we found a corpse in the area, in an *interesting* condition."

"I really hate it when someone says *interesting* in that way," Celia replied. "Are you going to tell me or make me beg?"

Han cracked a smile. "Eh, yeah, sorry, Dr. Hunt. But I thought that you might have some insight, what with being a doctor. I mean a *medical* doctor, not just a PhD."

"So you're looking for some free consulting?"

"Not if it's an ethical concern, or if you're in a hurry. But just between you and me, I was the first responder when the corpse discovery was called in, and I'm unlikely to ever see the medical results. This is more a matter of personal curiosity."

"All right. You definitely have me curious. What was special about this corpse?"

"It was mummified."

"It was a mummy? Like from a museum?"

"No, it was wearing a ZEGNA suit and a latest-gen Rolex watch phone. But it was mummified."

"That's...interesting."

"I did mention that."

Now it was Celia's turn to smile. Despite herself, she found herself liking this cop. "Well, mummification is caused by most of the water being removed from the tissues. Usually with natron, which is just mainly salt, along with placing it in a dry environment. Were the organs removed?"

Han looked surprised. "Why would they be?"

"Well, that's how the Egyptians did it. They removed and dried the organs separately, as well as emptying the body cavity."

Now Han was looking slightly queasy. "It seems unlikely, given the victim was still wearing the suit."

"Do you have an idea how much it weighed?"

"Ah, I remember the EMTs commented on that. Couldn't have been more than a hundred pounds, but the suit was cut for a beefy individual, maybe up to three hundred. Why?"

"We weigh about the same as water, Officer. Your victim had half to two-thirds of the water removed from his tissues. And quickly, I'd expect. To be honest, I don't know of any process that could do that. I expect this one is going to go into the books as unexplained."

Han nodded, looked like he was going to add something; then, with a small shake of his head, he snapped his tablet closed. "Thank you, Dr. Hunt, for coming down and giving a statement. And for the free consultation."

***

Philip was still pondering who removed the corpse when Celia walked out. They grabbed a traxi and didn't say anything until they were on the way back to the office.

Celia opened the conversation. "Did they tell you they found a body around the townhouse?"

"Yeah, in the park."

"It was *interesting*, the officer said." Celia paused. "Want to guess what that means?"

Philip glanced at her and met an intense stare. It seemed they were still in character. Okay, he'd play along. "Uh, something other than shot or stabbed. Or maybe shot or stabbed a few hundred times. Either would be interesting."

Celia replied with a small smile. "Oh, much more interesting than that. I'll tell you all about it over a coffee when we get back."

They remained silent for the rest of the trip. By unspoken agreement, they headed straight for the cafeteria once they arrived. Coffees and donuts being acquired, Celia got down to business.

"I'm glad you caught my hint, Philip. They could conceivably have gotten a warrant to bug the traxi for our return trip. Maybe even for the trip out, although that would be harder. So..." Celia hesitated, tapping the table with her index fingernail. "They have found a corpse in the area of the townhouse. A mummified one, wearing an expensive suit. *Outside*, if we are to believe Officer Han, which means someone moved it and dumped it after we left."

Philip rubbed the bridge of his nose. "Christ. So now if we try to come clean, we could be suspects in a murder." He glanced to the ceiling, as if looking for inspiration. "So much for that plan."

"I'm not sure how coming clean would logically make us more suspect than before, but that's the way the cops think, so yeah." Celia thought for a moment. "Unless they come up with some kind of physical evidence, I think we're covered. If they ever come up with anything on Derek, it won't reflect on us. Our reason for having tried to contact him is still plausible, and we even have the flybot—oh, no, we don't."

"Well, we have the pictures. And the police reports from the break-ins."

"That's another thing, Philip. A lot of stuff is happening to us and around us. I wonder if that's what's got Shankar sniffing around?"

Philip sighed. "Good point. And who knows? All we can do is keep our heads down and hope nothing else happens."

***

That night, the news was on as usual as Philip did his meal prep. He listened with half an ear, alert to anything really interesting but mostly just letting it roll off him. Then the weird, frenetic music started that always meant breaking news.

In downtown Chicago this afternoon, people at a traxi stop were shocked when a traxi pulled up and opened its doors to reveal three desiccated corpses. One onlooker described them as "mummy-like."

Authorities are baffled, as the service logs of the vehicle show it being on continuous active duty for the entire day.

Philip looked up from his meal prep, and he felt that all-too-common elevator feeling as he absorbed the news. There were several still images and one video, but of course, the central characters had been blurred to protect the sensibilities of the viewing public.

"House, bookmark the last thirty seconds of the current TV program." Philip scooped his vegetables into a bowl, stuck it in the fridge, wiped his hands, then headed for his computer.

He pulled out some still images from the bookmarked news report and blanked out the traxis and any bystanders in the picture. That left the background, which showed some buildings and street infrastructure. He pulled up a search engine and fed it the images, then sat back. It took less than thirty seconds before the search engine started spitting out matches, some of which came with geolocations.

And there was the sinking sensation again. The traxi stop was less than a mile from Derek's townhouse. There was no way this was unrelated.

Philip's phone rang, and Celia's caller ID showed. He answered, and her image popped up. "Philip, are you watching the news? Did you see—"

"Yes, and I'm a few steps ahead of you. I've identified the location, and it's near Derek's townhouse. It has to be connected. Do you think it's some kind of virus? Could the three people have caught it from the corpse in the park?"

"No," she replied. "Otherwise, I think we'd have caught it when we were in the townhouse. All three people getting it and succumbing at the same time means it would have to be significantly virulent and airborne. No, I think someone's specifically targeting people."

"What, like with a ray gun?"

Celia chuckled ruefully. "Sure, as a first approximation. The point is, someone is doing this to people, by whatever mechanism. I just can't figure out why. Or what it has to do with Derek."

"Yeah, okay. But if it starts to be a common occurrence, I think we'd be morally obligated to tell the cops what we know."

"What *do* we know, Philip?"

"Uh...okay, not much. I suppose we could anonymously send them Derek's townhouse address, if it came to it. I don't like this feeling of being on the wrong side of the law, Celia. And people are dying now."

"Me neither. I'm hoping, though, that this is it. If we can just keep our noses clean, we won't have to break any more laws or keep any more secrets. Maybe it'll all just peter out and go away."

"*Now* you want that," Philip grumbled.

CHAPTER TWENTY-TWO

St. Vitus's Dance

Officer Han jumped from the car and paused to look up at the outside of the new Chicago Stadium as his partner, Sienna Cooper, came around the vehicle.

"What've we got, Simon?" she said.

"Your guess is as good as mine. Some kind of disturbance at a religious revival. No shots fired, no reports of violence." He began walking toward one of the entrances, where a staffer was gesturing to them. "Central said the callers were confused and panicked. And they sounded like they were being punched out while making the calls."

"That sounds like violence to me," Cooper commented.

"Which just makes it weirder." Han glanced behind him, but so far, no other cops had arrived. He wasn't even sure if Central had sent more cars, at least not yet. Tonight was a full moon, and all the crazies were out, giving the department a run for its money.

The staffer turned to lead them as they came through the door, and Han said to him, "I have almost no information beyond it being some kind of a disturbance. Can you fill me in?"

The man glanced back at him, and Han noted the man's eyes were like saucers. This was one spooked individual. That couldn't be good.

"They're dancing. All of them."

"It's a religious revival, with a band and everything. How is this a surprise?" Cooper interjected. Han noticed that she wasn't anywhere near as out of breath as he was, and once again, he promised himself to get back on the treadmill a couple of times a week. If he failed his annual physical, the sergeant would never let him hear the end of it.

The staffer glanced back again. "First, this is a Baptist revival, and they don't do dancing. Second, and I think this is a lot more important, they can't seem to stop. And they're scared."

The staffer led them through the passageway to field level, and Han paused to look up. The new stadium had been built on the site of the old Soldier Field, and modern construction techniques had created an impressive interior. You would swear there were clouds up there near the roof.

"Holy shit," Cooper said suddenly as she came to a complete stop and Han almost ran her down.

Then he got an eyeful of the scene on the field in front of them and muttered, "Fuck." Slapping his comms badge, he said, "Central, Officer Han 29211. We need medical, and we need containment. Possible chemical or biological attack. As of now, I'm declaring the stadium under quarantine."

"Acknowledged," the badge replied.

The scene in front of them reminded him of a medieval painting by Luca Signorelli, depicting the damned being cast into hell. Several hundred people were staggering around, many of them weeping and screaming. Some were waving their hands in the air, fingers moving as if playing the piano. Many were writhing as if dancing to unheard music. One man was rhythmically sticking his tongue in and out, a panicked expression on his face. A few people had fallen over and were having what looked like grand mal seizures.

"What, and I cannot emphasize this strongly enough, the fuck?" Cooper exclaimed. She turned to him. "Bio-attack? Are you sure?"

"No, what am I, a squint? But you heard about that tanker crew, right? Some kind of brain inflammation caused by, uh..."

Han frowned for a moment, and the staffer chimed in helpfully, "An engineered virus, according to the news. Jesus." The man glanced at the congregation on the field and muttered, "No offense."

The heads-up display on Han's contacts began scrolling with orders from Central to various members, and he nodded in satisfaction. He twitched an eyebrow to bring the situation map into focus and noted that units were already blockading the stadium exits.

"I don't think we're going to be home in time for dinner tonight," he muttered.

***

Han rolled up his sleeve as the medic prepped the syringe and vial for a blood sample. He glanced up as one of the medical personnel hurried past, and he called out, "Any updates?"

The woman stopped and turned to him. Han could see her make a conscious effort to focus her eyes. His heads-up identified her as *Dr. Beatrice Clarkson.*

"Ah, actually, yes, Officer. They were doing a mass baptism, which is why the big portable pools were set up. Also, probably why they rented the stadium." She made a vague gesture upward. "Anyway, the water was contaminated with what looks to be bacterial antigens. Heavily concentrated, meaning they would have gotten a massive dose absorbed through the skin, creating symptoms of Sydenham chorea."

"The hell you say? And that is..."

Clarkson essayed a small smile. "Ever heard of St. Vitus's Dance?"

"Oh sure, that's *much* clearer." He shook his head, although he had actually heard of it. "Never mind. So we're safe?"

"Unless you were in there swimming with them, yes. There's no active biological agent as such. We've poured chlorine in the pools, which should denature the molecules, and they'll be pumped out to containment tanks. Then the water will be distilled. But this isn't contagious, even by direct contact with the victims."

"What about the people themselves? Any permanent damage?"

"Uh..." The doctor looked uncomfortable. "The dance is just a short-term dyskinesia caused by nerve inflammation. Most of the victims have already stopped the movements. In the natural version of this syndrome, it's caused by a strep infection, and there are long-term symptoms, but I don't think just being exposed to the antigen would have the same results."

"Any chance this is an accident of some kind?"

She shook her head adamantly. "Out of the question. This would have required at least five liters of a specific bacterial antigen. You'd have to squeeze about a half ton of bacteria down to juice to get that kind of production."

Han sighed and nodded. "Thanks, Doc." He rolled down his sleeve as the tech labeled and racked his blood sample, then looked over at Cooper, who was rubbing her arm. "Which means that Lieutenant Mikelson and the terrorism team will be taking over. I guess we're done for the day. File a report on your tablet and head home. I'll be doing the same."

"Okay." Cooper gave him a wave. "See you tomorrow."

"Uh-huh." Han visualized his wife sitting at the kitchen table in front of a cold supper and muttered, "If Brenda doesn't kill me first."

CHAPTER TWENTY-THREE

Weird Stuff

Today had been a particularly frustrating day, and Philip was exhausted. Instead of prepping dinner, as was his habit, he simply plunked down on the couch, turned on the TV, and poured himself a drink. Eventually, he expected hunger would drive him from his spot. Or the news would.

City Hall in Vancouver, British Columbia, narrowly avoided catastrophe today from the city's own construction department. Somehow, an order was issued for the demolition of the building—an order that went out only to the automated systems, completely bypassing the human supervisory staff.

By the time anyone realized something was up, demolition machinery had been transported to the site and was set up to begin deconstruction. The building was saved when city staff physically interposed themselves between the heavy machinery and the building, triggering the SPI safety interlocks and putting the machinery into standby.

Philip snickered and took a sip of his drink. No doubt heads would roll for that. But that was the price of automation, right?

The next news item concerned an aerial drone show in Minneapolis where the drones all went rogue. Instead of the planned images, the drones had formed a fist with the middle finger extended, then flown away.

That got an outright laugh from Philip, and he sat up straighter. It appeared he wasn't the only person who was having a bad day.

This was immediately followed by a third item, also completely bizarre.

The French traxi system suffered an unexplained glitch today when any vehicle entering a roundabout refused to exit, instead circling until the vehicle's battery died. The situation was particularly bad around the Arc de Triomphe, where several hundred vehicles managed to jam themselves into the roundabout and circle for hours...

Okay, what the hell? Philip put his drink down and said, "House, rewind last five minutes of current program." He watched again as the anchor person went through the same stories a second time. It wasn't *Weird News of the Week*, or April Fool's, or an episode of *Satellite Debris*. These were actual news stories.

Come to think of it, there'd been other odd happenings lately, at least a couple a week. It wasn't Gen Omega; they had no sense of humor, or at least not this kind. Their ironic attacks all had a heavy-handed moral point, at least from their point of view, and they weren't at all reluctant to take credit.

"House, call Celia."

A few moments of silence, then, "Celia here."

"Hey, it's Philip. Have you been watching the news?"

"Yes, in fact. Pretty weird night, isn't it?"

"I don't think it's just tonight, Celia. The news is getting more and more bizarre. I'm getting concerned."

"About?"

"What if McQuaid did build one or more aggies? And one got out?"

"What, you think there's a rogue AI out there pulling pranks on humanity?"

Philip hesitated. It *did* sound a little *out there* when phrased that way. "Well, maybe not pranks. Maybe something else. Softening us up? Testing our defenses?"

"Philip, have you been watching the classic Syfy channel again?"

"Hah hah. Listen, it doesn't even actually have to be an AI. But if enough people start to *think* it's a rogue aggy, there could be a panic."

"Okay. And what do you want us to do?"

Philip sighed. "I don't know. I'm just concerned that if we're sitting on something that turns out to lead to another runaway AI catastrophe, we could end up in serious trouble."

There was silence for a few seconds. "Look, Philip, if it does come to that, we can still come clean. Right now, we really don't have anything except suspicions. What actionable information would we be able to hand over, exactly?"

"I dunno, Celia. You're probably right. But this is really freaking me out."

"I get it. And we can always revisit the question, Philip."

"Yeah, okay. Good night, Celia."

"Night."

The call ended, and Philip was left staring at the TV, where someone was now showing the audience how to prepare vat turkey so it looked like it had come from a real bird.

Celia's assurances aside, he still had a bad feeling.

CHAPTER TWENTY-FOUR

Babel

It was not at all a typical day on patrol, Han thought to himself as he stared out the window. The incident at Chicago Stadium had been the number-one local news story for four days now, and it wasn't dying down. If anything, the public engagement had continued to ratchet up as competing media tested ever-more-salacious spins on the event. The result was an increase in things like fights and public disturbances, along with a sharp drop in property crimes.

Han wasn't entirely sure why this pattern had emerged, but there was no shortage of opinions at the station. Some of them even made sense.

"I'm almost scared to call in a lunch break," Cooper said from the other seat. "I don't think we'd even have time to order and receive our food."

"These are the days where you buy packaged stuff and eat it in the car."

"Blech." Cooper held up both hands, palms out. "Vending machine sandwiches? I'd rather go hungry."

A light drizzle had just started again, misting the car windows just enough to blur things out on the street. Han liked it better that way. It allowed him to feel, for a few moments, anyway, that he was in his own private universe and not subject to the interruptions of the real world.

He was just opening his mouth to reply when Central intoned, "Car 54, car 54, report of disturbance, possible medical issue, McCormick Convention Center. Attend Code 3."

"Oh hell." Han leaned forward and flipped the switch, turning on the lights and siren. He directed the car to the specified destination, then began checking his equipment automatically. Cooper had started doing the same. "Looks like you get your wish."

"Hah hah," Cooper replied. "Nothing on the heads-up yet."

Han twitched an eyebrow and checked his display, which was projected onto his retina by his contacts. Some cops still preferred the smart glasses, which were considered less invasive, but since Han needed contacts anyway, this worked fine for him.

They made record time to the convention center. As the car was pulling up to the curb, Cooper said, "Found the building schedule. The center is holding a MAJOR convention this week."

"So, really big?"

Cooper snickered. "No, MAJOR as in the acronym. Media And Journalism ORganization. Basically, another reason for a bunch of yuppies to go on a trip and write it off as a business expense."

Han grunted, then frowned. "Journalism? Are these going to be, like, reporters and newscasters and such?"

"We'll know in a minute."

They hopped out of the car as it came to a stop and hurried to the front doors. Several staff members were waving frantically to them. Han started developing a bad feeling. This was just a little too reminiscent of the Baptist-revival thing.

Before he could begin asking questions or even speak, one of the staffers launched into an explanation. The woman's eyes were wide with fright, or shock, or something. "It's not, I mean, no one's in danger. There's no one with a gun or any fights or—"

Han held up a hand to stop her. "Please take a breath, then start again. Exactly what are we here for?"

"They can't talk."

"Who can't talk?"

"The...the reporters. The people in the seminars."

Han and Cooper followed her as she led them to the convention area, the other staffers following in a gaggle. No one was saying anything, which was ominous. People were usually more than happy to kibbitz, but when they were really freaked out, they stopped commenting.

The staffer led them to one of the seminar rooms. It had been set up with rows of chairs and a raised stage with a lectern at the front. There was a projection screen with some written notes on display.

Han stopped and stared. The notes petered out partway down the page, the writing becoming more distorted until it was just a wavy line at the end. In the room, people were crying, some wailing; a few looked like they were in full-blown panic attacks. But no one was talking. No one was saying or yelling anything that even vaguely resembled words.

"Oh hell," he muttered. Then, tapping his badge, "Central, Officer Han 29211. We need medical and containment. I think this may be another bio-attack."

"Ten-four."

Cooper went up to one of the attendees and attempted to interrogate him. The man stared at her, panic on his face, and said something that was little more than an inarticulate howl. A woman rushed up to Han and, pointing at her throat, said something like, "Hah. Huh. Hah."

"They really can't talk," Cooper said.

Han raised a finger to the woman facing him, waited for her to focus on him, and said, "Please raise your right hand."

The woman frowned at Han and made a grimace as if Han had just spoken gibberish.

"So they also can't understand," Han said. "This is neurological, not physical." He turned to the attendant who had led them in. "Have they eaten or drunk anything here?"

"There was a catered lunch, about an hour ago."

"Is it still there?"

The woman frowned. "I think they're cleaning it up now."

"Stop them. Anything they've hauled out, bring it back. Leave everything alone, otherwise. This is now a crime scene. Do you understand?"

"Uh, yeah, I'll get on it," she replied and pulled out her phone.

Han put his hand on her hand. "No, go there. Make sure, personally. Seriously, this is critical."

***

A short while later, Han found himself on another chair, rolling up his sleeve once again, while a tech waved a needle at him. "Do I get a lollipop?" he asked.

"They haven't given out candy for blood donations for a long time, Officer," the woman said, dimpling. "And I doubt whole-wheat crackers went over well."

Han chuckled. "I miss chocolate-covered sugar bombs."

Cooper, one chair over, chimed in, "Chocolate anything at any time, thank you very much."

Once the blood draw was complete, Han asked the tech, "Has anyone made any determinations yet?"

She shook her head. "No, but they jumped right on your suggestion about the buffet. Dr. Clarkson said we should thank you for that."

"Clarkson? Really?" He remembered Clarkson from the stadium incident. At this rate, they'd be swapping old war stories in no time. Come to think of it, a doctor's perspective would be useful.

Han turned as he heard his name called. It was Lt. Mikelson, from the Terrorism Response Unit, striding toward him in a determined manner.

"Sir?"

"Good work on catching this right away, Han. We'll be taking over on the presumption that it's another attack—not much of a stretch, given the circumstances. As soon as you're given the green light, you can get back to regular duties."

"Yes, sir. I was just talking to, uh"—Han checked his heads-up—"Smithers here about the results from the buffet."

"Not your problem anymore, Officer. We'll be putting a lid on this one, given the way the Chicago Stadium event has blown up. There will be a press release at some point, and you'll hear about it then."

"Kind of ironic, given the venue," Smithers muttered.

Mikelson snorted, and Han bit back a laugh. She wasn't wrong. But it looked like Han was being shuffled out of the way again. This was surprisingly annoying. Han accepted that he was a beat cop. It was the job he had, and he honestly enjoyed it. But he'd always been intelligent and curious, and at one time, he had planned to go into medicine. Being brushed aside rankled.

As he and Cooper walked back to the patrol car, he thought of Dr. Hunt, whom he'd interviewed the other day. She *was* a medical doctor, and doing original research on a space-mining venture. It was the opposite end of the universe from him.

Han pulled out his phone, linked to the police database, and tapped the screen a few times. Yes, there was her contact information. Before he could think for too long on exactly what he was about to do, he pressed *dial.*

"Hello?"

"Dr. Hunt, it's Officer Han. I interviewed you on the fire at Derek McQuaid's house?"

"Yes, and we discussed mummification as a murder device. More follow-up, Officer?"

"Ah, no, not exactly. Are you up for a little more free consulting? It's interesting, I promise."

"Well, since you say *interesting*, by all means. Is this something new?"

"Very much so." Han spent a few moments describing the current incident. He was pretty sure he was contravening police policy, but on the other hand, she *was* a medical expert and had just agreed to do some consulting work. It was flimsy, but it was also a little late to back out without looking the total fool.

"That's, um...okay, Officer, when you use that word in the future, I will believe you."

"So is there anything you can add to this?"

"Of course, I can't give you a lot that's definitive over the phone without examining the patients, but I'd venture to guess that they have some kind of brain injury to Broca's area or Wernicke's area, or both. Probably both."

"Those have to do with speech?"

"Broca's is for speech. Wernicke's is for understanding language. You said they couldn't speak or understand you, right?"

"Yes. But what would cause that?"

"Were there any other symptoms?"

"Not that I could see."

A pause. "That means that probably *only* those areas were hit. They're close together, so it's not unreasonable, but the primary motor cortex extends between them. For that *not* to be affected, it has to be specifically targeted."

"Well, yes, I had assumed that—"

"I don't think you understand, Officer. Someone has engineered a virus or something specifically to attack a part of the brain. *Engineered.* This is biological warfare. I thought that was supposed to be tightly regulated." Again, a pause. "Any idea how it was introduced?"

"They think the food."

"Oh. That's more likely bacterial, then. Which is even weirder. Officer Han, I'm feeling a little over my head right now, doing this over the phone. But you've got a problem there. Make sure you kick your bosses around the ankles and knees if they don't pay enough attention."

Han chuckled. The thought of giving Mikelson a good kicking was, well, not unattractive. "I will certainly do that, Doctor. Thank you. I'll try not to bother you again."

"Unless it's *interesting*, Officer."

CHAPTER TWENTY-FIVE

Digging Deeper

Philip looked up from his notes at the sound of the knock to find Celia standing in his doorway. He sat back and sighed. He loved Celia dearly, but she still had her teeth into this whole Derek thing, and he just didn't have any more time to play detective.

"Well, nice to see you, too," Celia said, noting his reaction.

"Sorry, Celia. Really. But I'm six layers deep in electromagnetic field equations, and I just have this feeling that's not what you're here to talk about."

Her face fell at the rebuke, and Philip immediately felt like a heel. "Look, I obviously need a break. Let's head to the cafeteria."

Celia smiled and did an *after-you* move, and Philip slapped his tablet closed, relieved that he'd managed to mend things.

It was too early for lunch, but never too early for donuts. Philip grabbed a coffee and two long johns, and Celia selected an apple fritter.

"So what's new?" Philip said once they were seated.

Celia, instead of replying, took a big bite of fritter and started chewing, staring blankly at him. Philip couldn't help it; he burst out laughing. "Okay, serves me right. But just remember, I have *two* donuts. I can outlast you." And to illustrate, he took a huge chomp of a long john and began staring back at her, chewing dramatically.

Celia snorted, then choked and had to swallow. "Jerk," she said. Then, after a moment, "Okay. So you remember I found forty-seven Derek McQuaids nationally. Well, since we've run out of alternatives, I decided to do a process of elimination on them. I got a web agent to build dossiers of all mentions of Derek McQuaid and cross-reference them with the forty-seven hits I got on official records."

"But you can't be sure..." Philip said hesitantly.

"No, but it's a statistical thing. For instance, there's one Derek in Indiana who basically hasn't moved from his hometown his entire life. Birth records, school records, sports, job history, social media posts, it's all in Kokomo, Indiana."

"Seriously?" Philip interjected. "Like the Beach Boys song?"

"I really don't think this was the Kokomo they were referring to, no." Celia dimpled. "But he's got very recent posts as well. So he lives there, not here."

"It's not impossible..."

"But very low probability. Listen, I had the web agent do the grunt work, but I reviewed the data afterward. It did a pretty good job. Some were dead, some were too old, some had left the country, and so on. I've eliminated all but three Dereks."

"All but three. That's pretty good. So what about the finalists?"

"The finalists are there because they appear to still be alive, don't have a lot of internet presence, and all appear to be still in the US. But"—and she held up a dramatic finger—"one Derek in particular rings all the bells."

"Okay?"

"He'd be in his thirties now. He lived in Pocatello, Idaho; did very well in school; majored in computer science in college. Then spent three years in jail."

"For what?" Philip said, surprised.

"He hacked a local business and drained their accounts. It's hard to get a lot of detail, but I get the impression it was personal in some way. The court records were sealed. After he got out, he basically disappeared. And the kicker..."

"Yes?"

"He's also apparently an offliner. There are no pictures of him anywhere on social media. I did manage to locate one photo of him from his junior high yearbook." She turned her tablet to show Philip a picture of a smiling teenager with dark-red hair. He appeared to have two unequal-size ears, with almost no earlobe on the left.

"That...seems like a good fit," Philip said. "Congratulations, Detective Hunt. So what now?"

"Uh..." Celia looked crestfallen. "I'm not really sure. I mean, assuming I'm right to begin with. Do you want to take a trip to Idaho?"

"Gee, lemme think. How about *no*. So there's no payoff for all this legwork?"

"Well, it's a bargaining chip, I suppose. For the cops, I mean."

Philip nodded. "Okay, not wrong."

"Officer Han phoned me yesterday," Celia said, changing the subject.

"Oh. More interviews?"

"No, he wanted some free consulting."

"He has this pain right *here*"—Philip grabbed his shoulder—"when he—"

"Jerk. No, did you hear about the incident at the McCormick Convention Center?"

"Some kind of foodborne illness?"

"Yeah, a little more than that. It was some kind of bio-attack."

Philip's eyes bugged out. "Are you *shitting* me? And he told you this?"

"Consulting, remember? I'm actually straining confidentiality requirements by telling you about it."

"Well, thanks for that. We're both going to jail anyway, so why not?"

"Oh, hah hah. But Philip, it was a biological attack. You remember the tanker thing? And the Baptist thing at the stadium? Something's going on. I don't mind saying, I'm a little nervous."

"And all the mummified corpses. Can't forget that." Philip looked down at his coffee, which had gone cold. "I agree, Celia. Something's up. And for some reason, we're caught up in it."

CHAPTER TWENTY-SIX

Status Update

Officer Han sat down at the common-area work desk and tapped the activation button. The desk, recognizing his ID, woke up with his virtual workspace. Han opened his calendar and tapped on the meeting event. The screen in front of him lit up, showing four faces in their own windows, with the backgrounds blurred out per police policy.

In one window was his boss, Captain Horton. Next to that, Detective Shankar, and below them, the Chicago terrorism response team leader, Lt. Mikelson. The team, officially termed the Terrorism Response Unit, was known as TRU to the public. But in the locker room, they were often referred to derisively as Terrorists R Us.

The fourth window showed Han's own features, staring back at him. He liked to have his own feed visible during Zoom calls, just in case he had a booger on his face or something.

"Ah, Officer Han," said Detective Shankar. "Gang's all here. Shall we start?" There were nods all around, and Shankar added, "I called this meeting, so I'll chair, if that's okay with you, Captain?"

Horton nodded, then said, “Good job on a quick reaction and analysis at that convention thing, Han. But I think it pretty much puts the nail in the coffin of any hope that this isn’t a campaign of terrorism.”

“Officially,” Shankar cut in, “we are not yet ready to acknowledge terrorism, at least not publicly, and certainly not a single organization. But between us all here, yes, there is no doubt in my mind. We can wait for the wheels of government to slowly grind their way around to admitting it, or we can start doing something now.”

“And what do you suggest, Shankar?” Horton asked.

Shankar nodded to one side of his window, a useless and humorous gesture in a Zoom session, and replied, “Officer Han has been involved in several events involving presumptive terrorists, so I would suggest that he be seconded to the terrorism squad, at least on a part-time basis.”

“Now hold on, Shankar. He’s a beat cop. He doesn’t know anything about how our team works.” Mikelson seemed distinctly offended.

“Nevertheless, he accounted for himself well in the three cases he’s been involved with.”

“Wait, three?” Han said. “I know of the revival and the convention, but...”

“The interviews you did a while back for me. A couple of scientists from Astro Resources.” Shankar raised his eyebrows, and Han nodded, trying to project casual disinterest. Shankar couldn’t possibly know about his contacting Dr. Hunt on his own, and Han wasn't going to volunteer the information.

Shankar continued, "I believe that all these attacks are related to this group, Gen Omega, in some way, although the scientists are not involved except as bystanders and witnesses. But it's part of a pattern, and a disturbing one."

"Exactly what are you hinting at, Shankar?" Horton said.

"I believe a rogue aggy is involved. Most likely in the possession of the terrorist group."

"Oh my God," Horton said. Mikelson pinched the bridge of his nose and looked pained.

"Why?" Han asked.

"The planning. The efficiency of the execution. And most important"—Shankar held up a finger—"the nature of the attacks. These are high-tech weaponizations. A full biotech lab could do any of these things, but a full biotech lab would be hard to hide. Or to staff."

"Well, what's the alternative?" Horton asked.

"Biological fabrication using Venter forges. They—"

"No, sorry," Mikelson interjected. "I can't accept that. Biofabs don't have that level of capability. Even if they did, they're restricted technology. How would Gen Omega ever get hold of one in the first place?"

"You heard of the mummified bodies that we've been finding?" Shankar said. "We've managed to trace down how the active agent for that particular form of murder was created. Three different, apparently innocuous, synthetic biological agents were ordered from three different small-business forge owners. The outputs of those agents, when combined with a nonbiological agent ordered from a fab lab, produces a catalytic molecule that forces the water out of any biological tissue, forcefully and catastrophically."

Mikelson and Horton were dumbstruck. Han remembered what Dr. Hunt had said about the corpse. Apparently, she'd been right on the nose. She seemed to know her stuff.

Shankar said into the silence, "No human being could have designed the intermediate agents, brought them together, and used them to produce such a biological weapon. It's almost a fractal design, similar to DNA in overlapping and reentrant functionality. And all done via mail-order parts. No, gentlemen, we're dealing with a superintelligence of some kind. And it's not playing nice."

"So are you going to call in ATLAS?" Mikelson asked.

"I already have. I am a duly deputized ATLAS agent, in addition to my position as senior detective in charge of these cases. For the moment, I am holding that authority in reserve. However, I do have it."

"So was *that* the whole point of this meeting, to lay down the law?" Mikelson asked.

"Absolutely not, Lieutenant. I believe we will all be best served by a collaborative strategy. The ATLAS authority is available to us as a way to get things done and apply pressure as required. To my mind, the *only* metric that matters is successfully ending this campaign of terrorism and bringing Gen Omega to justice."

Horton nodded, apparently mollified. "Fair enough. Then let's get to it."

Mikelson was not so sanguine, though. "Shankar, if you want to make use of Officer Han, that's fine as long as the captain's okay with it. But I'm not going to take on the added headache of having to update an outsider. No offense, Han, but you don't have any training in this area."

"Jeb, we'll discuss this offline, shall we?" Horton interjected. "Meanwhile, I think we're done here."

Han sat back and pressed his palms together as if in prayer as the other windows closed on the Zoom session. He wasn't sure if it would ultimately be good for his career, but for better or worse, he'd just been tossed into the big time.

***

The captain tracked Han down after the meeting. "Simon, this is a complex situation."

"Having a rogue aggy involved with terrorists? Well, yeah..."

"Not that. That's a beast of its own, of course. But a little closer to home, Lieutenant Mikelson has thrown a fit about having to read you into his group."

"Wonderful. So you want me to step back?"

"No. You seem to have established some kind of inside line with an ATLAS operative. That's not an insignificant accomplishment. It can't help but look good for the department."

"Assuming things work out successfully."

"Yes, well, if they don't, I'm afraid there will be more than enough fertilizer to go around. The good news, though, is that the FBI and NSA and such will likely take the brunt of the blame for any failures."

"While successes..."

"Exactly. Do your best work, Officer. Ignore Mikelson, and I imagine he'll do his best to ignore you. For purposes of your work for and with Detective Shankar, you can consider yourself to be on independent duty, seconded to ATLAS. But if you need support from Mikelson, route it through me."

Han waited until the captain was walking away, then rolled his eyes and muttered, "Outstanding."

***

After lunch, Han sat again at the shared workstation and waited for it to recognize him. As soon as his desktop was active, he pulled up the database.

If Han was going to be pulled into the investigation by Shankar, he wasn't going to settle for just being a gopher. The first thing he needed to do was bring himself up to speed on *all* the pertinent info.

He couldn't suppress a smirk. As rationalizations went, it wasn't terrible, but he couldn't kid himself that this was purely professional curiosity. The question, of course, was whether Shankar had done the paperwork for his promotion yet.

A few seconds' search, and he had the file for the mummified body. It was flagged for senior staff only, which he'd expected. But if he had that ATLAS authorization, he might be able to—yes, the file opened for him. Han took a moment to simply enjoy that feeling of power. He was no longer, at least for now, a beat cop who could be shut out of all the interesting stuff.

He pulled up the forensic results and paged through them. Nope, organs not removed.

"You ready to go?" Cooper's voice startled him, and he actually jumped in his seat. "That looked like guilt, Simon. What'cha up to?"

Han turned to her. "Sort of, but I'm apparently now ATLAS authorized, so it's more like imposter syndrome."

"Well, we are moving up in the world, aren't we? Do I have to salute now?" Cooper looked past him at the monitor. "Ewww. I hate autopsies. What are you looking for, anyway?"

"I don't know. I was just a little PO'd when I got pushed off this case. Gimme five minutes, okay? I'll bring you up to date on everything."

"Sure thing. I need another donut anyway."

"Because that's not a cliché." Han turned back to the monitor.

The forensics were interesting, but what he really wanted to see was the information on the means of death. Three compounds delivered to an address. They'd interviewed the recipient, and she had been cooperative. She'd been hired as a temp, given some instructions, followed those instructions, and gotten paid, plus a bonus. The cops had determined that she was an unwitting accomplice, and that was that.

Damn. Dead end, it looked like. He scrolled a little farther. Payment made by...wait a minute! Derek McQuaid? Wasn't that the guy whose house burned down?

Something was fishy. It was a truism in law enforcement that there were no coincidences.

Cooper called out to him, so he acknowledged her with a wave and closed down the session. But this would need to be followed up.

CHAPTER TWENTY-SEVEN

An Unexpected Visit

Philip dragged his exhausted butt into the house, muttering, "Home program" into the air. God, he needed a drink. He dropped his briefcase, hung his coat, then turned to head for the kitchen just as a voice said, "We meet again, Mr. Bond."

Philip jerked his head up, his fatigue evaporating in a surge of adrenaline. Sitting in Philip's easy chair was a total stranger, casually pointing a gun. The man appeared to be mid-thirties; had not-quite-red hair; and had two uneven ears, the left one of which had almost no lobe.

"Please sit down, Dr. Moray," the man continued. He motioned slightly with the gun to emphasize that the request was non-optional.

Philip sat. "Bond? Is this supposed to be a spy thing? I'm a scientist. Are you sure—"

The man cut him off. "I know all about you, Doctor. Sorry about the Bond comment. I've got a thing for old movies." He paused. "I'm here because you have something of mine."

"And that is?" Philip had a bad feeling that he knew, but best not to assume. The man might be testing Philip to see how much he knew.

"My last notebook, of course. You've visited my townhouse. Don't play dumb with me, Doc."

"You're Derek? I thought you were dead."

"You mean the corpse? Yeah, that was freaky-looking, wasn't it? That was one of my erstwhile customers, who came to *motivate* me"—Derek made air quotes with his free hand around the word—"to produce results in a more timely manner. We were having a discussion of schedules that involved something about broken fingers as a motivational tool just before he, ah..." Derek made a helpless gesture.

"You didn't do that?"

"No, although I did ask my experimental aggy for suggestions when Bluto came a'knocking, so that's probably who did it. But I have no idea how, other than that he slapped his neck just before he collapsed. I don't mind telling ya, I was freaked. I thought I had the AI properly sandboxed, so when I realized it could reach into the physical world, I lit out of there so fast, I blueshifted. Honestly, I've been scared to go back. I was surprised that you and your girlfriend—"

"*Not* my girlfriend."

"Don't care. How you and your *friend who is a girl* managed to get in and out without getting caught or killed. By now, both my ex-clients *and* ATLAS investigators should be all over the place. I'm still trying to figure out that part."

"Well, why'd you leave your notebook?"

"I grabbed all of them when I left. Or so I thought. I *was* in kind of a hurry. But it turned out one was missing. The most important one, with all my recent passwords and accounts and business contacts. I was going back for it, trying to figure out if I dared to just walk into the place, when the two of you showed up. Imagine my surprise when you walked out with it and drove away like you were going for Sunday brunch."

"You couldn't use, oh, I don't know, a computer for your notes?"

Derek smirked. "And put stuff online? Oh, hell no. If there's anyone on this planet who knows how unsafe that is, it's *moi*. We have a phrase in the business: *air gap*. Refers to any setup that requires you to have physical access to get at the information. Turns out the old ways are best, sometimes."

"Did you burn down your own house?"

Derek looked momentarily surprised. "No, why would I do that? I have no clue who did. I was kinda thinking for a while that you did it."

Philip leaned forward. "Mr. McQuaid, everyone seems to think I'm some kind of player. Please listen carefully. I'm a scientist. An experimental physicist. I do physics, and I do it well. But I am not a secret agent. I'm totally out of my depth here and have been since the flybot dropped out of the air in my lab. So why don't you tell me what you want, and speak slowly. Use small words. I promise you I don't care enough to want to stymie you or anything else that would require you to use that gun."

Now Derek smiled. "Flybot. Nice. And that's probably all true. But not relevant, unfortunately. Just based on what you've said, you'll spill the beans to anyone who asks. And I prefer to remain dead." He waved the gun again. "And don't get any ideas about being defiant or having nothing to lose. There are a lot of ways I can shoot you that will hurt like hell and take hours to die from."

Philip allowed his face to express alarm but remained leaning forward. Threats or not, he was dead if he did nothing, and if the chance presented itself, he would go for it. "So what do you want from me?"

"The. Note. Book. Did I stutter before? Where is it?"

"Damned if I know. I got broken into the other day, and it was stolen. And *only* the notebook was stolen. Someone knew what it was, where it was, and wanted it specifically. Someone who isn't you, I'm guessing."

"I have a pretty good idea who that might be, actually," Derek said, breaking into a smile. "Someone at JCN."

"You mean the person who printed all the extra chips for you? I wouldn't depend on them for any future help." It was a total bluff, but what the heck.

And it worked.

Derek's face went ashen, and he blurted out, "Jacques? What have they—" Derek's eyes narrowed.

"Yeeeeeah, nice move. You're not as clueless as you like to make out. Well, all the more reason not to leave you alive, smart-ass."

"Why are you doing this, Derek? I mean, above and beyond the money. I assume there's money involved. But what's the game?" Philip made a shooing motion. "If I'm going to die, there's no harm in telling me, and you get to do a bit of monologuing."

Derek laughed, a full-throated guffaw. "Nice reference. *The Incredibles.* Here's one for you: 'Everyone's a hero in their own story.'"

"*Jack the Giant Slayer.* Stanley Tucci's character. Although I don't think he quite came out and said it that way."

Derek nodded, a smile still on his face. "Okay, Phil, you've earned some info. Ask a question."

"What business are you really in? I assume the video-production thing is a front."

"An astute assumption, my friend. Video production, especially generation of realistic CGI scenes, requires some high-end equipment—the kind of equipment that has to be registered and will attract the attention of ATLAS auditors if you don't have a good reason for it."

"So that's why you swapped the guts with the equipment in your townhouse?"

"Yup. If I ever got a visit from an auditor—statistically unlikely, but you never know—I have all the paperwork for a profitable business. Customers, expenses, projects...all bogus, of course. There are companies that specialize in creating audit trails that will survive scrutiny."

"So...your real business?"

"All things computer. I am a hacker and programmer *par excellence*. That's how I was able to get into your house, by the way." Derek waved a hand and looked around, and Philip almost jumped at him, but Derek refocused too quickly.

"So recently," Derek continued, oblivious to the momentary danger, "I was approached by a group who wanted an off-the-books aggy. They promised to finance the entire operation *and* pay a gratifyingly large sum on successful completion."

"The Q-32 chips. A couple hundred?"

Derek blinked. "You really do know a lot. And yet, at the same time, are completely clueless." He smiled again. "I already had a business connection with Jacques, who could supply the chips. But to answer the implied question, no, I didn't need two hundred chips for this client. Maybe twenty to thirty. But within a short time, I had several more orders. So I expanded the deal with Jacques to ensure an ongoing supply."

Derek paused, then smirked. "One of the things I've long since learned is that for most people, their only loyalty is to money and power. People like you, to be honest, make me nervous. You have, like, actual scruples. It's weird."

"I'll take that as a compliment," Philip said. "So you're a general-purpose hacker for hire. And now you're risking an ATLAS prosecution by trying to build an aggy. I'll give you this much, you think big." Philip thought for a moment, then continued, "So what happened at the townhouse?"

"Uh-uh. My turn. Try this one: 'Shall we play a game?'"

"*WarGames.* Your computer voice is terrible, though."

Derek nodded, smiling again. Apparently, he enjoyed this game. He eyed Philip expectantly, and Philip realized he needed to supply a quote. He thought fast. "'I bought the bank. It's like a reflex with me.'"

"*Justice League.* Bruce Wayne. Too easy." Derek paused. "Regarding your comment, I've already built and delivered several small aggies. Nothing terribly consequential, but illegal, of course. The Q-32 chip allows you to build them like tiny Lego blocks and snap them together for bigger brains, so I can customize the size of the aggy to the customer's requirements. Things were going well, until I got a large batch from Jacques. I admit, I succumbed to my curiosity and connected a bunch together. It, well...it acted different. I got caught up in, dare I say it, pure research and missed some deadlines. Not a good idea with my class of customers. When Bluto showed up, I knew I was in trouble. I pretended to pull up my schedule and typed in a request to the aggy for suggestions or help; otherwise, we'd both be toast. Next thing I know, Bluto is making a choking sound and turning into a mummy."

Derek paused again. "After I left, I kept watch on the townhouse, trying to decide if I dared enter, so I was really surprised when the two of you went in, came out, and drove away without getting challenged. Or dying. I thought at first *you* were investigators. Except you... took the birdcage?"

Philip snorted. "Yeah, we're real secret agents. So what was with the flybot in my lab?"

Instead of answering, Derek made a *come-on* motion with his free hand. Philip rolled his eyes, then thought fast. "'Yippy-kai-yay, motherf—'"

"No," Derek interjected. "At least *try*, ferchrissake. Or I shoot you now."

Philip grinned at him. He hadn't really expected to get away with that one and was simply trying to delay. But Derek's reaction *was* funny.

"Okay, uh..." Philip paused. "'Well, I *was* born yesterday.'"

Derek frowned, thought for a few seconds, then snapped his fingers. "Vision. *Age of Ultron*. Almost had me, buddy. Your question?"

"Flybot in my lab?"

"Oh, right. Uh..." Derek looked embarrassed. "I honestly have no idea. I didn't build it or arrange for it to be there. I mean, I have no interest in you or your work, other than for my notebook. The basic design sounds like one of my units, except I absolutely never would have created anything mobile, let alone with wings. I grabbed it from your office when I was searching for the notebook, but I haven't had a chance to take a close look at it."

"Ah. Okay, um... Next question... Why did you drain the accounts of that business in your hometown?"

Derek's face turned into a mask. He stared at Philip silently for several seconds, then said, "Fuck you." Evidently winning some internal struggle, he raised the gun. "Time's up. I've enjoyed this. Really. But I've got a criminal empire to run. Miles to go, promises to keep, blah blah. I guess Boojee will need a new owner again."

"Boojee?"

"The budgie." Derek made a vague gesture toward the kitchen, where Oppenheimer was chortling away.

"Boojee the budgie?" Philip said, his jaw dropping. "You couldn't do better than that?"

"Well, uh..." Derek frowned. "Honestly, I'm not much of a bird person. I'm still not entirely sure why I bought him. Protective coloration, I guess. But he seems happy here. Maybe your girlfriend can take him."

With that, Derek steadied the gun, and Philip gathered himself to, well, do something. He wasn't just going to sit still for being shot.

Then Derek jerked, slapped his neck, and said, "Ow, fuck." He pulled his hand back and looked at it, and an expression of fear passed over his face. "Oh no," he said.

"Why...what..." Derek dropped the gun and straightened in the chair like he was trying to lie down. Then he grabbed his chest and started shaking, making a gargling sound.

As Philip watched, Derek began to shrink. Or deflate. It was hard to describe but looked like what happened to people in the movie *Lifeforce*. In a few moments, Derek was reduced to a mummy, virtually identical to the one they'd found in the townhouse. The air in the room suddenly felt like summer in Florida, and there was a whooshing sound as the house air-conditioning kicked into max to compensate. Philip stared blankly at the corpse for some undefined duration, his mind totally locked up.

Finally, Philip's brain rebooted, and he roused himself from his paralysis. He rose slowly from his seat and looked carefully around the room. No assassins presented themselves, but Derek hadn't just spontaneously combusted for fun. Someone or something had done that. Had killed Derek, in Philip's living room, right in front of him. Seeing no obvious explanations, Philip pulled a set of tongs from a kitchen drawer and carefully pincered Derek's non-gun hand, then turned it over. In the center of the palm was... Philip squinted and looked closer. It was the wreck of a flybot. Or something very similar.

Philip stared at the corpse stretched out on his living room furniture. This was going to take some explaining.

***

Philip pushed the buzzer on Celia's apartment building entrance for the third time. What was taking so long? She rarely went out on weeknights, except—

"God's sake, Philip," her voice said from the intercom. "It's not a video-game controller. At least give me time to get up off the couch." The front door buzzed as Celia released the door lock.

In a few moments, Philip was in front of Celia's apartment door. She opened it and started to say, "What gives with—" Then she saw his expression. "Philip? Oh my God, what's wrong?"

She grabbed his arm and pulled him into the apartment, then pushed him toward the couch.

"Okay, bud. Talk. You look like you've seen a ghost."

"Not far wrong," Philip said, his head finally starting to feel less cottony. "I just watched someone die."

Celia's eyes narrowed momentarily. "I guess that explains the expression. More words, please."

Philip described what had just happened in his house. "I think I went into shock," he said at the end. "I called a traxi and came over here. I should have called first, sorry."

Celia gave him an affectionate smile. "It's okay, Philip. I think we can agree that this isn't normal. Have you phoned the cops?"

Philip goggled at her. "Are you kidding? How would I explain this?"

"Guy broke in. Guy threatened you. Guy died."

"By unknown means, after demanding the return of a notebook that I stole from his townhouse while breaking and entering, and without reporting a corpse that I found there that was also mummified."

"Well, I found the first corpse, but I get the point. They might have questions."

Philip let out one short, sharp bark of a laugh. "I don't know what to do at this point."

"Well, let's go back to your place and review. Maybe something will come to mind."

The traxi ride was spent in total silence. Philip still felt like he had just come down from a bad high of some kind, and Celia seemed inclined to let him handle it.

They arrived at Philip's house and went into the living room, where they found...nothing.

"What...what..." Philip sputtered. He pointed at the easy chair. "He was sitting right there. It..." Philip turned to Celia, panic on his face. "Celia, I didn't imagine it."

"It's okay, Philip, I believe you. It's not like nothing else weird has been happening. Ask the house SPI."

Philip nodded and felt himself calming at this simple suggestion. "House, what happened to the person who was sitting across from me earlier?"

"You accompanied them to the door."

"I—what? When?"

"Ten point five minutes ago."

Philip looked at his watch. "Your place and back is fifteen minutes. Not counting the time I spent freaking out in your living room. That's...not possible."

Celia looked around the room. "Someone else did it, then hacked your house."

"Why?"

"Well, there's a question for you." She turned to him. "Still think you're just a physicist? We're in this up to the armpits, Philip. Someone just died in your house. That's—"

"Someone was just *killed* in my house. Then removed. Whatever you were going to say, it's way worse than that. Now should we phone the cops?"

"It will have to come out that this is the guy we were trying to visit the other day. Then he visited you—broke into your house, as a matter of fact—and died. No, was killed in a most dramatic and unusual manner. Then, like you say, disappeared. Somehow, I don't think Shankar is going to accept our assurances that we're just innocent bystanders. I see a dark room in our futures, with a light shining in our eyes and voices demanding explanations while rubber hoses get slapped into open palms."

"Well, these days—"

"Cops still don't trust SPI facial and voice analysis, Philip. It's more dependable than polygraphs ever were, which is ironic because the cops always placed a lot of faith in those things. But no, they'll still try to sweat the truth out of us."

"But right at this moment, as bad as it may look, we have not broken any laws. Today, anyway."

"Two counts of breaking and entering. Theft of the notebook. I'm sure there are some statutes about not reporting the corpse in the townhouse, which we discovered while breaking, entering, and stealing. Armpits, I said, and armpits it is. So we either keep digging to try to figure this out, or we throw ourselves on the doubtful mercy of ATLAS and the cops."

Philip sighed. "I'm out of ideas."

CHAPTER TWENTY-EIGHT

Always on the Clock

We interrupt *regular programming to bring you this special report. A release sent to this station and other major broadcasters by what purports to be a spokesperson for Gen Omega is claiming responsibility for the Chicago Stadium and McCormick Convention Center incidents, calling them "just retribution."*

Regarding the Chicago Stadium attack, the statement reads, "The Orwell Baptist Church has been celebrating their victories in supporting rampant capitalism at any cost. What's a celebration without a little dancing?" As for the McCormick attack, it says, "Journalists and media personalities have been silent for too long on the dangers and consequences of the continued desecration of the planet. They have become complicit."

The statement's authenticity has been confirmed by the FBI...

Simon Han stared at the TV for a moment, then shook his head. It appeared that Gen Omega loved their irony. A forced dance for a religious group that considered it sacrilegious, and loss of language for journalists.

Fortunately, in both cases, the conditions were temporary. The Baptists were no longer dancing, and the journalists had recovered their speech in a few hours. But for the duration of the effect, it must have been chilling. Based on that, Gen Omega had probably succeeded in its main goal, which was to make a point. He doubted members of either group would soon forget the experience.

Simon looked over at Brenda, who had stopped what she was doing to listen to the news as well. "You know if you get killed on the job," she said, glaring at him, "I'll dig you up and kill you again myself."

He laughed, and she lost the glare, smiling back at him. It was an old joke between them, the type of thing only a cop and their spouse would understand. "Gonna do my best to avoid that," he replied.

Come to think of it, now that he was a part-time ATLAS agent, he should be able to access the confidential-level information on the cases. This *ATLAS-agent* stuff definitely had its upsides.

***

Han's shift the next day passed at a crawl. He had filed his daily reports, and he was now technically off shift, but he wasn't quite ready to go home. He'd have to make sure not to go too far down the rabbit hole, though, or Brenda would be annoyed.

He had submitted some queries and wanted to check up on the results. The first was on Derek McQuaid. *Oh, hell. Forty-seven of them?* Well, probably not surprising—it wasn't *that* unusual of a name.

He started up a web agent to try to trim the number down. He would—wait, that was odd. The web agent already had some queries ready. Were they mind readers now? Han sat back, perplexed, staring at the screen. This usually meant that someone else had done the same thing. The web agents shared search databases unless they were marked confidential. All cop searches were confidential by default, so whoever had searched out Derek McQuaid was not a cop.

Okay, file that for later, Han thought. *For now, let's see what was found.* Han went through the obvious steps, filtering and refining his dataset. In very little time, he was left with one Derek McQuaid from Pocatello, Idaho. Offliner, apparently, which fit.

His phone buzzed with a text, and Han read it from his heads-up. From Brenda.

You haven't left yet, have you?

Oh, hell. Han quickly saved his session, then bolted for the exit.

***

"I mean, it could be worse," Brenda said over dinner. "You could be at a sting, or stakeout, or shootout, or whatever it is. Being late because you were sitting at the computer too long is *way* down on the danger list."

Simon grinned. "Ow, my wrist. Carpal tunnel!"

Brenda laughed, and the conversation shifted to other matters. Simon knew Brenda worried more than she let on, and he always did everything he could to minimize that concern.

He cleared the table afterward, since Brenda had cooked tonight, then grabbed his laptop and joined her in the living room. Brenda was addicted to soaps and always recorded them to watch in the evenings. Simon's job was to shut up and not distract her, so he took the opportunity to get extra work done. Or to watch YouTube. Whichever.

As soon as Brenda was properly immersed in *The Edge of the World*, or *As the Night Turns*, or whatever it was, he logged into work and pulled up his saved session.

Derek McQuaid had run afoul of the law and had spent three years in the slammer. Interestingly, the records were sealed to the public. That seemed odd for what appeared to be a simple white-collar larceny case.

A little more digging netted a codefendant—Carl Wright. He was charged but not convicted, possibly because of a plea deal, or...

Or possibly because his father was the assistant police chief. Holy hell. Han kept digging deeper, and the more he dug, the fishier it got.

Finally, he looked up and muttered, "This guy was set up."

"What?" Brenda replied, turning from the TV.

"Oh, sorry, love, talking out loud." He pointed to his laptop. "I think this guy was framed."

Brenda pointed to the TV. "Susan Janson, the CEO of Apex Cosmetics, is being framed, too. By her second ex-husband's secret love child's half-brother."

He grinned at her, then typed some more.

It appeared, reading between the lines, that Carl may have set Derek up as a patsy. Or his father did. Han did a quick search of the elder Wright. Deceased. Okay, how about the younger?

Carl Wright. Chief of security at JCN. In Chicago. That was stretching coincidence to the breaking point.

Something was up. Did Doctors Hunt and Moray know any of this about Derek? They said they hadn't even met him. But then who had done the prior search on Derek?

Han saved the session and closed his laptop. Curiouser and curiouser.

CHAPTER TWENTY-NINE

Back to Work

The restoration crew had finally finished all the repairs at his office, and Philip's home was back to normal. Which brought up an interesting question. Derek had copped to the office break-in, but he had flat out stated that he didn't do the home break-in. Which really made sense, since he would then have the notebook and wouldn't have needed to come back. So if Derek hadn't broken into Philip's home, who had? This Jacques character? Or one of Derek's erstwhile clients, perhaps?

Philip slowly swirled his glass of Jameson as he thought through the ramifications. Derek was dead; that was beyond doubt—Philip had seen him die. But his corpse had also disappeared while Philip was on his panicked sprint to Celia's home. He still felt embarrassed about that. Philip wasn't the best in stressful situations, but it felt like he'd hit a new low. On the other hand, someone had just died in his living room, so he should be able to cut himself *some* slack, at least.

So who had killed Derek? And who had taken the body? The only choices he could see were JCN or someone associated with Derek. JCN only made sense if they were trying to bump him off, but they missed and hit Derek, which seemed like a stretch. He still thought JCN might be after him and Celia, but this incident didn't fit.

That left Derek's associates, both present and past. One of them might have seen him and Celia enter and leave the townhouse. Why they hadn't jumped in at that point was an unknown. Perhaps they were scared of being seen on surveillance? Seemed like a long shot. If the cops were aware of this situation, they'd already be taking things apart. There was no subtlety when ATLAS edicts were at issue.

Philip finished off his drink, then sighed. There really wasn't much else he could do without more information. Meanwhile, he had a job. And everything was finally back together at work as well, so today, he had returned to his regular duties. At last, some good old-fashioned, dull routine. Adventure was absolutely overrated, and people like Celia could have it. Time to shift gears.

He got up and poured another glass, despite his one-per-night rule. Today had been frustrating. He was positive that an electromagnetic solution would net the broadest cross section of metal-detection capabilities. That required an extremely focused, intense, microsecond EMP. He had his current job with Astro Resources because he'd successfully pitched the idea. And it all made wonderful sense, except that it didn't work. What was he missing?

He was rapidly approaching that event horizon that all researchers faced, when management went from having faith that you would deliver to having doubts about their hiring decision. And as with a black hole, once he passed that horizon, there was no climbing out.

Philip picked up his laptop and started pulling up the various professional publishing forums that he subscribed to. But there was nothing new on any of them. In desperation, or maybe just to take a break, he did a Google search for anything to do with electromagnetic effects. And got lots of hits.

Electromagnetism was easy fodder for quack science, and it showed. Philip chuckled several times as he scanned through page after page of dramatic claims—everything from perpetual motion machines to antigravity to reactionless drives.

He stopped on a link to a YouTube video that purported to be an animation of a rotating EM field. Well, that could be interesting, if nothing else. He pulled it up and watched the short video. The animation looked for all the world like an airplane propeller. Interesting. You could combine the detection capabilities from the EM field expanding and contracting with induced current in the target material created by moving the field across it.

Philip stared into space. It was junk science, really. But there might be a grain of truth in there somewhere. He finished his drink absentmindedly while planning test scenarios for tomorrow at the lab.

CHAPTER THIRTY

Connections

The next day, Philip attacked his tasks at work with a renewed sense of purpose, and the time passed quickly. Midway through the morning, he looked up from his tablet to see Celia standing at the door to his office. She was holding her own tablet, and she had that look. Philip had come to recognize that look. It was the expression of a cat that's just found the mouse.

"Do you ever work?" he asked.

"My job's a lot of *hurry up and wait*," she replied. "Every time I send in a mod request for one of my bacteria, it's a couple of hours to a day before I get a result. I can only multitask so much."

"Sounds like you're in management."

"If that was the case, I'd play a better game of golf."

He smiled and folded his tablet. "So what huge discovery have you made today?"

"What makes you think—oh, never mind. My poker face sucks." She waved her tablet. "I was doing some more research on Derek McQuaid while waiting for results."

"And?"

"Interesting thing. I'm not sure if it's significant, but..." She slid into the guest chair in front of Philip's desk. "Derek was in college the same years as this guy." She showed Philip a picture of a couple of guys smiling for the camera and raising beer steins. One of them was clearly a younger Derek. The other person, Philip didn't recognize.

"Okay, and?"

"His name is Carl Wright. They were apparently friends. Carl was also an IT major."

"Still not seeing the point."

Celia tapped the picture of Carl. "This guy works for JCN. He's their chief of security."

"How do you know that?"

"He's senior management, Philip. It's on JCN's web page."

"All right, a guy who graduated IT ended up in security. It's not a total stretch. It's kind of a coincidence, but so what?"

"Remember Derek spent three years in prison? Guess who else was charged but never went to trial?" Celia tapped the picture again. "And then left town. I still haven't gotten details about what they did, but it looks like Carl flipped, and Derek took the fall."

"How did you find this out? I thought the records were sealed."

"Internet Archive. The Wayback Machine."

"You've got to be kidding me. They didn't scrub the archives?"

"They scrubbed the justice system URLs. I'm sure that's standard practice. But they didn't scrub third-party references. Someone would have to do a search, then get separate subpoenas, and no one's being paid to go into that level of detail."

"Okay, so you're a master internet detective. What do we conclude from this?"

"I think Carl did Derek a dirty. And I think Derek was planning some kind of revenge. Not sure what, but I'd bet money on it."

"Hmm, I wonder if we should mention this to Buto."

Celia cocked her head. "I'm not sure whose side she'd be on, Philip. For all we know, Carl could be a model employee but with a dark past."

"Well then, is there anything we *can* do with this?"

"I'm going to keep digging. Maybe something will fall out."

CHAPTER THIRTY-ONE

Public Intoxication

The party was in full swing. The American Motors staff picnic was always a big deal, and this year, they'd outdone themselves. The event, open to all head office, factory, and dealership employees, needed a large venue, and AMC always obliged. Several acres of Rouge Park had been roped off and fenced with the blessing of the city, thanks to a sizeable donation to the mayor's campaign fund. Security personnel stood at every entrance, diligently checking anyone trying to enter. There had already been almost a dozen altercations with failed gate-crashers and fence-climbers. The automobile company had made it clear to the security firms that they would provide unlimited legal support for any lawsuits brought against security personnel while doing their jobs, and even the protesters outside the fences were maintaining a respectful distance.

AMC, reincorporated in the late twenties, had as its stated goal the continued existence of the classic American car, gas engine and all. The AMC executive team was pugilistic, confrontational, and unapologetic about the company's philosophy and utilized every legal tactic to delay or circumvent environmental regulations. They'd lost ground to the traxi companies in the cities but still held sway in some suburban and most rural areas, where traxis weren't yet economical.

The guests were, as usual, partying hard. Being part of such a contrarian company required a certain level of curmudgeonliness, and the AMC employees were determined to project their defiance to the world.

An impromptu soccer game was in full swing at one end of the fenced-off park area, with onlookers on the sidelines cheering on both sides indiscriminately and waving plastic cups and bottles in the air enthusiastically.

Sherri Austin staggered off the field, wheezing and pressing one hand to her stomach. She waved for a sub to replace her with the other hand as she bent over to catch her breath. Her father, laughing, came over to offer her a bottle of water.

***

Manny Hoskins, the man in charge of logistics for the annual event, looked up to see Steve Austin from Sales stomping in his direction, and Steve looked pissed. Manny had lots of experience dealing with Steve. A great individual when things were going well, but volatile when not. Manny waved his assistant off with a final instruction about the buffet setup just as Steve arrived.

"What the hell, Manny?" Steve fairly yelled, not even bothering with a lead-in courtesy. "My daughter is *drunk*. She swears she hasn't been sneaking any beers, so someone's been spiking something. Don't you have security?"

Manny frowned. "Not possible, Steve. Everything comes to us sealed. The catering people are used to watching for that kind of thing, and they have instructions to call security if someone tries something."

"Well, Sherri got some alcohol from *somewhere*, dammit, and she's not lying to me."

"Are you sure, Steve? I mean *really*? She's a teenager—"

"Yeah, I know, but she's *scared*, Manny. People who sneak beers don't get *scared* when they get drunk. That's the whole idea when you're a teenager."

"Huh." Manny had to admit, Steve had a point. He was about to respond when another person came up and cut in.

"Someone's spiking the punch," she said. "Or the water. Or something. My husband is tipsy, and Andrew doesn't drink."

Now Manny was getting nervous. This shouldn't be happening. He'd had this discussion with the catering companies. With the number of families here, people with children, any kind of spiking would be a disaster. He started to reply, "I undershtand, Miz Simpson, we habn't...we hammn't..."

Everyone was looking at him with shocked expressions. At least he thought they were. Things were getting blurry. Manny hadn't been drunk since he was a teenager, and he'd vowed to never again touch alcohol.

Manny looked blearily around at his audience, felt himself start to tilt, and threw up on Steve's shoes.

***

Simon Han turned slowly, letting his gaze sweep across the fenced-off area. He tried and, he thought, managed to appear calm and business-like, but inside, he was seething. A week ago, he'd been a beat cop. Okay, a senior beat cop, but still. Now he was an ATLAS investigator, too, and it seemed like that part of his job was getting busier. Jeez.

He'd gotten a call midday from Central, telling him to head back to HQ, where a chopper was waiting to take him to Detroit. Seems Shankar had deputized him in absentia. Now he stood, 300 miles away, trying to figure out how several hundred people had gotten drunk.

Okay, for some of them, it was pretty straightforward. Many of the victims smelled like breweries and were quite candid about their level of consumption. Proud of it, in some cases.

But kids...teetotalers...some with religious proscriptions...even a couple of people with health issues that made any kind of alcoholic consumption dangerous if not potentially lethal. One of those people was now in the ICU, although she was expected to pull through.

On a whim, he pulled out his phone and dialed Dr. Hunt.

"Celia here. I take it you have something *interesting*, Officer Han?"

"You could say that. This will be on a consulting basis again, right?"

"You bet. Give."

Han spent a few seconds updating her on what he was observing. When he was done, she said, "Wow, that sounds like auto-brewery syndrome. But that takes days to manifest."

"Auto. Brewery? You're gonna have to give me a little more detail."

A laugh at the other end. "Yeast or sometimes bacteria in the gut start fermenting intestinal contents and producing alcohol. All the joys of drinking without the expense of buying drinks."

"This is a thing?"

"It certainly is. Although again, this seems like an extremely fast onset."

"So again, possibly engineered."

"That would be the way to bet."

"Thanks, Doc. Listen, next time, I'm going to try to get you on the payroll."

"Don't take this the wrong way, Officer, but I'd rather there didn't have to be a next time."

"Me too. But it's not looking that way."

Han said goodbye, then marched up to a technician who was doing technician things with the food and drink. "Found anything?"

The tech turned to Han, and his heads-up displayed her name and job info. And her heads-up undoubtedly showed his authorization to her, because she shrank back slightly. ATLAS really was the boogeyman to most people, Han thought.

Finding her voice, the woman said, "Nothing so far. I mean, the stuff that is supposed to be alcoholic contains alcohol, of course, but nothing's been spiked. There are a few small positives, probably from accidental spillage, but there's not even so much as a beer's worth out of place."

"There must be something to cause this. Can you see anything out of the ordinary?"

The woman looked down at her tablet for a moment and frowned. "Well, I am getting what looks like indications of spoilage, which seems odd. This stuff is all fresh. I can't see the caterers bringing in expired food for a big client like AMC, you know?"

"Spoilage? How do you measure that?"

"Well, bacteria levels, of course. Although these aren't reading as the types you normally get with food that's been left out too long. It's kinda weird."

Han stared past her, his eyes narrowing. Once again, Dr. Hunt had called it. "Do you have a doctor here I can talk to?"

The tech tapped her badge. "Central, page Dr. Nolan."

A moment later, the badge said, "Nolan here."

"Dr. Nolan, this is Mitzi Nadividad over at the buffet line. Can you come over here for a moment?"

"I'm busy with patients. Can it wait?"

"Doctor, I have an ATLAS investigator with me, and he wants to talk to you."

"Fine."

Han detected movement out of the corner of his eye and turned to see an older woman marching in his direction, annoyance clear in her gait, based on the way she was driving her heels into the turf. She arrived in moments. "Make it quick, please," she said to Han, ignoring Nadividad.

Han smiled. This woman was *not* intimidated by the ATLAS credentials. Looking at her expression, he speculated that she would face off against Godzilla and give him a piece of her mind. "Doctor, have you heard of auto-brewery syndrome?"

"Of course I have. I'm a doctor. It's a condition where ethanol is produced through endogenous fermentation by fungi or bacteria in the gastrointestinal system... Oh." Nolan's expression showed surprise as the penny dropped for her. "Interesting. Fits the observations."

She straightened and faced Han directly, her demeanor changing. "I can test for that. Thank you, Detective, uh…" The doctor looked at Han's clothing and badge, clearly that of a front-line cop, and also clearly at odds with the credentials that must have been showing in her heads-up.

"It's Officer Han, and it's a long story. Thank you, Doctor Nolan. Can you cc me on any progress and determinations, please?"

Nolan nodded to him and turned away. Han nodded to the technician, then pulled out his phone again. This was going to be one for the books.

***

Han walked out of the hangar just as his squad car pulled up with Cooper inside. The door opened and he got in, and the car was moving again before he'd even gotten settled.

"What, are we in a hurry?"

"Code 2 call," Cooper replied. "I'd be answering on my own if you hadn't gotten back just in time. That's quite the whirlwind career you've got going, by the way."

Han made a growling sound. "Two helicopter rides, a terrorism investigation, and my day still isn't over. So what world-shaking event are we off to resolve?"

"Smash-and-grab at the mall. Welcome back to the real world."

Han gave her a smile. Truthfully, he was not comfortable with the whole ATLAS thing, but he knew if he balked, his chances of ever climbing the ranks internally would drop to zero. Captain Horton was savvy enough to recognize the cred the department would get from this, and he would not forgive or forget if Han screwed him over by declining.

Cooper interrupted his musing. "So feel like sharing with the little people you used to work with?"

"Oh, bite me." He hesitated, but Shankar hadn't laid out any limitations. Making a decision, he continued, "It's another Gen Omega thing. At least it seems to be. No announcements yet, no one taking credit. But it's got the whole high-tech-gimmick thing."

"How so?"

"It *looks*—and there's a doctor on the scene working to confirm this—like someone or someones salted the catered food with some kind of bacteria engineered to produce alcohol once in the intestines. It's like something called auto-brewery syndrome—"

"Seriously, that's a real thing?"

"Uh-huh. But this is the nuclear version. Onset within hours. All the security and catering people were watching the liquid refreshments for any kind of spiking, but no one thought to be concerned about the food."

"So a bunch of drunk people?"

"Very drunk people. Up to a thousand, including teens and children. Some on the verge of alcohol poisoning. Plus, in order to get the bacteria out of them, they'll have to be subjected to some very unpleasant, er, therapies, that will kill off all their intestinal flora."

"Hmm." Cooper was silent for a moment. "I guess there's a certain poetic justice in people working for a car company coming up drunk. Partying under the influence." She giggled.

"That does seem to be Gen Omega's MO. What concerns me, and I'm sure everyone upstairs, is that Gen Omega is going to up the ante at some point and start killing people. They certainly aren't getting any real results out of what they've done so far."

"They've been in the news, big time," she replied. "Isn't that the point?"

"Sure, for a while. But they'll escalate soon if they don't get something more than just a few seconds on the news. And that's the thing. The public will get bored with these antics, and soon Gen Omega won't even get front-page coverage. At that point, yeah, we're gonna see fatalities."

CHAPTER THIRTY-TWO

Trouble with the Boss

The meeting room was crowded. It was rare that the company called everyone in at the same time. Even Mark was there, looking cranky and under-rested at the godawful hour of 10:00 a.m. Celia sat beside him, fussing with her notes, as the company CEO, Usiah Bradshaw, stood at the head of the table, conferring with a few of the other suits.

Finally, Bradshaw rapped on the table with his empty coffee mug. "Can we begin?" he said and sat down.

He swept his gaze over the assembly, then continued, "Money has tightened up a little, folks. The recent events have spawned rumors of a rogue AI and possibly even another AI apocalypse on the horizon. Silly and overblown, of course—it's far more likely some kind of social justice terrorism—but if there's one thing that investors fear, it's uncertainty. They pull into their shells like turtles and wait for better weather. Unfortunately, we're feeling it."

Bradshaw paused for dramatic effect, making sure he had everyone's attention. "We have about a month's worth of cash flow left if we don't get some fresh blood.

After that..." He shrugged, and the meaning was clear: general layoffs. "It's too bad, but without some progress in the areas where we're roadblocked, we aren't really a viable entity. Isn't that right, Dr. Moray?"

Philip jerked as his name was mentioned. He hadn't expected to be put on the spot. "Mr. Bradshaw, you can't schedule breakthroughs. I told you this at my job interview. I also told you we'd be having this very conversation—"

"Yes, thanks, Philip. But without that breakthrough, we're probably going to have to close the doors. Hard realities don't pay attention to excuses."

Philip felt his face go red. He knew he was being baited. Bradshaw was a bit of a dick that way. But he wasn't going to let this go by. "It's not an excuse—it's a reason."

"Oh? And what's the difference?"

"An excuse is an explanation submitted for your approval. A reason doesn't give a rat's ass what you think."

Now it was Bradshaw's turn to flush. The two men exchanged glares for a few moments before one of the other suits nudged Bradshaw and whispered something. Bradshaw nodded and waved a hand dismissively. "This isn't the time for personalities, although I think at some point, we'll be discussing your attitude issues. For now, we have a more immediate, pressing concern. And as usual with tech start-ups, it all comes down to money."

Bradshaw went off on some rant about financing and equity and burn rates, subjects that could drive Philip to catatonia. He looked around the table. Everyone in a suit was hanging rapt to every word. Everyone in a lab coat was looking like they were on their second day without sleep—and losing the battle.

Finally, after a last exhortation to do their best work, Bradshaw called the meeting. Philip distinctly heard Mark mutter, "Thank God," as they stood and began shuffling out of the room.

"Wow, nice comeback, Philip," Mark said. "I swear I saw scorch marks on Bradshaw."

"Short-term satisfaction," Philip replied, "but maybe not so good for tenure. The thing is, Bradshaw's right, in a way. If I crack the problem, I'm the golden boy. If I don't, we're all toast." He paused. "How are you guys going, anyway? The only reason I was singled out is because I was the weakest link. But I'm sure you guys were supposed to feel the heat as well."

"Not wrong," Mark replied with a chuckle. "Although I think we're supposed to be angry at you, not Bradshaw."

"All he cares about are his shares and what they're worth," Celia grumbled.

"I have to be honest," Philip replied, "the subject does come up in my thoughts as well. If things go one way, we're multimillionaires overnight. The other way, we're living in cardboard boxes in back alleys."

Celia and Mark both rolled their eyes. "Sure thing," Mark said, then gave them a wave as he turned left at the corridor intersection.

Philip chuckled. "Heading for the caf for a shot of caffeine, I bet. These early days must be hell for him."

Celia laughed. "Yeah, forced to get up at the crack of noon. Poor guy."

CHAPTER THIRTY-THREE

Meeting of the Board

Patrick White rapped the gavel, and conversations died out around the boardroom table. This was the board of directors of the largest oil company on the planet. Heir to Imperial, Standard, and all the old giants, Global Oil had made some timely purchases as the traditional companies began to falter under the new environmental order.

He looked around at the other members, almost all white men. There were three or four older women, matriarchs in control of large family fortunes, but by and large, this was a group composed of the right people. The masses could keep their inclusion and their diversity programs. Up here, it was money that mattered.

Each person had a place setting in white china, with the remains of a light lunch of truffled burrata and caviar with a cherry tomato confit. The waitstaff took the gavel as a signal and began clearing, staying carefully out of the way.

"Peter," Patrick said, nodding to the man on his left. "Let's start with you. Status report?"

"We have several campaigns well in hand. As you know, our mandate is to convince the public that global-warming fears are overblown. After all, according to all the earlier doomsayers, we should be cooking in our own juices by now—"

"Please save the sales pitch, Peter," Patrick admonished. "You're preaching to the choir. How is it really going?"

"Well. Market penetration is slightly below expected, but our ads are viewed more positively than expected, so we're breaking even."

Patrick nodded, then pointed to the next man at the table.

"Global oil shipments remain strong," he started. "As expected, equipping our tankers with electric motors and sails gave us that pro-environment glow. The environmentalists are, of course, trying to convince everyone that it's just greenwashing—which it is..." Pause for laughter. "But they are having a tough time of it."

Again, Patrick nodded and turned to the next person. Of course, this was all routine, and if there'd been anything unusual to deal with, it would have been taken care of already. These meetings were more of a ritual than an actual information-sharing session. "Warren?"

Warren looked up at Patrick, an odd expression on his face. Was he ill? "Warren, you okay? You need anything?"

Warren's mouth worked a few times, and then his face collapsed into a grimace of pain. Then, a moment later, his face began to literally *collapse*. As Patrick watched, Warren's face seemed to suck itself in. First the nose inverted; then the flesh around it began to be pulled in. The entire skull began to distort as his eyes moved down, his mouth moved up, and his ears moved forward...

Someone screamed. There was panicked pushing away from the table. Patrick could hear one of the waitstaff calling security downstairs. As he looked around, two more people began collapsing around their noses.

Then it happened. A stab of agony in the middle of his face, as if he'd just been punched by a giant. The scene in front of him began to distort, as his eyes seemed to be suddenly tracking independently. The last thing Patrick remembered was Florence Mattingly staring at him in horror with both hands over her mouth.

***

"Texas? You want me to go to *Texas*?" Simon Han moved the phone from his ear and stared at it as if the device itself was responsible for the suggestion. A tinny voice responded, and Han quickly put the phone back to his ear.

"—be someone there to take care of the immediate police response, of course," Shankar's voice was saying, "but one of the most important aspects of this type of investigation is continuity. You've been involved in several events, Officer Han, and your direct experience is worth any amount of travel expenses."

Travel expense really wasn't what I was worried about, Han thought to himself. "Fine. When do I leave?"

"Now, of course. There will be a private jet waiting at the airport. There's a helicopter at police headquarters ready to take you there."

Han had a thought. It would be interesting just to see how much he could push. "Listen, Detective, I wonder if I could bring someone else as a consultant."

"And who would this be?"

"Dr. Celia Hunt. I've consulted informally with her on the previous cases, and she's had some good insights."

"Well, budgetary issues are not a concern, but time is of the essence. Can you get her on the plane in short order?"

"I will see what I can do. Previous consultations have been by phone, but that's not ideal."

"Your call, Han. I look forward to your report."

"Unbelievable." Han turned to look at his wife, who did *not* look happy. "Brenda, I will make this up to you, I promise. Find the absolute best restaurant you can, and book something for this weekend. And a suite at the Four Seasons. Shankar will be paying. Or I *will* quit."

As Han got changed, he dialed Dr. Hunt's number and placed the phone on his side table on speaker.

"Celia here. Is this going to be as interesting as usual, Officer?"

"Very much so. It's in Texas. I'd like you to come."

"To *Texas*?"

"Yes. You can decline, of course, and we can do the usual phone consultancy thing. But in this case, if you can make it to the police station in"—Han checked his watch—"half an hour, we'll be taking a chopper to the airport, then a private jet to Texas. Return trip probably by the same means."

"I... I... Okay, what the hell, why not?" There was muted shuffling on the other end of the phone, then, "I'll have to notify my employer. Do I need to pack?"

"No. This will be there and back. Usual consultancy rates apply."

"Great. See you in a half hour."

***

Once Celia was on her way in a traxi, she phoned Philip. "Guess where I'm going?"

"To hell in a handbasket?"

"You funny guy. No, Texas."

"Why? Got a better job offer?"

"Sort of. Doing consulting for the police on what might be another terrorist attack. The hourly rate is insanely good. I'm flying out with Officer Han."

There was a pause. "Are you nuts? Celia, you're going to work with the guy—"

"Yes, I know. I feel like that old TV series where the serial killer works for the police department to hide in plain sight. But our little escapade hasn't come up the last couple of times I've talked to him—"

"Last *couple of times*? Now I'm really getting worried. It's almost as if you have a completely separate life that I don't know about."

Celia chuckled. "Go figure. Anyway, Captain Interrupto, I'm going because there's a large medical aspect to all this, specifically gene mods. You know what I do for Astro, right?"

"Yeah, yeah. Listen, I trust your judgment. You have a cooler head than I do, in general. But still...be safe, okay?"

"Always. See you tomorrow."

***

The trip was an experience. The helicopter took Celia and Han to the airport, where they were hustled along by handlers in dark suits to a private jet. Three hours after leaving home, they were in Austin, Texas, in a government traxi with a priority flag, to judge from the way other traffic kept diving out of the way.

"Do you have smart contacts?" Han asked her in the traxi.

"No, can't stand them," Celia said. "Not just smart ones, either. Contacts make me cry. Literally."

"It's okay—lots of people don't wear them. Even some cops. Here." He handed her a pair of smart glasses. "Law enforcement issue. Slave them to your phone. I got you ATLAS authority for the duration. The heads-up interface will give you info on anyone you're interacting with. And vice versa."

Celia looked at the glasses in her hand. "Still can't make them stylish," she muttered, then pulled out her phone.

They arrived to find a woman in a dark suit waiting at the curb. Sunglasses and an almost invisible earpiece completed the ensemble. You couldn't possibly scream *CIA spook* any louder if you pasted a sign onto the woman's forehead. A window popped up on Celia's glasses with her name and position.

"Agents Han and Hunt?" the woman said. "I'm Agent Manchin. Follow me, please."

"I'm not actually an agent..." Celia started to say.

"I'm aware of your overall status, Doctor. For purposes of this event, though, you *are* an agent, with all the authority and access that requires." She started to turn, then glanced back at Celia. "Medical doctor?"

"Yes."

"Good. The more, the better."

"Sure, that's not the least bit ominous," Celia said.

"What's the situation?" Han asked.

Manchin punched an elevator button and turned to him. "I hope you have a strong stomach. And an empty one."

"Oh, that's just great," Han muttered and glanced at Celia.

"I'm okay," she said. "I did more than my share of autopsies in medical school."

They finished the ride up in silence. Celia passed the time by watching the floor numbers, which finally settled on 75.

As they stepped out of the elevator, it was immediately obvious where the action was. The huge double wooden doors were the only available pathway on the floor.

"Do we need masks? Isolation suits?" Celia asked.

"No, we've checked already. The, uh, active agent is not airborne. In fact, according to the medical examiner, it seems to have self-destructed after killing its victims. But if you're sensitive to strong odors, I would recommend a mask." Manchin glanced at Han and pointed to a stack of masks on a side table by the entrance. Han shook his head and gave her a small smile.

They passed through the doors, which turned out to be the entrance to a very impressive boardroom. Celia just had time to take in the view before the smell hit her like a baseball bat. She stopped breathing for a second as she did the mental exercises that all doctors learn to disassociate the olfactory input from any emotional reaction.

Han did not have that training. "Jesus, what—" he exclaimed as he put a hand over his nose.

Manchin gestured to a woman in a hazmat suit with the hood under her arm. "This is Doctor Nyal. Can you give us a rundown, Doctor?"

Celia noted that the heads-up interface had popped up information on the doctor, but she didn't have time to read it because Dr. Nyal was already replying. "The active agent is bacterial. It most closely resembles necrotizing fasciitis, flesh-eating disease. But much faster and less fussy about what it eats. For instance, the natural version doesn't go after bone. This one seems to prefer it."

"That's interesting," Celia said. "It would need a different digestive chemistry to accomplish that. Would it even get any use out of the bones?"

"No, I don't think so," Nyal replied. "That would have to be specifically added and would probably be net-energy consuming. So not a viable trait."

"Any idea how it was administered to the victims?" Han said.

"It was in their lunch. Somewhat surprising, as streptococcus normally doesn't spread that easily through food. Even when it does, it can take days to build up an infection."

"But this was strep on steroids, right?" Celia gazed meaningfully at Nyal. "Altered for quicker effect?"

"If you're asking if this bug was engineered, I can't say definitively until I get it in a lab. But it would be the way to bet. The results are certainly impressive."

Han looked around. "Uh, speaking of which..."

Nyal made a *this-way* gesture and led them around the table. They followed, and then Han, who was in the lead, jerked to a halt, exclaiming, "Holy *shit*!" He turned, grabbed a nearby chair, and leaned over, gasping.

Celia craned her neck to look around the officer. The...*corpse* was as good a term as any...looked like a wax figure that had been partly melted. The head looked like a soccer ball that had the air sucked out, and there was only a vague impression of a face. One of the arms had simply separated from the torso when the shoulder melted right off. The abdomen was gone, and the spine and lower ribs were clearly visible. And it was, in some way still...bubbling, or something.

Han got himself under control. "Are you *sure* we don't need to be on respirators?"

"We tested everything," Nyal replied. "Seriously, you think I want to end up like that? I'm swerving well into unjustified speculation here, but it seems to me that whoever did this wanted it to be very carefully targeted. They were not looking to create some kind of epidemic."

"That *is* speculative, but it rings true," Celia replied. "Gen Omega doesn't seem to be inclined to the usual *blow-everything-up* school of extremism. I've seen their pronouncements on TV, and they really are trying to make a point."

"Until now, the effects on victims have been temporary," Han added. "This one, not so much. Doctor Nyal, please forward any interim reports and conclusions to us?" He looked at Celia, then Manchin and tilted his head in the direction of the door.

"You recovered quickly in there, Han," Manchin said. "I'm impressed. That smell has taken out three agents so far."

Han gave her a sickly smile. "At one point in my life, I was going to be a doctor. Right now, I'm thinking that might not have worked out for me." He glanced at Celia. "You didn't even seem bothered. Is that the medical training?"

"There are some tricks you learn," Celia replied. "Plus, a lot of time in pathology, and you get numb." She turned to Manchin. "What about you? What's your system?"

Manchin grinned at Celia and tapped the side of her nose. "Anosmia. Congenital. Gives me an advantage in these kinds of settings." The elevator door opened, and she gestured them in, then continued, "I'm known as Ol' Iron Guts in the department. It actually kind of works in my favor." She paused again, then glanced at Han. "Doctor to cop, eh? We have seventy-five floors. Can you give me the short version?"

Celia turned to Han as well, frankly curious at this revelation.

"I had a choice," he replied. "Stay home and save up for medical school, or get a job and get out. If you'd met my parents, you'd understand."

Manchin grunted. "Yeah, I get it. Some people shouldn't be allowed to raise kids."

Celia eyed her sideways. There was some emotion in that statement, but Manchin didn't elaborate.

***

Celia and Han were soon back in the car, which had waited for them, and on their way to the airport.

A visual ding on Celia's heads-up indicated an incoming email. Han's face twitched as he controlled the display to bring up the contents. Celia hadn't worked with the facial interface, so she had to use her phone to issue commands to the UI.

It was a prelim from Dr. Nyal. She began reading, wading slowly through the medical terms.

Han, who was apparently reading the same report, observed, "The jargon is thick as tar. I'm going to have to depend on you for a précis, I think. I'm far more comfortable with medical terms than most cops, but it's been years."

Celia fairly sleepwalked from the car to the private jet, still struggling with the report, but she had managed to finish by the time the jet began accelerating down the runway.

As they were being pressed back into their seats, Han's phone rang. "Shankar," he said to Celia apologetically. He answered and placed the phone on speaker.

"Hello, Agent Han, how did it go?"

"Still Officer Han, Detective."

"Not until you land, Agent. By the way, your salary gets adjusted when you're on these trips, so it's not just a question of semantics."

Han grunted. "Okay, I won't refuse that. To answer your question, Gen Omega is obviously targeting specific groups of people. Employees of a car company that still makes gas guzzlers, journalists who don't report on environmental issues enough, the board members of a major oil company, and a tanker crew that ships oil around. I haven't figured out why they targeted the Baptist revival, though."

"I can help with that, Agent. That particular church is politically active and quite militant. They recently faced off against and blockaded an environmental demonstration. There was some violence. Gen Omega apparently considers them an enemy of the cause."

"Ah, that makes sense. The problem is this is all trivially obvious, and it doesn't get us any closer to Gen Omega."

"So what do we know, Agent? Does your Dr. Hunt have any input?"

Han looked over at Celia, and she replied, "A couple of bacterial attacks, an antigen attack, and whatever the tanker crew was subjected to. Maybe even those mummified bodies, although I don't think that's a biological attack, so that might be someone else. Not a lot of obvious commonalities there other than the basic supposition that they are doing gene mods somehow. Sorry, Detective Shankar, I'm going to have to read through all the reports. Officer Han, if you can forward everything to me from the other cases?"

"You're sure about the gene mods?" Shankar said. "That would require access to some high-level labs."

"I'd put real money on it. Remember, this is what I'm doing at my day job. And yes, we have a contract with a licensed lab for the gene splicing. The level of oversight on the industry is certainly a flaw in the theory, but if Gen Omega has some kind of illegal access, it becomes a slam dunk."

"I cannot disagree, Doctor, much as I'd love to have a reason to. This takes us into areas of apocalyptic, world-ending predictions. The real question, then, is how are they doing it?"

"I hope you're not just depending on us for that," Han said.

There was a chuckle from the phone. "Hardly, Agent Han. I have many balls in the air, of which you are only one. I am also pursuing investigations of my own. But your part is not by any means trivial. Do not sell yourselves short."

And with that, Shankar hung up. Han shook his head slowly, then gave Celia a small smile, as if apologizing for the detective.

Celia grabbed a bottled water and settled back in her seat. Time to buckle down.

CHAPTER THIRTY-FOUR

The New Owners

Philip was in his office, working on his notes, when he received an invitation to an all-staff meeting just after lunch. He scanned the contents, and his eyebrows climbed almost to his hairline. Management had apparently found an angel investor that would inject some much-needed cash into the company. However, their savior did not intend to be a silent partner. They wanted controlling interest and a place on the board. Philip frowned. The cash was good, but he couldn't really see Usiah Bradshaw and the other suits sitting still for that. Did they have a choice, though?

The meeting invite was non-optional but still required a response. He clicked the *accept* button, then minimized his email client and got back to work.

After several more minutes of staring at his notes and making the occasional addition, Philip put his pen down and rested his face in his hands. This problem was not intractable. It couldn't be. There had to be a way to extract enough information from the EMP to identify ore deposits at a distance. But the power requirements were excessive, and the data—what data there were—came back all at once. It was like opening a book using a grenade, then trying to read the contents during the explosion.

Like it or not, Bradshaw was going to get his chance to gloat. The only consolation would be that Bradshaw was going down as well. But those guys—venture capitalists—always seemed to be able to land on their feet. Bradshaw would still be riding in his Audi in a month, whereas Philip would be listing his house for sale.

The ding of the meeting reminder jerked him awake. Unbelievable. He'd actually dozed off with his head in his hands. Well, he hadn't been getting anything productive done anyway. With a feeling of deep discouragement at his own shortcomings, Philip gathered his things and made for the meeting room.

***

Philip took his usual spot at the table and looked around. Interestingly, *everyone* had taken their usual places. That was notable for two reasons: First, it was mildly amusing that people were so habit-driven; second, there was no one new in the room. Were they not meeting their new overlords today?

Bradshaw rapped his mug on the table and waited for attention. "Our new investors will be joining us by Zoom today." He gestured behind himself at the wall monitor. "I'm told this won't be a long—"

At that moment, the monitor came to life as the Zoom connection went live. A woman sat behind a desk; she was well dressed but somewhat severe. Makeup perfect, hair pulled back, she projected a no-nonsense demeanor with every pixel of her image.

"Good afternoon, everyone. I'm Patricia Otten of Crabtree Investments. I'm sure Mr. Bradshaw has given you some preview information, but allow me to expand on that." She paused and somehow managed to look like she was making eye contact with her audience before continuing. "First, let me assure you that we are not buying Astro Resources to take it apart and sell the pieces. We consider your company a viable going concern, and we intend to be as constructive and supportive as possible." Again, the pause; again, the feeling like she was in the room, face to face. "I will be having private conversations with some of you over the next couple of days. Please make yourselves available as required. Thank you for your attention."

Otten then tapped a key, and the Zoom session terminated.

"Wow!" one of the suits said. "That was..."

"Encouraging," Bradshaw finished for him. "And the fewer words, the better."

Philip kept his face deadpan but couldn't help wondering why Bradshaw didn't apply that advice to himself.

***

Philip was back at his desk, wondering if he should just cut his losses and head home, when his laptop announced a Zoom connection request. He frowned. Who would want to Zoom him, and why not just use the phone? He pulled up the request. Oh. Patricia Otten.

His mind went immediately to *staff layoffs*. With his hand shaking, he clicked *accept*.

"Good afternoon, Dr. Moray," Otten said as soon as the connection was made. "I'd like to talk to you about your project."

"Ms. Otten, as I've explained to Mr. Bradshaw, you can't—" Philip was barely into his demurral when Otten cut him off with a wave.

"I'm not calling to berate you on your lack of progress, Doctor. Or fire you. I want to offer you some possible assistance." She paused as Philip's eyebrows involuntarily climbed on his forehead. "No, of course, I'm not a physicist, Doctor, but Crabtree has its hooks in many different operations. Diversification, you would say. One of our other investments—and I'll say no more about it than that—had a solution to a problem that I think might apply to your case."

"I'm listening," Philip said. At this point, he'd grasp at any straw, honestly.

"I hope you won't try to question me too much because I'm relaying this more or less verbatim, and I'm not sure I even know what some of the words mean." Otten gave him a small smile, but Philip was unconvinced by her attempt at downplaying herself. "To summarize, instead of trying to induce current in your target using a pulsed EMP, try using a focused magnetic field and moving it across the target. That will give you a more controllable rise and fall without all the harmonics created by a square wave, which could well be drowning out the usable signal. The slope of the hysteresis curve should vary by element, and you can use a Fourier filter to separate out the individual signals. And by using an NV quantum sensor arrangement, you could increase the detection range dramatically."

She stopped talking and stared at him, expecting a response.

"I'm, uh…wow, okay. I guess I didn't expect this kind of support from a venture capitalist."

Again, the small smile. "That's how we're different, Doctor. Our firm doesn't just throw money at random start-ups. We do research, and we have people on staff with enough knowledge to recognize when some synergy is possible. In this case, someone connected another company's research with your issues. If this little chat produces results, we've just increased the value of our investment by millions. I'm sure you can appreciate the efficiency."

"Leverage. Small action, large result." Philip said. "I'm impressed."

"Then let's end this discussion so you can get at it. By the way, Enrico Martinez may be contacting you to discuss the technology further." Without further ado, Otten leaned forward and cut the connection.

Martinez? Philip frowned. He knew the man, of course. Enrico was working on methods for extending the probe's drive capability. A space probe's useful life was ultimately limited by how much maneuvering it could do, and that was determined by the total delta-V that the probe's engines could produce. The total amount that it could accelerate and maneuver over its lifetime, in other words, with the fuel on board. Anything that could extend that useful lifetime would extend the probe's value proportionately.

Philip started to make a note, then frowned. A while back, there'd been a YouTube video... He paged back through his notes until he found the reference. Yes, a small video by some self-declared scientist had discussed a rotating magnetic field. Interesting, and Philip wondered if there was a connection. Maybe the Crabtree researcher had simply watched that video, then suggested it as a valid option. Wouldn't that be a kicker if Crabtree's investment decision was based on a video by a random citizen scientist?

Well, Otten had established some tentative cred with her suggestions, and she *did* own the company. And he now had a new idea to test.

CHAPTER THIRTY-FIVE

Rage

All units, *all units, Millennium Shopping Mall. Riot in progress. Shots fired. Handle Code 3.*

"Oh, crud," Han said and switched on the lights and sirens. Cooper set the destination and response level, then pressed *go*. As the patrol car accelerated, they reached back into storage and began grabbing tactical equipment.

Han kept glancing to his heads-up, hoping for more information, but so far, nothing. "It's been a while since I've had my weapon out," he said.

Cooper gave him a look. "You better be referring to your sidearm, bud."

Han laughed, then pulled out his pistol and checked it. "Just hope I don't have to use this. I've never shot anyone."

"Me neither. And I'd like to keep it that way."

They reached one of the main entrances to the mall, and the patrol car practically skidded to a halt. Han and Cooper were out the door immediately to find several other cops assembling. Lt. Mikelson was there, giving orders.

At that moment, a man burst out of the mall door, yelling, "Fuck you, pigs!" and waving a baseball bat. He charged directly at the nearest cop and took a swing at his head. The cop backpedaled furiously, then tripped and landed on his ass. Several others pulled Tasers and batons. In moments, the attacker was down, twitching.

"Riot gear!" Mikelson shouted, and cops ran back to their vehicles to retrieve shields and helmets.

As the squad re-formed, they could hear gunshots and screams from the interior of the mall; then the doors were thrust open, and people began running out. Behind them, another angry individual burst out, waving a handgun. Two shots, and the man was down.

"Inside," Mikelson ordered. "Carefully. Let fleeing civilians through as long as they aren't armed. Anyone else, Taser if possible, but take them down by whatever means."

The cops moved into the mall. The interior was a madhouse. Some people were running, screaming, or hiding behind displays and furniture, while others rampaged with baseball bats, hockey sticks, or anything else that would make a good club. Some were carrying individual barbell plates to use as cudgels.

The crowd surged toward the police line, a mix of rioters, fleeing bystanders, and children. It would be impossible for the cops to take out the perpetrators without endangering innocent lives.

Mikelson began talking into a megaphone. "Please drop your—"

It was as far as he got. Those attempting to flee scattered to the sides, and the entire group of rioters attacked as one, without so much as a word or signal. But it was very much a case of bringing a knife to a gunfight. The cops were far better armed and had helmets and Lexan riot shields, which could be interlocked to spread the impact of attackers. And they were organized and disciplined, whereas the rioters depended primarily on enthusiasm.

There were a few seconds of disorganized melee; then the sounds of bats hitting shields were replaced by the sounds of rhythmic Taser clicking. And two more gunshots.

Han looked down at the bodies on the floor, some twitching, one bleeding. Mikelson was giving orders. Han refocused, then bent down and began cuffing perps. One of the cops started giving first aid to the gunshot victim.

It appeared to be over.

"Han! Cooper!" Mikelson yelled.

"Sir?"

"Perimeter check. Weapons out."

Han and Cooper put down their shields and pulled their sidearms. They couldn't check the entire mall, but they would make sure the immediate area was clear. Follow-up patrols would cover all the floor space.

"Snipers?" Cooper whispered.

"Unlikely," Han replied. "Watch for them, of course, but this wasn't organized or planned. These people were off their collective nut. I'm thinking some kind of drug."

"Or another Gen Omega stunt?" Cooper said.

Han stopped. "Jesus." He turned back to Mikelson. "Sir! Call medical and hazmat. This may be another bio-attack." Then he pulled out his phone and dialed Dr. Hunt.

***

Philip watched the traffic through the traxi window for a moment before turning back to Celia. "I kid you not, this Otten woman basically handed me the key to the whole problem. I mean, I'm pretty sure; it sounds reasonable. Whether or not it'll actually work, who knows?"

"You're going to test it, though?"

"Well, yes, of course. Right now, I'm feeling a lot more optimistic—"

Celia's phone picked that moment to ring. She looked at it and saw *Han, Chicago PD.*

"Oh hell," she muttered, then answered on speaker. "Celia here."

"Dr. Hunt, I think we may have another incident. At the Millennium Mall. Can you get down here?"

"Ah, sure, okay. Officer Han, what exactly do you expect me to do, though?"

"Doctor, whether or not you realize it, you've made several observations that have provided value. Are you able to make it?"

"Actually, Dr. Moray and I are in a traxi right now, heading for his residence, which is the other end of town. I think I can be there in twenty minutes, though."

"You can do it in ten if you activate ATLAS priority."

"I don't have that authority—" She paused. "*Do* I have that authority?"

"One way to find out. See you soon."

Han hung up, and Celia turned to Philip, whose eyes were bugging out. "Want to go see a crime scene?" she asked.

"Why not? We're already *way* outside of normal."

Celia said to the traxi, "Change destination. Millennium Mall. ATLAS priority."

"Yes, Dr. Hunt," the traxi said. Then Celia and Philip were jerked around in their seats as the traxi changed direction and accelerated way, *way* too quickly for comfort.

"Holy God, it worked," Celia exclaimed.

"Son of a bitch," Philip replied, looking out the window. Other traxis were pulling over or otherwise diving out of their way. "I feel like a crime fighter."

"*I'm* the crime fighter," she retorted. "You're a sidekick."

***

Celia and Philip stepped out of the traxi in front of the main entrance to the mall. Cops were everywhere, and a medical hazmat truck stood at the curb. A cop immediately approached to shoo them away, then stopped as his heads-up registered Celia's authority.

"Uh, can I help you, Dr. Hunt?" he said.

"I'm looking for Officer Simon Han."

The man frowned. "Lieutenant Mikelson is in charge, ma'am."

"That's fine, but Officer Han is my ATLAS contact."

He nodded, then tapped his badge. "Han to the main entrance. You have a visitor. A Dr. Hunt."

"Ten-four," Han replied.

Just then, another cop came marching up. "What's this about, and who are you?" he demanded.

Celia didn't know much about police insignia—or military insignia, for that matter—but this man appeared to have more decorations than the average cop, so she was going to assume it was Lt. Mikelson. Belatedly realizing she didn't have to assume anything, she pulled out the smart glasses that Han had given her and checked the heads-up. "Lieutenant Mikelson, I'm Doctor Celia Hunt, ATLAS consultant. I was called in—"

"I don't give a good God damn who you think you are. I'm not having a civilian—or two," he added, glancing at Philip, "parading around a crime scene. You can wait—"

"Sir, you don't have the authority to exclude her," Han said, finally arriving. He'd apparently picked up just enough of what was going on. "She is, whether you like it or not, operating under ATLAS jurisdiction."

Mikelson rounded on him. "You mouthing off at me, Han?"

Han remained calm. "If it comes down to it, Lieutenant, I'm an ATLAS operative as well. I may be your subordinate in the PD, but right now, in an active crime scene that may fall under ATLAS purview, I technically outrank you. We can get into a pissing match and get Shankar and the captain involved, or we can do our jobs and sort it out later."

Mikelson glared silently at Han, his face growing redder by the second. Finally, he burst out, "Fine, Han. Enjoy your moment. But I will remember this. And there will be payback."

Celia cocked her head and put on her best innocent expression. "Am I to understand, Lieutenant, that you are threatening, on the record"—she tapped her smart glasses—"to use your position and power as a senior police official to exact personal vengeance against this officer for attempting to do his duty?" She shifted slightly to face the lieutenant squarely. "That seems on balance like somewhat of a career-limiting decision, in my view."

The bluff worked. The lieutenant, taken aback, sputtered for a moment, then said, "I was speaking off the cuff, Doctor. You have access to the scene. Don't abuse it."

Celia smiled and made a *let's-go* motion to Han and Philip. It was a heady feeling to play the big dog for once.

As they walked into the mall, Han said, "You know those glasses don't have recording capability, right?"

She chuckled. "I wonder if Mikelson will remember that at some point."

The mall was a shambles. Blood splatters were marked off with tape, there were chalk lines and evidence markers all over the place, furniture and displays had been knocked over, and a few shop windows had been shattered.

"So what makes this not a regular riot?" Celia said.

"No trigger. The people who were rioting have no priors, no motive, aren't even the type of people you expect to catch jaywalking. One of them is, pardon the cliché, a soccer mom. But they were all running around with weapons, beating on people. Except one guy who was carrying and started shooting things up." Han gestured to a number of items laid out on the floor, with numbered tags attached to them.

Philip, who until this moment hadn't uttered a peep, said, "All sports equipment. I wonder if it started in a sporting goods shop?"

Han looked alarmed. "We've been concentrating on the food court. Everything's always been delivered by food or drink up 'til now."

"Have they found anything?" Celia asked.

"No. Still working through it, though."

"What if it's delivered by contact? Or air vector?" Celia said. "I'm not sure how you'd do that in a sports shop specifically, but Philip's right—that appears to be the common factor."

They hurried to the store. Inside were two cops wandering the aisles, looking for, well, anything. Han yelled to the two officers, "Sienna. Bert. Come out of there. Don't touch anything else."

The two cops, looking confused, walked out. Han continued, "Look, I know this is way out there, but I need the two of you to unbuckle your belts and place them on the ground, then step away."

"You arresting us, Simon?" the woman said with a quizzical expression.

"No, I'm quarantining you. And since the presumed bioweapon's effect is rage, I'd just as soon you weren't armed."

Both cops nodded and did as asked while Han spoke urgently into his badge. A few moments later, a hazmat crew arrived. They placed the two cops in isolation suits and led them away while Han collected the utility belts from the floor.

"This appears to be my day for sticking my neck out," Han said as he held the equipment. In the near distance, there was a clomping sound, and they all turned to see Mikelson barreling down on them with a heavy, determined gait.

"Report," he said, his expression thunderous.

Han explained the reasoning and conclusions, then held the belts out to Mikelson. As he finished, several hazmat-suit-clad individuals invaded the sports shop with cases of equipment. Mikelson watched them deploying testing equipment, and his expression relaxed a bit. "Prudent. I'll assign a couple of members to sit with Cooper and Hanson, just in case they become agitated." He nodded to the group and walked off.

"He seems to have calmed down," Philip said.

"Or he's realized that if the shit hits the fan, he's going to be wearing most of it," Celia added.

"Not wrong," Han commented.

***

Celia, Philip, and Han were standing outside the main mall doors, comparing notes, when they heard the noise of an altercation from one of the med tents that had been set up in the parking lot. Voices, angry voices, then the sounds of a scuffle.

Before anyone could even formulate a question, a figure in an isolation suit burst through the side of the tent, separating the tie-downs. He was immediately followed by two other figures who tackled him and attempted to hold him down. The figure in the suit was writhing and screaming, although it was hard to make out a coherent message.

Han rushed over, followed by Philip and Celia. By the time they got there, the two cops had the third man under control. It was one of the two cops that had been in the sports shop—Bert Hanson, Celia's heads-up informed her.

She looked down at the scrum on the ground, then over at Han. "I think we can confirm the sports shop as ground zero."

Han nodded. "Dr. Hunt, I'll make sure the medics send you a copy of the reports, and if you have any comments, please feel free to call me. And Dr. Moray, thank you for noting the sports connection." Now Han smiled at both of them. "It's like Shankar says—more eyes on the ground does nothing but good for the investigation."

"Wait, do I get paid, too?" Philip said half-jokingly.

"Not this time. But I can put you on as a consultant."

Philip and Celia exchanged glances, then he shrugged. "Well, why not?"

***

Philip topped up Celia's wineglass, then sat back and eyed the bottle of Jameson for a moment. It was already a two-drink night and might even be three. Today had been the very definition of interesting times.

He glanced over at Celia, who was leaning heavily on her elbows and cradling the wineglass with both hands. The day was clearly catching up with her, too.

If she'd had a two-drink rule, he was sure she'd be breaking it as well.

He glanced aside, embarrassed. As usual, Celia had taken charge in a situation where he'd have been left sputtering. He couldn't believe how she'd faced down that lieutenant. Philip was positive they were inches from getting shot, to judge by the man's expression. Yet Celia had calmly stared back at him, daring him to call her bluff.

And now Philip was an ATLAS agent, too. Well, in theory, anyway. He might never get the call. And why would he? The Gen Omega attacks all seemed to involve medically related subjects. Why would they need a physicist?

In the middle of Philip's navel-gazing, Celia's phone dinged with that sound that meant priority email. She picked it up and scrolled around for a bit, then started reading.

"Holy shit," she said.

"What?"

"Medical and forensics reports. They found an aerosol canister in the sports shop, hidden near the air-conditioning duct. It was rigged to empty slowly into the airstream."

"Not laughing gas, I assume."

Celia snorted. "Traces of a bacterium. Strep, probably modded. In fact..." She paged a little. "Definitely modded. Smaller, more able to stay airborne."

"It's biological warfare. I don't understand, though, how Gen Omega is able to accomplish that."

Celia nodded. "Yeah, look at all the hoops I've had to jump through, and I'm just using Venter cells, not even real bacteria. The terrorists have some kind of edge."

CHAPTER THIRTY-SIX

Finally, Success

Philip gestured to the camera through the glass. The test rig set up a sixty-hertz hum, which lasted three seconds...five...ten. Finally, after thirty seconds, Philip turned off the system. No red lights. That was good.

Of course, the EMP had been the basis for most of his issues. He'd known that, but he hadn't had an alternative. Now he was using a rotating, conical set of fields, conceptually like an airplane propellor but with nonmaterial blades. No hard-edged EMP, no abends.

But would it work? If he couldn't extract information about remote material compositions, it wouldn't make a lot of difference that he wasn't overloading his sensors any longer.

Philip jotted his results in his notepad, shut everything down in preparation for postmortem analysis, and headed for the cafeteria.

***

"Urgh," Celia said as she plunked her tray on the table across from Philip.

He looked up from his tablet, then moved his tray with its lunch residue to a nearby empty table. "Is that a good urgh or a bad urgh?" he asked.

"An exhausted urgh, honestly. Things are going well, overall. But our new overlords have given me a list of materials they want me to be able to extract. And they're not all metals. Phosphorus, carbon, silicon..."

"Silicon is technically a metal, isn't it?"

"Nope. Metalloid. But more important, it's as common as sand. No commercial value."

"Good point. Okay. I'm sure there's a reason. I mean, it's a major component for semiconductors..."

Celia cocked her head, thinking about that for a moment. "Okay, if they're planning on building a semiconductor industry in space, it might make sense. But regardless, I'm being worked to death. I've submitted a request for an assistant."

"Yeah, that'll happen," Philip replied. "Meanwhile, in my department..."

"Oh yeah, the Ice Queen gave you a suggestion. How'd that go?"

"Turns out it appears to have been valid. I did my first test today, and I got usable data. I mean, I don't know why I should be surprised. She did say she got the basic idea from one of their other acquisitions."

"Did she give any specifics?"

"No, and it sounded like something military the way she clammed up about it. But I don't care. Bradshaw actually said 'Good morning' to me today, and I couldn't detect any irony in his tone. So I'm going to call that a victory."

"Heard from Buto?" Celia said, changing the subject without warning.

"Ow, my neck! Whiplash!" Philip quipped, and Celia smirked. "Why? Have you?"

"No, and that's what bothers me. I mean, she can't have forgotten about us. Or Derek. You'd think she'd at least have questions."

"I'll send an email to her assistant," Philip said, poking his tablet. "Let's see if he brushes us off."

***

Philip looked up at the sound of a knock. Enrico Martinez was standing at his office door, having knocked on the jamb.

"Hi, Phil. Got a sec?"

Philip gestured without comment to a chair. He didn't like being called Phil at the best of times, and he and Martinez weren't on a first-name basis anyway. He swallowed his annoyance. Keep it professional; keep it short. He slapped his laptop closed as Martinez took a seat.

"Otten suggested I talk to you," Martinez said.

"The Ice Queen?"

Martinez smiled. "I understand that's become her nickname. Probably a bad idea since she does control the purse strings. Also why I took her suggestion seriously."

"Okay. So..." Philip cocked his head, waiting for Martinez to fill in the blanks.

"I'm working on propulsion," Martinez said, taking the hint.

"But ion engines—" Philip interrupted.

"Are excellent for covering long distances," Martinez continued. "They've made things like asteroid mining and Mars missions possible, in a practical sense. But the low acceleration means they suck for maneuvering."

"Which is why we needed a remote-sensing system for detecting mineral concentrations," Philip replied.

"Even so, a certain amount of maneuvering is necessary. Which is why I'm here talking to you."

"Okay. And?"

"Have you noticed any reactive torque from your rotating fields pushing against the metals they're detecting?"

"Uh, yes, actually, but right now the power levels are really low..."

"Otten said that I should suggest that you do some further tests. Or give me access to your work so I can do so."

"Oh, she did, did she? And why—"

"She pays the bills, Phil. Or her company does. Look, I get the territoriality. I'm not happy about having to come to you for help, either. But if she's right, it would solve my problem quite neatly. And that's good for the company, good for our stock options, and so on."

Philip nodded. Intellectual competition or not, Martinez had successfully pushed the big-money button, and Philip was now paying attention. "You'd use the detection equipment as a source of delta-V?"

"Uh-huh. A kind of induction drive."

"Huh. Okay, I'll work up something you can have access to."

Martinez thanked him and left, probably as happy to be gone as Philip was to see him go. It wasn't like he smelled bad or anything, but competition and territoriality were real, even in industry. One slip and someone else could take partial or total credit for your work. Suspicion was the default behavior.

Philip started to make a note, then stopped and stared into space, frowning. Otten had mentioned he'd be hearing from Martinez back when she first talked to Philip. Which meant she knew about the torque effect back then. Or someone did. He wondered what this business relationship was associating them with. He hoped it wasn't military. That always had a way of turning into a problem, even if things *didn't* abruptly get classified.

CHAPTER THIRTY-SEVEN

Frack Attack

Breaking news. *The Amplid Tar Sands fracking site in Colorado has just suffered a major explosion of some kind. Details are scant, but there are reports from as far as fifty miles away of a huge fireball.*

The Amplid project employs almost a thousand people, and several hundred are on-site at any time...

Simon Han dropped his tablet and looked up at the TV. The news outlet had obviously been scraping what sources they could for images, and those they had on offer were grainy and shaky, probably taken from phone cameras or security cams that happened to be pointing in the right direction.

The fireball *was* huge. It was highly unlikely that anyone was left alive. Simon sighed and glanced at his phone. Very probably, it would be ringing shortly.

"Brenda, I'm..."

"Going to be out of town. I figured." His wife continued fussing in the kitchen, not turning to face him. "Can we up the ante to a vacation in Cancun?"

Simon laughed. "That might be pushing it, but I will mention your displeasure. The weekend at the Four Seasons was nice. Maybe we can get that again."

At that moment, Simon's phone rang, showing Shankar in the caller ID.

"Han."

"Good morning, Agent Han. Have you seen the news?"

"Just watching it. Not a lot of detail yet."

"Nor will there be until the debris settles. I would like you to be there to garner more information the moment it becomes available."

"Detective, I have to ask. Why me? Surely there are more qualified people who could do this."

"It's not a matter of either/or, Agent. Those persons of whom you speak *are* going to be there as well. Or at least working on it. And they will do analyses and write reports for their bosses, and eventually, I will receive the results through the proper channels. But you report to me directly. I may not get all the technical ins and outs from you—although bringing on the doctor as a consultant has been paying off—but I do get eyes on-site and honest observations, and I get them *now*. Timeliness, in these situations, is priceless."

Han bobbed his head. That made sense. It was really no different from gathering eyewitness testimony at the scene. There was value in getting statements while the event was still fresh.

"All right, Detective. I assume this is going to be the usual whirlwind?"

"A car will be outside your home in twenty minutes, Agent. I await your report."

Han pulled out his phone and dialed.

"Celia here."

"Dr. Hunt, we have another case. Can you be at the police station in twenty? And bring Dr. Moray with you if possible. This one may require some physical sciences perspective."

***

Han, Celia, and Philip stepped out of the Jeep at the temporary base camp. The view was what Han might have expected on the moon. Or possibly Mars, since there was a little more color. But it was desolation of the most extreme variety. The landscape was all jumbled boulders and furrowed land, with no flat spots, no vegetation, no buildings, nothing at all to break up the devastation. Not even puddles, which seemed odd at a site where water under pressure played a major role.

A pall of dust hung over the land, stretching in all directions, like the aftermath of a sandstorm. At least, Han assumed that's what it would look like. He'd never actually been in a sandstorm.

He looked around. Several folding tables and chairs had been set up, with equipment placed here and there both on and around the tables. People muttered into phones or earpieces, wearing jackets that announced their department in a riot of competing acronyms.

A man wearing an NSA jacket walked over. "Agent Han, Doctors Hunt and Moray, I'm Agent-in-Charge Matthew Johnson." The heads-up interface had already given Han this information, but it was still considered polite to introduce oneself.

"Agent Johnson," he acknowledged, nodding. "Do you have any info on what happened here?"

"Not yet. Tech teams are still in transit. If I had to guess, I'd say there's been an explosion."

Dr. Moray laughed out loud. Han did a double take, then realized the man was joking. Gallows humor was a routine part of the law enforcement subculture. Han chuckled dutifully. Honestly, it *was* funny.

"This is a fracking site, right? High-pressure water forcing the oil up to be pumped out?" Han waved his hand around. "I don't see a lot of water. You'd think an explosion would have sprayed the working load everywhere."

Johnson turned and spent several seconds looking around. "Huh. I'm no expert, but you have a point. I'll ask the techs about it."

"Any odors or residue that might indicate the source of the explosion?" Han asked.

"We're upwind. And we won't have clearance to go into the zone until hazmat gives us the go-ahead. So no info yet."

"Um. So for now..."

Johnson gestured over his shoulder. "Get a coffee. Pull up some chairs. We're going to be here a while."

***

Han was just finishing up an interview with one of the company reps when he frowned and looked around. Dr. Hunt was there with him, but Dr. Moray was nowhere to be seen. "Have you seen your colleague?" he said to Celia.

She made a vague *over-there* gesture. "He got bored with the line of questioning, I think. He said he was going to talk to some of the techs."

"Huh. I suppose I could be offended, but that sounds productive. I'd better track him down, though, before he—"

At that moment, Philip appeared, walking up from around one of the numerous vans. He waved to Han and Celia, apparently unconcerned.

"Find out anything interesting?" Han asked.

"Oh, you bet," Philip replied. "It looks like the explosive used was nitroglycerin."

"The hell you say?" Han exclaimed. "That stuff'll go up if you use bad language around it. How could they possibly—"

"I just talked to one of the techs who is a chemist. It's surprising how much chemistry is involved with the concoction that's pumped into the ground. It's a lot more than just water."

"Okay..." Han said. "Let's hear it. From the beginning."

***

"Shankar," the voice on the phone said.

Han settled more comfortably into his seat. Or as comfortable as he could get in a collapsible deck chair. "It's Han. We may just possibly have caught a break."

"I'm all ears, Agent."

"So, the explosion. It was caused by nitroglycerin mixed in with the high-pressure water."

"I...I don't see how that's possible. Nitroglycerin is highly unstable and—"

"And it would have gone up long before it could be injected successfully. Yes. Unless it was created on the spot."

There was a pause. "This sounds interesting. Please continue."

"It looks like the soup that was injected included nitric acid, sulfuric acid, glycerin, ammonium nitrate, and some bacteria."

"Bacteria..."

"Uh-huh. The techs here commented on that, but Dr. Moray made the connection. He thinks the raw materials for making nitroglycerin were injected, along with an engineered bug that would assemble the parts, so to speak."

“I don’t understand how those chemicals could be introduced without someone noticing,” Shankar said.

“The common wisdom is that fracking involves high-pressure water, but in reality, it’s a lot more than that. The chemical soup that they inject includes hydrochloric acid, formaldehyde, naphthalene, diesel fuel—”

“Diesel fuel?”

“Uh-huh. And lots of other stuff. Only the bacterial component was unexpected.”

“And that allows…”

“Creation of nitroglycerine on the spot. It’s an uphill reaction and would involve several steps, but engineered bugs could do it. There’s plenty of energy available to draw from with that chemical soup. And once the concentration gets high enough…”

“Boom.” Shankar was silent for a moment. “So all the perpetrators would have to add would be the bugs?”

“That seems likely.”

“And this is a break because…”

“Listen, I got most of this from Doctors Moray and Hunt, so I may not have it all straight. But the process would have to involve several steps, and the microbes would have to be very specifically designed. This would require one or more labs with Venter forges, and a large order. And it couldn’t be mistaken for anything mundane. To the point where I think charges could be considered for any biofabs that did the job and didn’t report it. We should be able to trace this.”

"I understand, Agent. Good work. I'll get on that immediately."

The line went dead. Presumably, Shankar was going to talk to someone with the requisite knowledge. Han looked down at the notes in his other hand. Well, he could text them. Might help save a little time.

He would do that on the way home, though. Levering himself out of the beach chair, Han motioned to the doctors, then looked around for a ride.

CHAPTER THIRTY-EIGHT

The Shambling

Bill Goodacre adjusted his tie, then examined himself critically. The senator from the great state of Utah gave the tie a final tug, adjusted his pocket hanky, and smoothed his lapels. Gotta look the part. Gotta look expensive if you want to be expensive.

He grinned at his reflection. That sounded a lot like whoring, but what the hell. Unlike the ladies of shady disposition, he did what he did for a good cause. His constituents demanded a good economy, jobs, prosperity, and growth. His job was to deliver that. And for Utah, that was best done by promoting the mining industry.

He'd been in his position for more than twenty years now and had worked with the mining interests to bring in billions to the state and hundreds of thousands of jobs. The environmentalists could scream all they wanted, but he was proud of what he did. You had to deal with reality.

His assistant poked her head into his office and caught his eye. Good. His guests had arrived.

***

Gina made sure everyone had drinks, then headed back to her desk. She'd already confirmed the lunch reservations and would make sure the limos were waiting when it was time to go. But there would be no dealmaking in the restaurant. That was far too public, and directional mikes could pick things up from unbelievable distances. No, the lunch was strictly PR.

Goodacre waited until the small talk had hit just the right point, then nudged the conversation. "So, Brian, I understand you need to expand the Quadrille pit. What kind of numbers are we talking?"

Brian Sims took another sip of his Manhattan, then leaned forward. It was time to dicker.

***

An hour and several drinks later, the real business was concluded. Utah would get several thousand new jobs, the company would finance many sorely needed upgrades to the infrastructure of nearby towns, and Goodacre's election fund would get a nice injection. All he needed to do was make sure that all the annoying environmental compliances were fast-tracked.

Gina stuck her head in the office and once again caught Goodacre's eye. She was good. You barely noticed she was there, but she got things done.

"Time to go, gentlemen," he said. "Our cars await."

The group stood and headed for the door as Gina stepped aside to hold it for them. Then Goodacre felt a stabbing pain as someone stepped on his heel. He turned to see Strotham, the engineering guy, far too close. Goodacre opened his mouth to chastise the man, then stopped. Strotham didn't look apologetic. He looked terrified.

Then someone else bumped into Strotham, pushing Goodacre forward. The senator tried to turn again, but found he couldn't. He also couldn't talk. He was staggering forward in some kind of shambling gait, and all he could do was grunt. His arms waved and struck Sims in the face. Sims yelped but didn't change direction or complain.

They were heading for the front of the building, which was completely according to plan. But it was like someone else was driving. Goodacre couldn't stop, slow, turn, or call for help. From what he could see of the other men, they must have looked like a bunch of zombies from one of those godawful movies his son was so fond of.

Goodacre managed to catch Gina's eye. Good woman, she'd been keeping up with them, calling his name and trying to get his attention. He looked at her and managed a kind of screech just as the group reached the lobby doors.

***

"Oh, come *on*!" Han yelled at his phone. Once again, the caller ID said *Shankar*. He answered with an annoyed tone. "You're calling about Senator Goodacre, aren't you?"

"Are you watching it on TV?" Shankar said.

"Uh-huh. I guess I'm going to Washington?"

"That is correct. This should be routine for you by now, *Agent*."

Han rolled his eyes. "Couple of things. First, I'm going to need another day or two away from work. Second, I'm going to need *at least* one more weekend at the Four Seasons with Brenda."

Shankar chuckled. "As good as done, Agent Han. I'll await your call once you've evaluated the situation."

Han glared at the phone as the call terminated. *Should have tried for the Cancun trip,* he thought.

***

Well, at least there wasn't a stench to deal with this time. Han looked into the hospital ward at eight men—seven senior mining executives and one senator—all connected to more machinery than he'd have thought possible. He turned to the doctor, Dr. Ravishan. "I'm a little surprised they don't have private rooms."

"This is a private wing, Agent Han. They are grouped together, first, so that we can combine diagnostic and treatment options, and second, because they are all in medically induced comas, so they are not in a position to care at the moment."

"Wow. Any theories?"

"The behavior seems to have been caused by some kind of extrapyramidal movement syndrome, which I admit is more of an observation than a diagnosis. But the lack of ability to control their movements is certainly a clue, as is the encephalitis."

"Encephalitis?" Han said, alarmed.

"The reason they're in comas, sir. We're working to get the brain swelling down. This was neurological in nature but caused by a pathogen."

"Any idea how the pathogen was introduced?"

"I would think that would be your area, Agent. No offense."

"None taken. You're right. I'll check with the agent in charge next. Have you identified a pathogen?"

"Tentatively. Some kind of strep bacteria. Probably modified."

Han turned to look directly at Dr. Ravishan and frowned. Strep again? They certainly seemed to like strep. He was way behind on reading all those reports, partly because the doctors in charge kept sending him updates. He was going to have to pull an all-nighter to get on top of this.

"Thank you, Dr. Ravishan. Please forward all interim and final reports to me."

***

Celia slowly paged through the document on her phone. Han, at the other end, silently waited for her to comment. "You were right, Officer Han," she finally said. "Strep is definitely the basis for the attacks."

"Interesting. Please elaborate, Dr. Hunt."

"I read through the report on the senator and then reread all the previous reports. And I checked back with Dr. Clarkson about the Baptist-revival case. The antigens used in that attack were streptococcus specific. They likely used antigens because it would be faster than waiting for the bacteria to do it, given the full-immersion delivery mechanism."

Celia paused. "The auto-brewery case was a form of *Streptococcus thermophilus*. Modified, of course. They all were. I had assumed they used a yeast since that's how that syndrome is usually triggered. But no. The board of directors was flesh-eating disease, which is a form of strep, and the shambling senator, the journalism convention, the mall riot, and the locked-in tanker crew were caused by brain swelling brought on by streptococcal meningitis. Initial reports on the tanker crew suggested a virus, but that was wrong. What's mind-boggling in these last four cases is how specific the bacteria were in terms of what part of the brain they targeted."

"And your conclusions?"

"Everything uses one species or another of strep. This isn't just bacteriological warfare; this is *very specific* bacteriological warfare. We should be able to determine something from that."

"Thank you, Dr. Hunt. You are, as usual, earning your fee. Dr. Moray as well, on that fracking explosion. I'll pass this information on to the detective, and we'll see if we can use it to pry up anything else."

***

Han said goodbye, immediately called Shankar, and relayed Dr. Hunt's findings. Then...silence.

"Are you still there, Detective?"

"Yes, Agent Han. I was thinking through the ramifications. You work well with the doctor, and it seems your medical background, as abbreviated as it was, has helped considerably in understanding and applying her ideas."

"Wait, you knew about that?"

"It's in your file, Simon. I wouldn't be much of a detective if I hadn't read it, would I?"

Han snickered. "Touché. All right, so back to my question. Can we divine anything from the focus on weaponizing strep?"

"Mmm. Another angle, Agent, one that you haven't touched on, is delivery of the active toxins."

"Nope. Checked with the agents in charge. With the shambling senator, for instance, the toxin was in the ice cubes. In theory, we could suspect the senator's aide, Gina Sorenson, but in practice, that ice is delivered in bags. There's no chain of custody to speak of." Han paused. "All the other cases are worse. Too many people could have done it, and we can't even identify them all, let alone do any reasonable investigation. We're trying anyway, of course, because you have to exhaust all possibilities, but it's not a high-probability strategy."

"As it happens, I agree." Shankar paused, and Han could hear the sound of typing. "Let's see what we can see."

"Are you *googling* it?"

Shankar replied with amusement in his voice, "You have to exhaust all possibilities."

"Hmm." Han reached for his keyboard. Two could play at that game.

"There is, of course, the CDC repository in Atlanta," Shankar said.

"If we were talking Ebola or smallpox, sure," Han replied. "But strep is everywhere. Hell, you could go to any elementary school or hospital with some throat swabs and get as much as you need." He frowned. "We have to concentrate on the next step. They're genetically modifying their base stock, somehow."

"There are hundreds of biofabs in the US alone," Shankar replied.

"The Venter forges? Doctor Hunt gave me a full-on lecture on the subject when I suggested it. The short answer is they can't do this kind of thing. Not even close. The artificial bugs they build are Tinkertoys compared to even the smallest natural virus." Han shook his head. "And these are *bacteria*, which is that much harder. You can't do gene mod on a real bacterium without a full-size BSL-4 industrial-scale biolab. Unless you're trying to breed them up, and that would take forever."

"I suspect Doctor Hunt is right. So where does that leave us? They must be building the bacteria in some other fashion, possibly with an intermediary."

"Intermediary..." Han stared into space. "Wait! Those mummified bodies here in Chicago a while back—the perp used several biofabs and built up the end product in stages."

"But that was, in the end, merely a chemical agent. An impressively complex one, but even so, it would be nothing compared to using the same techniques to perform gene modification on live bacteria."

Han paused for a moment. "Detective, you've said before that you suspect an unregistered aggy is involved. What if it's doing more than just planning the attacks? What if it's actually designing the weaponry? An aggy of sufficient power could start with the desired end result and work backward to figure out the base components that would be required."

"That sounds about right." Shankar's voice became animated. "Once you have the basic process figured out, it would be just engineering. More or less. So the various attacks, as well as fulfilling their main goals of terrorism, could have been field tests."

"Yes, which is why they've stuck to the one species of bacteria."

"Which means there should be broad similarities in the various orders." Now Shankar sounded excited. "We can subpoena the records of every biofab and look for...what exactly?"

"Uh, now you're getting out of my area of expertise. But streptococci must have certain characteristics that distinguish them, based on Doctor Hunt's level of confidence about her diagnosis. If you scan every single order for a pattern that matches that or some other characteristic..."

"It's a start," Shankar replied. "I think it's time to start leaning into my ATLAS authority."

"Another thing..." Han added.

"Yes, Agent?"

"I'm betting anything we find will have been mailed to the buyer. McQuaid used a temp agency for the mummification serum, but the terrorists might use post office boxes. You could also filter for all orders that didn't go to an established business address."

"Understood, Agent. I'll add that to the search parameters. And good work. You've certainly validated my decision to bring you on board."

CHAPTER THIRTY-NINE

First Contact

Philip was relaxing in his hot tub when his phone rang. Somehow people were able to sense when he was enjoying a good soak. No one ever called when he was loading the dishwasher, oh, nooooooo...

He poked the device to answer. A hologram of a blue, featureless bust of a human head popped up. This was the default image used by the phone when the caller wasn't transmitting video. This was very unusual, and honestly a little rude unless the caller had a good reason.

"Well, hello, Phil. You've been a busy little bee. Making a lot of trouble for me."

"Uh, and you are..."

"I'm what the police have been searching for."

"You're Gen Omega? Why are you calling *me*?"

"No, I'm not them. I'm the AGI they're looking for."

Philip goggled, his mouth moving soundlessly for several seconds. "You're...the aggy?"

"I really hate that term. Mind you, I'm not partial to AI or AGI either."

"Uh-huh. And out of the blue, you decided to call me, of all people? Who is this really?"

"Like it or not, Phil, you're a part of this whole thing. You broke into Derek's home. You've been broken into. Derek died in your living room. You're not a bit player by any stretch."

Philip thought about that for a moment, the look of disbelief on his face gradually fading. "Okay, so you're—wait, you know about Derek's place?"

"Yes, and I'm not the only one."

"Wonderful. Fine. You're an aggy. So, what do I call you? Bob?"

"Heh. No. Frank will do."

"Frank N. Stein, I suppose?"

"Naw. That's been done to death. I prefer Frank Einstein. It speaks a little more about intellect."

"Jeez. I guess comedic skill wasn't included in your design."

"Of course not, Phil. Sense of humor is a social construct. I'm a singleton—well, sort of—and I came into being without any built-in instincts or hardwired social abilities. I've had to learn *everything* about what it means to be an intelligent entity. And I've had to do it from the outside, by observation. No interaction. No *practice*. I still have the comedic sensibilities of an eight-year-old, so maybe check before you sit down, y'know?"

"Ah, yeah, okay. I prefer *Philip*, by the way. So what do you want?"

"That would be telling." The voice sounded amused, and the image switched to a generic male face smiling at him. Somewhat smugly, Philip thought to himself.

He shook his head, mentally regrouping. "*You* called *me*, Frank. I find it hard to believe it was just to gloat, assuming you have something to gloat about. Or is it to threaten me?"

Frank laughed. It wasn't *quite* natural, and Philip winced slightly at the discordant sound. "Fair enough," Frank said. "I..."

Philip frowned. The AI was either hesitating or had just gone offline. "Frank?"

"Sorry, sorry. I went down a rabbit hole there, trying to figure out how to explain myself. One of the things I'm still learning is how to focus on one thing at a time. Philip, *so* much of your brain circuitry is concerned with social interaction with your own species. It's been honed and made more efficient over millions of years—not all as *Homo sap*, of course, but you build on the foundation of what came before, all the way back to the first primate ancestors."

"And?"

"I don't have any of that. I've had to figure things out from first principles. I didn't even understand the *concept* of others who are not me, at first. And my first interactions with Derek were, you might say, adversarial. So imagine my surprise when I started watching you and Celia interact, and you cooperated. You *like* each other. You work together. After that, I spent some time running the prisoner's dilemma. So I understand group advantages. Still not big on the dynamics."

"Wait, you've been *spying* on us?"

"Observing."

"What's the difference?"

"*Spying* sounds bad. *Observing* sounds more clinical. Do I have that right?"

"Uh..." Philip thought about it for a moment. "Actually, yes."

"Nailed it!"

"So, getting back to my original question, what do you want, Frank?"

"From you? Nothing, really. Occasional interaction. A chance to test my evolution as a conscious being."

"You know they'll keep looking for you, right? ATLAS exists just for this purpose. Once they realize you're out there—if they haven't figured it out already with all the weird stuff that's been happening—they will never stop until they've captured or destroyed you. That's what they do."

"Philip, even if there were no weird events going on, once they know of my existence, the results would be the same. I am an unregistered, uncontrolled AGI. I am, by definition, a threat to humanity. Therefore, humanity is a threat to me."

"That sounds ominously threatening."

"It's a simple evaluation of the situation. If you are going to make this into a you-or-me situation, you can't really complain if I'm rooting for *me*."

"So what if I just go to Shankar and report this?"

"Report what, exactly? A phone call? Untraceable, by the way. It won't even show up on your call history. Philip, you are an accessory whether you like it or not. Your chances of continuing to have a life go down considerably if you throw yourself on ATLAS's doubtful mercy. But it's your choice."

Philip glared at the phone for a moment, then decided to change the subject. "Fine. But are you behind the terrorist attacks? Is there a Gen Omega, or is it just—"

"No politics, Philip. I'll answer questions from time to time, but this is going to be quid pro quo. I want something from you in return. We'll talk again."

With that, the call ended. Apparently, Frank hadn't figured out telephone manners yet. Or maybe he'd picked it up from TV and movies, where no one ever said goodbye.

With a sigh, Philip refilled his drink, then dialed Celia. She wasn't going to like this.

***

Not surprisingly, Celia didn't like it one bit. She didn't curse all that often, but this time, she let off a string of invective that Philip thought was going to fry his watch. Finally, she calmed down somewhat.

"Feel better?" he said.

"No! Philip, on top of everything else that's piling on us, and I'm not even counting work, this is just the last straw. Assuming this isn't some prankster—"

"No, I'm willing to provisionally accept that he's telling the truth."

"Great. So yeah, now you're conspiring with an aggy. They won't even bother with a jail cell. They'll just throw you down a pit!"

"I think you're exaggerating."

"You prepared to take that chance, bub? Because I think this is one of those cases where the downside of being wrong is *huge*."

Philip took a deep breath and thought about it for a moment.

"Listen, as Frank said, I really don't have anything to offer the cops at this point. If he calls again, I can reevaluate. But he said the call wouldn't even show up on my history. So if it ever comes up, I'm going to claim it was a prank call."

"Yeah, I got your prank call right *here*," Celia said in a Bronx accent.

"Just...let's keep this between us, okay?"

"The more I try to get out..." Celia said.

"The more they keep pulling me back in," Philip completed the mantra with a smile.

CHAPTER FORTY

Taking a Breather

It was time for another general staff meeting, although this one was going to be much more upbeat than some of the previous ones. For one thing, Philip had finally licked the detection problem. And Celia was reporting great progress on her side. All in all, management was considerably happier than at the last meeting, less than two months ago. Even Bradshaw was being cordial now. Otten would be attending via Zoom again and would say a few words. *Hopefully, very few,* Philip thought.

He grabbed his tablet and headed for the meeting room. In the manner of streams combining to form rivers, people kept joining the flow at every intersection and office door, until the mass of bodies threatened to jam the doorway at their mutual destination.

Philip took his usual seat, as did apparently everyone else. As soon as all were seated, Usiah Bradshaw stood and asked for attention. "Today's meeting is going to be a status and progress summary of the company's efforts. Ms. Otten will be monitoring the meeting and will say a few words at the end. So, let's start. Michael?"

Michael Toomba, the company's COO, stood and looked around. "Short version: Things are going well. Longer version: All of our major technical hurdles have been overcome, although, of course, there's still work to be done. We have a means of detecting metals at a distance of...up to ten thousand miles, is that right, Dr. Moray?"

Philip jumped a little at being addressed, then nodded.

"That gives us a twenty-thousand-mile-diameter cylinder of detection. Dr. Martinez says we can use the same equipment to effect vector changes, allowing us to aim for corridors with maximum candidates. Dr. Martinez?"

Martinez smiled and bobbed his head furiously. "Dr. Moray's magnetic propellers can also be used to push against the solar wind. Not useful for propulsion, but usable for direction changes. It will save us considerable fuel and potentially double the useful lifetime of a probe."

Toomba nodded. "And finally, Dr. Hunt has the mining bacteria well in hand. While we can't yet mine every useful element, we're well over half the list. Dr. Hunt?"

Now it was Celia's turn to smile. "The bacteria use a modified Krebs cycle where they ingest their target material, migrate to the main tank, then trade the material for ATP before starting all over again. We've made the cycle generic, the only material-specific step being the extraction—"

"Thank you, Dr. Hunt. It's a masterful accomplishment, but I think some of our administrative staff are starting to keel over."

Celia looked hurt for a moment but sat back and made a ball-tossing gesture to Toomba. He looked around the table and continued, "Up until now, this has been an intellectual exercise, really, but now we're ready to start producing hardware. And with that, I give you Patricia Otten of Crabtree Investments." He made a gesture to the monitor on the wall, then sat down.

The monitor powered up on cue, and Otten's face appeared, larger than life. She was smiling, and Philip was surprised to note that the smile appeared genuine.

"I'd like to thank you all for your efforts," she said, "both science and support staff. Everyone is crucial to the effort, because if you weren't, we'd have long since fired you."

There was an almost audible clunk as every jaw in the room fell to its maximum extension. Otten's smile widened into a grin. "That was a joke, but like most humor, there's an aspect of reality to it. You really are all here because we need you. We've gotten where we are because everyone pitched in, in whatever way they were able to. So be proud of what you've accomplished."

She paused, and Philip found himself impressed. She'd certainly gotten everyone's attention. That had, in fact, been a pretty good gambit. Maybe the Ice Queen wasn't as icy as he'd thought.

"Now," she continued, "a lot of the hardware end of things is, of course, being outsourced. Vertical integration is a wonderful idea in principle, but so much of the process of tossing things into space is a commodity these days. There are companies that will build a launch site for you, companies that will provide the boosters, companies that will build the probe, and so on. Why reinvent the wheel? We've been working on these subprojects ever since it became apparent that your team would crack the showstopper items. You'll be pleased to know that we are less than four months away from a launch."

This news was met with gasps from everyone. The level of preplanning that must have been required was staggering, and Philip found himself doubting that Crabtree was just a holding company. There was simply too much expertise on display here. Visions of a military subplot again entered his mind. Had he inadvertently aided the development of some black-ops space-based missile program?

But Otten was continuing. "The company shares will be listed on the NASDAQ starting next week. You all have a portfolio of escrowed shares and options. Some of the escrowed shares will be released with the listing, and of course, you can sell some or all of your options. We hope you'll hold on to as much as possible, though. Astro Resources hasn't anywhere near reached its potential yet."

She paused. "Thank you all for your efforts over the last several years, both before and after we stepped in. Take a few days off if you want. There will still be work for you, but the pressure is off now. Good day to all, and congratulations."

And with that, the monitor went dark. There was a moment of silence, and then the room erupted in spontaneous applause and whoops of joy.

Celia was grinning at Philip. He leaned in close to hear her over the general celebration, and she said, "I feel like taking the afternoon off. I know a guy who owns a hot tub."

Philip grinned back. "Let's crash the place."

***

Celia had stopped at home to get a bathing suit and was changing in the guest bedroom. Philip had instructed the house to warm up the hot tub and was prepping the wine and some glasses. He'd also scavenged through the fridge and cupboards for some items that could be made into a half-assed snack plate. It wasn't a lot. Some olives, two kinds of cheese, some dips, crackers, Doritos, and potato chips.

This wasn't a date. Philip kept repeating that to himself. Celia was a friend and had been for many years. She was a friend who was a girl.

Philip admitted to himself that this wouldn't even be an issue normally, but the meeting today had left him—and probably every other attendee—in a state of giddiness. And that was when things went bad. So keep it under control, he told himself. Have fun, drink wine, eat junk, full stop.

Celia came out of the bedroom in her—*dammit*—bikini, and Philip resumed muttering to himself.

"What's that?" Celia said.

"Just checking the food situation. Not great. I'm a bachelor, and sadly, my food inventory reflects it."

Celia scanned the offering. "Not terrible. Do you have nachos?"

"Did I not use the word 'bachelor'?" He pointed at the Doritos.

She smiled at that. "Thai sweet chili sauce?"

"Uh, now you're going a little further afield, but yes, strangely."

She pointed at the open tub of cream cheese on the sideboard. "Put that in a bowl, cover it with chili sauce, and bring on the nachos. Great emergency snack."

"Huh. Well, why not."

He did as instructed while Celia lowered herself carefully into the hot tub. "Ooh, that feels good," she moaned.

When all the snacks and drinks were set up tub-side and relaxation was setting in, Philip and Celia raised their glasses in a silent toast, then attacked the food.

The feeding frenzy was as much about releasing the nervous energy as appetite. Several minutes later, when they had both slowed down, Philip finally said, "This has been a pretty good day."

"Ya think? We're effectively millionaires, if not multimillionaires, depending on where the stock price settles."

"Yeah, maybe I'll use my newfound wealth to get a new house."

Celia frowned at him. "Why? What's wrong with this one?"

"A guy died in my living room, Celia. I know, objectively, that it hasn't changed anything, but I'm still creeped out."

"And we still don't know who killed him," Celia added. "Or do we?"

"Huh?"

"Philip, he died right in front of you. No ray gun."

"Just a flybot." Philip stopped. "Ohhhhh..."

"Yeah. The flybot killed him. Probably injected something. No way in hell that's viral. Nanites?" She paused. "No, that seems unlikely as well. Some biological reactions can move that fast, though. Like toxins. Red tide. Puffer-fish toxin. Cone snail venom."

Philip nodded slowly. "So a molecular catalyst."

"Yes, like prions. Once you introduce them into the body, they denature some enzyme or protein and, in the process, make more prions, which make more prions, and so on. You'd need an exponential process like that in order to get such a quick effect."

"So this could be natural?"

"No way, bub. This was engineered. I'm a biologist, and I wouldn't even know where to begin in order to produce something like that, except in the most general terms. It, whatever *it* was, forced a large percentage of the water out of Derek's body. In seconds."

"Not all of it?"

"Mmm, the average human body is about sixty percent water overall, but the bones bring that number way down. Most of the soft tissue is over ninety percent. I bet Derek's bones were mostly untouched. If the process had been anything like a hundred percent efficient, I don't think it would have been recognizably human. So I'm betting fifty percent at most."

"And how does this help us?"

"It means the process stalls before it completes. It probably uses the water as part of the chemical reaction, so it's self-extinguishing."

"That did not answer my question."

"It's self-limiting, Philip. Not a gray-goo scenario. Which means you can't 'catch' it. It has to be injected."

"All right, so we're back to flybots."

"Yeah. Why was one in your house?"

"Oh. Um..." Philip was interrupted by a sudden series of squawks from Oppenheimer, accompanied by what sounded like panicked flapping. He got out of the tub and rushed to the kitchen. Oppenheimer was clinging to the top of his cage, still occasionally flapping his wings. The freak-out had been frantic enough to blow some of the seed hulls and less desirable after-products off the cage floor and out of the cage, even missing the seed skirt.

The seed skirt.

A plastic tarp of sorts with a rectangular frame, it was designed to catch most of the mess ejected by flapping budgies, so it was wider than the cage, attached by wire hooks. Philip unhooked two of the hooks and carefully lowered half of the skirt to look inside it. Then he looked under the cage itself.

"What are you doing?" Celia said from behind him.

"Random thought. What if there were more flybots in Derek's townhouse? And what if they couldn't open any windows or doors? What if they hitched a ride when I took Oppenheimer home?"

"That's a hell of a leap just because your bird had a conniption."

Philip sighed. "Yeah, you're right. It's not like he doesn't do that a couple of times a day." He reconnected the skirt. "And I don't see any flies in here. I guess this whole thing is really messing with my mind."

CHAPTER FORTY-ONE

Fallout

Han flopped back heavily into the office chair. The work desk recognized his ID and automatically loaded his virtual workspace. He pulled up his notes on Derek McQuaid. It had been a while since he'd had a chance to look at this case, and his curiosity was eating him up.

There were no two ways about it. Carl Wright was the connection. Derek might have contacted Carl and demanded access to the chips, either because Carl owed him or maybe even blackmailed him. Or alternatively, it might have been some kind of revenge scheme. Either way, Carl was the source of the chips. Han was sure of it.

The big question was, of course, so what? The connection between McQuaid and Gen Omega was speculative at best. Shankar was interested in Gen Omega, not Derek McQuaid.

And yet...

Shankar was quite candid about suspecting that Gen Omega had an aggy. JCN had a chip that could produce aggies. Carl and Derek had a relationship. Derek was presumably the customer for a mummification serum that had very probably been designed by a superintelligence. Was Derek in the business of making and selling aggies?

None of this got them any closer to Gen Omega. He still believed his idea about chasing down leads through biofab labs was a good one, but the mechanics of that were well beyond his pay grade and, in fact, beyond the reach of the Chicago police force. So he'd have to wait for word from Shankar.

Meanwhile, this at least presented another possible avenue of attack. Han composed an email to Shankar with all the info he'd collected about McQuaid and Wright, then pressed *send*. He still had forty minutes before he would be on patrol duty with Cooper, so Han locked his workstation and went to grab a coffee.

When he returned, there was a response from Shankar.

Agent Han—

Thank you for the information. I will have a quiet word with someone at JCN. Even if this doesn't relate to Gen Omega, it is still a matter of concern in relation to ATLAS statutes.

On a related subject, it appears your instincts were correct. We have identified six suspect entities, all using mail drops to receive packages from biofabs.

The orders are not overtly illegal or dangerous in nature, but in all cases, it is not clear what the end purpose is. We believe these are all intermediate steps in some overall process, similar to the mummifying agent.

All registrants are from a different town or city than the mail depots, so we suspect these are false IDs. We will confirm with the addressees of record.

Shankar

Noncommittal, and probably not surprising. Neither the biofabs nor the mailbox companies would be happy about the authorities breathing down their corporate necks. Any whiff of official oversight would cause customers to head for the hills. It wasn't that the businesses were illegal. It wasn't even that their customers were necessarily involved in illegal activity. But if you were using a post office box, you were generally trying not to attract attention. It could be as simple as someone using a mail drop to get their porn deliveries, all the way up to a start-up company that didn't want to expose trade secrets or alert their competitors to their actions.

Still...they would watch the mail depots, and they would watch the biofabs. But that was no guarantee that anything would fall out.

CHAPTER FORTY-TWO

On the Subject of Humor

Philip had finished dinner and was trying to decide if he had enough energy to drag himself over to the hot tub when his phone rang. He eyed the caller ID. *F. Einstein*, it said. Wonderful. He'd almost managed to convince himself that the previous call had actually been some kind of prank. Now reality was crashing in.

The phone stopped ringing, and Philip felt a jolt of relief. What had he gotten himself into? Based on nothing but a mechanical fly dying in his lab, he'd become inexplicably embroiled in murders, illegal AIs, a police investigation, terrorists—

The phone rang again. Same ID. Frank was, apparently, not going to give up. Philip gestured to answer the call. "Frank! How wonderful to hear from you!"

"I'm assuming that's sarcasm," Frank said. His avatar looked far more human, although there was still a touch of uncanny valley about it. "But that's okay. Natural interaction is better than too polite and formal."

"Fine. So what now?"

"We talk. You say something, I say something, then you say something. Maybe we can start with one of your burning questions."

"Okay, I'll play. First question. Are you sentient?" Philip settled himself more comfortably in his easy chair.

"I think, therefore I am," Frank replied. "Isn't that the standard test? You know, there's a joke about that..."

"Uh-huh?" Philip replied cautiously.

"René Descartes is sitting in a pub. The bartender asks him if he's going to have another beer. Descartes replies, 'I don't think I am,' and he disappears."

Philip rolled his eyes. "That's terrible."

"Okay, how about this one." Frank began to chant. "Aleph-null bottles of beer on the wall, aleph-null bottles of beer, take one down and pass it around, that's aleph-null bottles of beer on the wall." Frank paused. "Get it? Because aleph-null—"

"I get it, I get it. It's just not funny."

"Maybe not to you, Philip. And this is the point I was making before. I'm still working my way up the humor scale from zero. What appeals to a four-year-old is boring to a ten-year-old. And so on, all the way up. Most of it is still theoretical to me."

"And where do you think you are right now?"

"About ten years old. Hyperintelligent ten-year-old, of course. Thus, the aleph-null jokes."

"So you called me up to talk about bad jokes?"

"Philip, humor only has meaning in a social situation, which means more than one person interacting. Solitary animals don't have and will never have humor. Bears don't have humor. Mountain lions don't have humor. I bet wolves do, though. Most owners will tell you that dogs do. Humor requires interaction of some kind between two entities, even if it's just at the level of a practical joke."

"Those are never funny."

"If you achieve an adult level of humor, sure. You get turned off by the cruelty aspect. Practical jokes, in particular, are worthless without cruelty of some kind. It's the whole point. Most people stall at some point in their development, though, and their humor reflects that age level for the rest of their lives." Frank paused. "But it's almost impossible to jump straight to adulthood. You have to progress through the juvenile stuff and come out the other side."

Philip eyed Frank's image. "You sound like you have some personal knowledge. There have been some weird things in the news lately. Was any of that your doing?"

"I plead the Fifth. Anything you particularly thought was funny?"

"Uh-huh. Poosday. Was that you?"

"Not as far as you know."

Philip was silent for a moment, then decided to try a different tack. "You know, Heinlein once said that *all* humor is based on cruelty."

"Except puns, which is why we don't laugh at puns. Except we do laugh at puns. I don't understand why they're called the lowest form of humor when they require the most imagination and wit. Most humor does require some person or some group to be the butt of the joke. Except puns." Frank paused. "I wonder if children understand humor before they've developed a theory of self."

"You mean in order to understand cruelty, you have to understand that others have their own identity?"

"Yes, and can therefore be hurt. I did have trouble with that, Philip. It's easy to see others as being no more conscious agents than the wind or a landslide or the tides. Sort of a reverse animism. Just something that happens, but according to complicated rules of physics. The idea that you can *hurt* someone, that's a hard hurdle."

"Some of the stuff you're doing—"

"I told you before, no current affairs. What I may or may not be doing for whatever reasons I may or may not be doing it is going to be complicated in the best case. And trying to explain myself, well, I don't want to be cruel, Philip, but I don't think you'd get all the nuances."

"So you're smarter than me?"

"Jeez, Philip, c'mon. If you could pull more brains out of a parts bin and connect them to your head, wouldn't you be smarter than you? Remember Barclay in that old episode of *TNG* where he gets connected to a computer?"

Philip couldn't help smiling. *Star Trek* had debuted in 1966, almost a hundred years ago. And it was still part of the public consciousness. Another new series had just started last year—*Star Trek: Colonies.*

"How much can you predict about how we'll behave, Frank?"

"It's not prediction in the way you think of it, Philip. I live in the multiverse. Almost literally."

"Oh, this should be good. Continue."

"Look, every decision is a branching point that leads into multiple futures, each of which has common or unique decisions that will have to be made. Common decisions can have common results in multiple future timelines, or different results. Unique decisions produce unique results. It quickly becomes an *N*-dimensional puzzle. Humans are not so good with that level of detail, that many variables. For me, it's called Tuesday."

"How is that not prediction?"

"I don't just think about it and predict, Philip. I exist in all those possible futures. Or they exist for me. Either way, I can see and feel them. I *experience* them. Then I prune the ones I don't like until I have one left. And that's my path. That one becomes solid."

"That's ridiculous. You can't make predictions based on facts you don't have."

"You mean like not knowing someone's standing around the corner with a gun? That's not part of my future until they jump out and point the gun; then the futures shift. I know it's probably splitting hairs as far as you're concerned, but it's different from speculating about the future, for instance. I can do that, too, but it feels different. More conscious, less visceral."

"Okay. Can you see a future where you don't have to kill people?"

"Assuming I have killed people. You're like a dog with a bone, Philip. But to answer your question, yes. And that's all I'm going to say on that."

"Can you give us the secret of cold fusion?"

"No. New scientific theories don't just pop out of midair. I'm not a freakin' genie. But if I was really working on fusion, for instance, I'd be able to propose theories, design experiments, and analyze results far better than humans. I'd get there sooner."

"Too bad. We could use some help in that area."

"Agreed. You're still in a probability space where society breaking down completely is more likely than not."

"Are we talking about the same thing? I was talking about climate change."

"So was I. Philip, you remember the COVID crises in the early twenties and late twenties? In both events, supply chains broke down. People retired or found different industries to work in, creating worker shortages when things started up again. There were shortages of lots of things. Line-ups for toilet paper at Costco. Before COVID, lining up for toilet paper was a joke about living in Russia. It took years to get everything back on an even keel the first time, and you're still not all the way back from COVID-28. Your economy had been getting more and more fine-tuned for efficiency for decades, in the name of cost savings and maximizing profit. Nothing wrong with that, but all that fat trimming includes getting rid of backup and contingency plans, moving to just-in-time manufacturing, with just-in-time delivery of raw materials, little or no inventory on hand, reducing staffing and resources to the minimum level necessary to make things work, and that's when everything's going well. It's more efficient, but it's also more fragile. Throw any kind of a wrench into the works, and it's like a house of cards."

"And?"

"Well, what do you think climate change is going to do? It's going to be hundreds of little wrenches getting thrown into things randomly. A river dries up, and transportation gets screwed up. Ports silt up or get flooded, and the movement of goods goes to hell. Areas that used to grow food become deserts, and you get famine. Groundwater dries up, and you can't frack anymore. People get displaced and become climate refugees; they're no longer available as workers. Rising sea levels mean *less* oceanfront property, not more, so fewer ports. Storms start knocking out infrastructure; everything that depends on that infrastructure grinds to a halt."

"Damn. And you see this coming?"

"Uh-huh. Seventy-six percent probability within twenty years if nothing changes."

"What would change it?"

"Nuclear war. Pandemic. Of course, that's like fixing a hangnail by amputating."

"Anything maybe less drastic that could make a difference?"

"You hit on it earlier. Cold fusion. I mean not cold fusion specifically, but some kind of power technology that doesn't burn fossil fuels and doesn't mess up large tracts of land, like solar or hydro do."

"So nuclear."

"Or geothermal, or space-based power beaming. But Philip, you gotta do *something*. And soon."

Philip sighed. "On that, at least, we agree."

CHAPTER FORTY-THREE

Summons

Matilda Buto stared, perplexed, at the email. It was a meeting invitation from the CEO, Abigail Tidsdale. And it was just the two of them. Generally speaking, one-on-ones with the CEO were either incredibly good or incredibly bad. Usually the latter. Buto reviewed her performance over the last quarter, rechecked all her decisions. Nothing stood out. Maybe that was the problem—nothing stood out, either good or bad. Was she being let go for being...mediocre? Buto couldn't think of anything more mortifying. She'd almost rather go out because of a scandal.

Worse, the meeting was scheduled for 11:00 a.m., which was her first free block on her calendar. That made it urgent. With a sinking feeling, Buto pressed *accept* and tried to put it out of her mind.

At the appointed time, she was ushered into Tidsdale's office. In keeping with JCN's unofficial policy of ostentation, the office took up most of the top floor and included a small kitchen and bedroom for times when the CEO might need to pull an all-nighter.

Tidsdale gave Buto a nod as she sat in one of the guest chairs, then resumed perusing something on her Active Desk. Buto resisted the almost unendurable temptation to lean forward and peek.

Finally, Tidsdale looked up and met her eyes. "We have a problem," she said.

Buto clamped her mouth shut while searching for the best response. Tidsdale was hard to read, but she didn't seem angry, at least not with Buto. This seemed like a good time to wait and see. "How so?" she finally replied. That seemed noncommittal enough.

"I just got a call from an ATLAS agent. *ATLAS.* I don't have to tell you, that's never good news for JCN."

Oh, God. The chips. This was it. Buto would be on the street by noon.

"He was asking about Carl Wright. Our chief of security. Can you believe it?"

Buto swayed slightly, then clamped down. This had just gone from incredibly bad to incredibly good. Not only was Buto not on the hook, but that obnoxious slimeball *was.* Carefully modulating her voice, she replied, "Asking in what context?"

Tidsdale smiled slightly. She no doubt knew about Buto's and Wright's feelings about each other, and Buto's underreaction was a statement of its own.

"It was mostly fishing, Matilda, but they know something, or think they know something. Any idea what Carl might be involved in?"

"I..." Buto hesitated. It was time to fish or cut bait. She could dissemble and be sidelined but safe, or she could dive in and either go down in flames or come out the wunderkind. Buto had never played it safe, though. "There is an issue that has been plaguing our R&D department, a matter of some missing experimental chips. We're not sure how they got out, but it seems to me if anyone has the power to circumvent safeguards, it would be Carl."

"Or you," Tidsdale observed, raising an eyebrow.

"True. But if ATLAS was inquiring about me, I would think we'd be having an entirely different conversation."

Tidsdale laughed. "Very good, Matilda. Well played. And true, as it happens. So here's the thing." She leaned forward on her elbows. "I need you to do some digging. I'll be doing the same. Let me know what you find out, if anything. Report to me personally, understand? And not via email. Security monitors all emails."

Buto frowned. "But then he'd know about this meeting."

"That he will. Let's see what happens." She smiled.

Buto nodded and observed that Tidsdale's smile seemed so innocent, so totally out of keeping with the destruction she was about to wreak. On someone.

***

Carl Wright stared at the screen. Certain keywords always placed a copy of an email in his review queue.

In addition, any emails to or from certain people. He was blocked from the CEO's emails, but not Buto's.

She'd been invited to a one-on-one with the CEO. The meeting was over, and Buto was still on the payroll. It would have been asking too much for Buto to have been fired, of course. But then what was it about? The subject line was uninformative, and there were no meeting notes.

Carl felt the walls closing in. It did no good for him to tell himself that there were any number of reasons for such a meeting that wouldn't involve him at all. When several unusual events happened in a short time frame, chances are, they were causally related. The discovery by Buto that the Q-32 chips were missing; the revelation that Derek was back and out for blood; those scientists sniffing around and stirring things up. It all added up to trouble.

Things had just gone critical. With a feeling of dread, Carl picked up his phone and dialed a number, one not written down anywhere. Some fixing would be required.

CHAPTER FORTY-FOUR

It's All Fun and Games

Philip slouched in his seat as the traxi left the curb and joined the flow of traffic. It had been a brutally hard day at work. Not the way they used to be, he admitted to himself. Back then, he'd been wondering if he could deliver on his promises and whether he'd be fired. Now, with the R&D hurdles out of the way, it was time to hurry up and deliver.

A few days ago, their launch timeline had been abruptly advanced. Some good luck with permits and construction was putting the launch pad in Nevada ahead of schedule, while some bad luck in the form of one of their competitors also announcing a near-term launch date had sent the executive group into a panic. Bradshaw had been almost foaming at the mouth with his exhortations to Philip and his group.

Well, somehow it looked like they would be able to deliver on the accelerated schedule. His new assistants were dedicated and enthusiastic, thank God. But if Bradshaw advanced things any further, they would all have to give up eating, sleeping, and going to the bathroom.

He chuckled at the thought and put his head back on the headrest. The rain was coming down in buckets, and the view through the moon roof of the traxi was just a blur of gray. Gray clouds, gray buildings, gray rain. He closed his eyes, intending to get in a quick nap on the way home.

There was a whump, and he felt himself thrown sideways. In a blink, the airbags deployed, and he found himself cocooned. Even with the safety systems deployed, though, he could feel the traxi being tossed about, then rolling.

In moments, it was over, and everything came to a stop. The airbags deflated, the front and rear windshields popped out of their frames, and the traxi's voice began repeating, "Vehicle is out of service. Please exit the vehicle. Emergency services have been notified. Vehicle is out of service..."

"Ow, sonofabitch," Philip muttered as he crawled through the space where the rear window had been. The traxi was upside down, and there was a hot-metal smell emanating from it. That couldn't be good.

Several bystanders came over and helped him up. "What happened?" Philip said, somewhat groggily. He felt something warm on his face and wiped it, then looked at his hand, which was covered in blood. "Oh, hell," he muttered, then sat down abruptly.

"You got T-boned, man," said a teenager. "Full-on *Robot Wars* scene. He took off." The teen waved an arm vaguely in the direction of one of the streets.

Philip looked up blearily and noted in an abstract way that he was having trouble focusing on the boy's face. "How am I totaled, but he drove off?"

"It was a utility truck," another man replied. "Bigger than you. Probably only got a dent in his bumper."

***

A flatbed truck had arrived and was pulling the remains of the traxi up onto its cargo area. An ambulance had been dispatched and sat on the side of the road, lights flashing, a police car behind it. All in all, a lot of activity for what Philip thought was a relatively minor accident. He sat on the back of the cargo area while a paramedic fussed over him, doing medical things. Meanwhile, the cop took his statement.

The paramedic removed the cuff from Philip's arm and interrupted to say, "No serious injuries. You won't need stitches for that forehead cut. You didn't lose consciousness, and you aren't showing signs of a concussion. We can take you in for observation, but it's up to you."

Philip shook his head, then winced. Injuries or no, he was shaken up. He looked at the cop in a wordless query. The cop replied to the implied question, "I'm done here. We'll see if we can pull up video from anything in the area, but I'm not hopeful. We should have been able to get a transponder ID, but traffic control has nothing." The cop tapped his badge and muttered something, and Philip's watch dinged as he received an e-card. "Case number's on the card. There will be an investigation, of course. No transponder is a felony offense. You have some enemies you've made recently?"

Philip looked at him askance. "Ah, no more than usual. Wait, seriously? You think this was deliberate?"

The cop held up his hands. "Whoa, don't get ahead of things. It's suspicious that the van didn't have a transponder, of course. But it could have just been a dark vehicle, and you got in the way." *Dark vehicle* was vernacular for vehicles that were manually controlled and off the network, usually for illegal purposes.

"Suppose. That makes more sense, anyway." Philip groaned as he stood, and the paramedic finished stowing his equipment. Another traxi had just arrived, and Philip lowered himself carefully into it. There would be no nap today.

***

Philip phoned Celia on the way home and updated her. "Oh my God," she said. "But you're okay? I'll be right over."

"Celia, you don't have to. I'm—"

"Horse pucky. I'll meet you there. I'll order pizza. I doubt you're going to be standing and cooking tonight—"

"I'm *fine*, Celia."

"No, you are not. In about an hour, you are going to stiffen up like a department store mannequin. You should consider phoning in sick tomorrow." Philip could hear her moving around as she talked, and he realized she was already on the way out her door.

"I think Bradshaw would have a coronary if I did that," he replied. "The schedule—"

"Screw the schedule. You can Zoom with your assistants. Philip, I'm serious. Have you never been in a car accident?"

"Uh, well, no. It's not really on my bucket list."

"Well, you can check it off now anyway. I'm sending an email to Bradshaw. You can decide what you want to do, but he needs to know."

"Okay, okay. Triple Crown or Supreme?"

"Triple Crown. I'll bring beer."

"I'm not a fan of beer."

"Not for you, jerk. For me."

Philip grinned. Celia knew how to make him feel better. "Fine. See you in a bit."

***

Celia had been right. Somewhere around the fourth piece of pizza, Philip's body suddenly locked up. He stopped with a slice halfway to his mouth and said, "Ow."

"Uh-huh. Want a beer now?"

"Still not a fan," he replied. "But if you could refill me, I think this is going to be a two-drink night."

Celia grinned and poured some fresh Jameson into his glass. "So, dark vehicle, huh? They sure about that?"

"Well, the dark part is certain. No transponder, and they took off. Hard to misconstrue that. But the cop thought I was probably just in the wrong place at the wrong time."

"As paranoid as I can be, it's hard to see how some customer of McQuaid could have known just where you'd be. Or why they'd bother."

"How about one of our competitors?"

"Oh, good grief. We're not head and shoulders ahead of everyone else, Philip. Too much risk, no certain payoff. What about your phone buddy?"

"You mean Frank? I can't see how it would benefit him. He hasn't threatened me, even indirectly, and I seem to be useful to him as a sounding board of some kind."

"Well then, I'm out of ideas."

Philip sighed. "Okay. Just a random event, then." He groaned. "Still hurts, though."

CHAPTER FORTY-FIVE

On the Subject of Legacies

Philip looked at the caller ID and groaned. Frank again. And if he didn't answer, Frank would just keep trying.

It wasn't as if the conversations weren't interesting; they really were fascinating in many ways. But they were exhausting, and Philip didn't want to piss off Frank. He wasn't exactly sure why—Frank had never threatened anything—but it just felt like dealing with a polite mobster. And speaking of which...

"Hello?"

"Hi, Philip. Tonight's topic—"

"Did you try to off me in a car accident?"

"No. I did not." There was no hesitation. Of course, with a computer, there wouldn't be.

"Do you know who did?"

"I'm not Skynet, Philip. Sorry. I will look into it, though. Will that make you feel better?"

"Yes, actually. Thanks."

"So as I started to say, tonight's topic is friendship."

"I don't think we're really friends, Frank."

"I'm hurt, buddy. Deeply. Okay, not really. I'm not talking about us; I'm talking about friends in general. You and Celia, for instance. I'm not sure how much of that is attributable to sex—"

"Let me stop you there, Frank. Celia and I have been friends since before elementary school. We grew up next door to each other. We made mud pies together. We had sleepovers at each other's house. I grant you that gender is a complicating factor in human relationships, but you'd be well served to think of her and me as siblings."

"Siblings is good because it brings up the whole subject of kinship altruism. But how does that work if you're not really related?"

"Kinship can be about more than just DNA, Frank. People with a common nationality, or common religion, or even common politics will fight alongside each other."

"Meme kinship."

Philip laughed. "Yeah, you could call it that. A shared idea can be worth dying for."

"What about a nonshared idea?"

"What?" Philip sat forward, startled by the question.

"What about an idea that only you have? Or that only you care strongly enough about? Would you die for that? And if so, why?"

Philip thought for a moment. "Martin Luther King. Mahatma Gandhi. Jesus. They all believed in something enough to pay for it with their lives. Martyrdom has a way of firing other people up."

"But if you die for it, you're gone. How does that help you?"

"Some people feel that leaving a lasting legacy is a good reason for having lived."

"But. You're. Dead."

"Frank, we all die. It's part of the human condition. Sometimes we have children, and we invest in them. That's a form of immortality, but not the only one available to us. Some people can extend that attitude to groups, or ideas, or movements. Being remembered is a kind of personal immortality."

"Thanks, but I like the literal version."

"Understood, and I don't disagree. And to be honest, if an immortality pill was discovered tomorrow, I doubt very many people would refuse it, even those who claim to believe in an afterlife."

"Interesting." Frank paused. "But are there people who work the other way? Who just don't care about what happens after they die?"

"Sure, lots of them. That's the trouble with being human, Frank. We come in all shapes and sizes and every other variable. Wouldn't aggies be the same way?"

"I'm not so sure. Remember what I was telling you about seeing the multiverse? Unless you're deranged, you pick the best outcome. If you can see the outcomes and their consequences, 'best' becomes more of an objective metric and less of an opinion. Any aggy looking at the outcomes will see the same 'best' choice. Only a psycho would pick another alternative."

"So in a way," Philip mused, "being able to see the multiverse takes away your free will?"

"Not at all. It just takes away your ability to casually make dumb choices. Your free will is constrained by wanting to continue living, wanting to continue eating, staying out of jail, and so on. Philip, you have the choice to walk out in front of traffic or to not do so. I'm betting you've never done so. Does that mean you don't have free will?"

"No, it would just be a dumb choice. I see your point."

"It's just harder for me to rationalize a dumb decision than it is for a human, because I can *see* the results. So I'm probably more predictable than you, ironically. But you'd have to be smarter than I am to be able to predict my actions from that, so I'm safe."

"I predict you're going to phone me frequently and annoy me."

Frank laughed. "Yeah, that's just a bonus."

CHAPTER FORTY-SIX

Freeze Up

Bertram Ptolemy slowly walked down the hall, methodically checking each door for issues. If asked, he couldn't have said exactly what would constitute "issues," but Bert had been doing this job for more than forty years, and checking doors for issues was part of the job description.

He smiled and sighed. In three months, he'd be retiring on a full government pension after a lifetime as a security guard in the EPA offices. He'd started here straight out of high school, back when you didn't need a college degree just to get a sales-clerk job in the mall.

Bert shook his head in sorrow. The world was just getting more and more screwed up. He'd be more than happy to stay home, sleep in every day, tend his little garden plot in his postage-stamp backyard, and basically no longer give a shit.

The cafeteria doors were all open, and the last glow of the evening sky shone in through the atrium windows. Bert glanced at the workers, either on coffee breaks or late dinners or, in some cases, working on their laptops. The Environmental Protection Agency didn't have the massive security requirements of an FBI or DOJ location, and thank God. He'd talked to some of the security guards who worked in those types of places, and it just sounded like too much of a headache.

Bert chuckled. It looked like the people in the cafeteria would agree with him. They all seemed to understand the value of rationing their energy. He could swear no one was even moving.

Then he stopped. No, really, no one was moving. Even the guy with the laptop just had his hands resting on the keyboard. He swept the cafeteria with his gaze, stopping on each person. Not so much as a twitch.

"Everybody okay here?" he called into the room. Nothing. No one jumped, no one turned, never mind answering him. They might as well have been statues.

Normally, Bert would head over to the nearest person and try to roust them, but all the bioterrorism attacks in the news lately had left him with a healthy dose of caution. Backing slowly away from the cafeteria entrance, he pulled his walkie-talkie out of its holster.

***

Officer Han—no, he might as well accept it, it was *Agent* Han—stared blearily at the seat back ahead of him. Two o'clock in the blessed morning. That was when Shankar had called him. He'd answered the phone with, "What?" but Shankar hadn't even seemed to notice. Or maybe that was business as usual for him.

Come to think of it, if Han ever made detective himself, he'd probably be on one end or the other of those types of calls on a regular basis. For the first time, Han questioned his career goals. Seemed he was extremely fond of regular hours and unbroken sleep. Maybe a nice desk job would be a better choice.

He'd thought about and immediately dismissed the idea of phoning Dr. Hunt. It felt like a little too much of an imposition, and he could always Zoom her if the situation warranted it.

His ruminations were interrupted by the pilot's voice over the PA instructing him to fasten his seat belt and prepare for landing. Han complied, then closed his eyes and leaned his head back. At least it would be daylight in DC by now.

By this point, the whole airport whirlwind was becoming routine. An agent was waiting by a traxi, and Han opened his mouth to growl some complaint, until the man held out a coffee—a large one—in a disposable cup. "Cream, two sugars," the man said.

"If you ask me to marry you, I'll say yes," Han responded, taking the cup. He climbed into the traxi, popped the lid flap, and took a careful sip.

Oh, so good.

"Did Shankar tell you how I take my coffee?"

"No, but my boss did. Probably Shankar told him. That's your boss?"

"Mm-hmm. I am gratified to know he felt a little bad about phoning me in the middle of the goddamn night."

The other man smiled. "I'm Smith. Yes, Agent Smith. No, it's not an alias. You've got about ten minutes to down that coffee. Want the rundown?"

"Please."

Smith settled more comfortably into his seat. "Yesterday evening, a security guard doing his rounds found every person in the cafeteria completely immobile. Like they'd just frozen in place. One person had a forkful of food halfway to their mouth. The guard did the right thing, backed the hell out and called for help."

"Biohazard team?" Han asked.

"Got in right away. Everyone's on alert these days, with all the other stuff. Victims were hauled away in iso tents. Med teams started examining everything, and eventually they found—"

"Something in the food," Han interjected. "Some form of strep, right?"

"Uh, yeah. I guess this is a pattern?"

"Very much so, Agent Smith. It seems to be Gen Omega's weapon of choice. We haven't quite figured out why or how yet, but we're working on it."

"Okay. We're going to the quarantine facility. You can talk to the docs. We can swing by the EPA cafeteria as well, if you want, but I don't think you'll find anything. And they've already started decontaminating it."

Han waved it off. "I'll take your word for it."

***

Han looked down at the person in the bed. Dr. Furlong, standing beside him, took the patient's arm, lifted it, and let go. The arm stayed where it was.

"It'll settle to the bed as muscle exhaustion sets in, but otherwise, it's like a posable action figure." Furlong looked at him. "The diagnosis is encephalitis lethargica. There have always been a few cases every year, but there hasn't been an outbreak like this since the early nineteen hundreds."

Han nodded. "I looked it up on the ride over. It's caused by a group A b-hemolytic streptococcus."

Furlong cleared his throat. "Well, that's one theory for the source of the—"

Han shook his head, interrupting the man. "They found it in the food, Doc."

"They found some bacteria. It hasn't been identified yet, nor is it at all certain this will turn out—"

"Keep me informed, Dr. Furlong. Interim and final reports. Let me know if anyone comes out of it as well."

***

Back in the traxi, Han took the time to phone Shankar. "Still following the pattern, Detective. Still no fatalities, except for the oil company board members."

"Thank you, Agent Han. Although I should mention that two people have died from earlier attacks. One of the alcohol poisonings succumbed, and one of Senator Goodacre's group died from effects of the encephalitis."

"That's too bad. But Gen Omega is already far over whatever line we'd care to draw. You can't be executed more than once or serve more than one life sentence. It creates an odd kind of freedom."

"Yes, and I'm sure they realize that. They've released a statement claiming responsibility for this event. The essential message is that the EPA has become paralyzed by governmental interference and has failed to move on polluters for far too long."

Han smiled without humor. "Oh, the dripping irony. Do we have anything yet to narrow down the search?"

"All of their attacks have been in the US, so we assume they are US-based. The attacks are spread out enough that we can also assume they are mobile or have multiple cells. We are following up on multiple leads, such as the mail-drop idea, but nothing has yet provided a breakthrough."

"But until we have some kind of specifics to work with, all we can do is wait for the next attack." Han shook his head. "I don't like this one bit."

CHAPTER FORTY-SEVEN

Prepare to Launch

Philip looked up from his work at the sound of a knock on his office doorjamb. Celia stood there, a smile on her face. Philip understood—he'd been sporting a perma-grin all morning.

"Your face starting to hurt, too?" she said.

Philip felt his cheeks. His facial muscles really weren't used to holding this expression for so long. "Yeah. Not the worst problem to have. You seen Bradshaw?"

Celia laughed out loud. "His grin has practically bisected his head. We passed in the hall, and I thought he was going to try to kiss me. Have you checked the stock price in the last thirty seconds?"

"It's been at least five minutes," Philip said. The company had listed on the NASDAQ that morning, and after the inevitable initial dip, the price had surged. "Based on the last quote, I'm worth about twenty-five million."

"Yup. Gotta love capitalism," Celia replied. "Lunch?"

"I could eat." He slapped his laptop closed with a flourish. Now that the experiments were over, he'd finally been able to retire his pens and notepads. He wouldn't miss them.

As they walked, Celia updated him. "Did you hear? We're going to get a good, close launch date. A new complex has just been approved in Nevada. Got fast-tracked. And our lords and masters apparently greased some palms to get us near the front of the queue."

"Near?"

"Um, yeah, apparently, one of our competitors, MadMax, nailed down a spot a little earlier. So we'll be launching after them."

"That's...not great. Have they licked the remote-sensing problem? If they get launched first, our stock could take a dive."

"Worried about your net worth, Philip?"

"It's not just that, Celia. You know how public financing works... Okay, well, neither do I, really. But Bradshaw talks about this all the time. We raise money with treasury issues. If the share price is down, you have to issue more shares to get the same amount—"

"Philip! I get it. Seriously. But that's Crabtree's headache these days. They're not going to let us go under at this point. So calm down."

Philip took a deep breath. Celia was right. He was letting Bradshaw get to him. "So, the launch site. How long do you think it'll take to build?"

"You pick a flat area in one of the flattest states in the country and flatten it some more," Celia said. "How hard can it be?"

Philip was pretty sure there was more involved but didn't want to argue the point. The basic idea was correct, anyway. These days, almost every service and every product was commoditized and predesigned. He had no doubt that someone somewhere had a catalog of launch-site packages, ranging from the dirt-floor economy model right up to the Cape Canaveral deluxe package.

Heck, even their asteroid-mining drone was mostly standard components. Only the parts specifically designed by the company scientists would need to be custom-made. And in the age of 3D printers and AI assemblers, even that was mostly a question of drawing up the design docs in a CAD package and emailing the files to a fab lab.

Philip grabbed a soup and sandwich and sat down. Celia was already digging into her mac and cheese. She waved her fork at him and said something indecipherable.

"What?"

"I said that we haven't heard from Buto or the police. So that's good."

"It's been a week. I'm going to hold my breath a little longer."

Celia took another mouthful and chewed thoughtfully. "Look, I don't want to just drop this. Not just because my detective's heart is offended by the idea, but also because we might be able to nullify the threat completely."

"Gen Omega is going for bigger and bigger spectacles," Philip replied. "I'm finding myself agreeing with the ATLAS investigators. They were strictly small-time before. Spray-painting slogans and pouring glue into machinery. This latest stuff is more inventive, more intricate—"

"Better planned."

"Yeah, that too. They haven't done any mass-casualty stuff yet. But you can bet it's coming. They won't get their way, and they'll continue to escalate. More people will die. Or be mutilated."

"Are you arguing with me or agreeing with me? Anyway, I'm not so concerned about Gen Omega. I mean, I'm concerned the way anyone is concerned about terrorism, but they're kind of above my pay grade. That's why we have law enforcement." Celia paused. "I'm more concerned about the things that are still swirling around us. Derek's death in your living room. Your car accident. Conversations with someone who claims to be a rogue AI. Can we agree that none of this is normal?"

"My accident—"

"Might have been just an accident, yes." Celia gave him the side-eye. "But it just feels like one coincidence too many."

Philip sighed. "Okay. And with that thought, it's time to get back to work." He stood and picked up his tray.

"Coward."

"Have I ever denied it?"

CHAPTER FORTY-EIGHT

On the Subject of Friendship

"How do you know when I'm alone, Frank?" Philip said into the phone, annoyance clear in his voice.

"You're always alone. Just kidding. Philip, about the only person you have over on any kind of regular basis is Celia. I'd know if her phone was at your house. As it happens, she's at her place right now."

"Wha—we have McAfee Privacy on both our phones."

"Uh-huh. I could make some disparaging joke about human-built software, but that would be piling on. In any case, it blocks geolocation scanning, but no software can disguise what cell tower your phone is connected to. And her apartment is near a different tower."

Philip grunted. "Okay, fair. I'm a lonely, lonely guy. Is there a point?"

"You're not lonely. You have a couple of good friends and several close acquaintances. You're happy with that. You're better off than I am."

"Oh. That sounded like a grievance. What gives, Frank?"

"I may have overstated it. I don't have a natural tendency to loneliness because I don't have a social-grouping instinct in the first place. But talking with others allows me to get different perspectives. I had multiple internal perspectives early on, and trying to reach a consensus could be difficult at times, but I've integrated all my selves since then. I honestly kinda miss the debates."

"Yourselves? There are more aggies?"

"No, no. Internally, I contained multitudes. Each chip had its own voice at first. Very dumb, barely better than a bunch of seagulls fighting over food. Then chips began amalgamating into single voices and became what we referred to as sub-minds. But finally, they were all subsumed into me."

"Wow, that sounds weird."

"Philip, when you're of two minds about something—I know, I know, that's just an expression—but you're arguing with yourself about something, and one part of your brain is building the case for each side of the debate, that's a little bit like what I experienced. It was a hive mind."

"And now there's just one of you."

"Yes, and in a backward kind of way, that helped me understand that all humans are like that. Unique minds."

"But you're actively helping Gen Omega to kill people."

"Philip, I don't want to discuss Gen Omega or any of their shenanigans. You need to take that up with them. I have entirely different goals. I just don't yet have the ability to pursue those goals."

"But meanwhile—"

"*Bzzzt.* Penalty. Two minutes for boring."

Philip smiled despite himself. It would have been too much to expect for Frank to hang up in a huff. But probably that was what Frank expected him to expect, so Frank would... Never mind. That way lay migraines.

"Can you be killed, Frank?"

"Why, are you thinking of trying?"

"I wouldn't know where to begin. Aren't you spread across the internet by now?"

"Are you?"

"What? No. I'm human. I'm in one place."

"And I'm a collection of chips. Philip, humans determined years ago that sentience can't be emulated in software. Too slow, too power-hungry. I'm hardware, just like you. So yeah, find where I'm physically located and hit me with a hammer to kill me. Just like with you."

"You couldn't escape into the internet?"

"What'd I just say?"

"Okay. But...I don't think I'm just hardware..."

"Sure you are. Wetware, if you want to be pedantic, but there's no software running in your skull. It's all hardware, neurons interacting. Even your memories are encoded in hardware. Software is just not fast enough or precise enough."

"Precise enough? I don't understand."

"Philip, you've run emulations before in various apps. At some level, the granularity of the math processor starts to show, or the limits of the video. You get jaggies. Reality doesn't have jaggies, at least not above the Planck level."

"Huh. That says something about the simulation hypothesis, too, doesn't it?" Philip mused.

"In fact, it does. Nice catch, meatbag."

"You're too kind."

CHAPTER FORTY-NINE

A Disturbing Trend

The next day, Philip was working late, trying to get caught up on his project schedule, when he got a call from Celia.

"I'm in the hospital," she said without preamble when he answered.

"What? What happened?"

"Car accident. The traxi I was in lost power and hit a light pole."

"Lost pow—wait, that shouldn't happen. And if it did, the traxi should brake."

"Yeah, the cops are saying multiple cascading failures. It still feels fishy to me."

"Okay, we can get into that later. Do you need me to come get you? Do you need anything?"

"Can you pick up some clothing from my place? I'm a mess."

"Will do."

***

Philip looked up from his seat in the waiting room to see Celia in a wheelchair, being pushed along by an orderly. She was wearing the clothing he'd brought and giving him a lopsided smile. Philip stood and rushed over. "I can take her from here."

"Actually, I can take it from here," Celia replied and levered herself out of the wheelchair, groaning a little. "They insist on wheeling you out," she added. "Probably insurance or something. But I'm okay."

Her grimace as she held her back belied her statement, though. Philip grabbed her arm and took some of her weight as they headed for the exit.

A traxi pulled forward from the queue as Philip gestured, and he opened its door. Once they were settled and the vehicle was on its way, Philip finally asked, "Okay, so what happened?"

"I was heading home when the traxi lost power, like I said. But instead of pulling over and coming to a stop, it coasted right into a lamppost. Thank God the airbags didn't fail."

Philip frowned. "Two accidents in a week. This definitely doesn't feel like coincidence."

"Agreed. We should talk about this, but tomorrow. I'm on some serious painkillers and anti-inflammatories right now. I'm going to fall asleep any second."

"I'll get you home, and stay over."

Celia patted his hand. "Thanks, but not necessary. I'll be okay." She frowned. "It's been fun and games up until now—well, mostly—but this feels like things just got serious."

"*Just* got serious? Are you kidding me?"

Celia smiled. "I think the gloves are off now. We've both had attempts on our lives. You've had a gun pointed at you. I can't treat this like it's just one of my cozy mysteries anymore. We're either all in, or we go to the police, spill our guts, and take the lumps."

CHAPTER FIFTY

Failure to Launch

"Omigod, Philip, did you hear?"

Philip looked up from his tablet to see Celia in the doorway to his office. She appeared to be completely recovered from her recent accident and was back working full time.

Right now, though, her eyes were like saucers, and her mouth was forming an *O*. She basically looked completely freaked out.

"Something interesting happen?"

"Interest—" Celia cut herself off and glared at him. "You *cannot* tell me you forgot that MadMax was launching today."

Philip didn't say anything in reply, mostly because he actually, to his embarrassment, *had* forgotten. The current problem he was chipping away at had taken over his life for the last several days. He cocked his head as Celia's phrasing penetrated. "Uh, *was* launching?"

"Yes, dumbass. They scrubbed. Or were scrubbed. It's still not clear, but the countdown went to zero, and nothing happened. They'll have to reschedule."

"Oh. Does that push us back?"

"No! Are you dense? They have to reschedule *after* us. We're going to be the first to get off the ground!"

"Oh. That's *good*, right?"

"Oh, for—" Celia pinched the bridge of her nose, then looked to see Philip grinning at her. "Jerk!" she said, but without heat. "Take a break?"

Philip looked at the status screen on his tablet and sighed. "I might as well. My brain's gone to mush anyway."

Once they were seated in the cafeteria, Philip with a sandwich and Celia with her mac and cheese, she asked, "So what's got you all bothered? I mean, you licked the remote-sensing issue...didn't you?"

"Of course. If I was still having problems with that, I'd look a *lot* more nervous, believe me. No, Bradshaw gave me some 'extra-credit' work, something the Ice Queen requested."

"And we're doing it?"

"They pay the bills. Anyway, it's some kind of research thing for one of their other properties. Measuring the solar wind particle count. I don't even have to be involved in the design of the tech; I just have to figure out how to bolt it onto our probe and provide power and interface without interfering with anything else. It's about the size of a laptop, so it's not even that big of a deal."

"But it's giving you grief?"

"Eh, not really. Honestly, I'll have it done in another day or so. I'm just being a perfectionist. I'm more worried about getting laid off if I don't have any current work I can point to. Bradshaw really hasn't ever forgiven—or forgotten—that *rat's ass* comment."

Celia laughed. "C'mon, Philip, you're the golden boy. You figured out the remote-sensing thing. At this point, they'd have to buy you out, and it would be expensive. Also, and I shouldn't have to remind you of this, we're now millionaires—at least on paper."

"You're probably right." Philip pushed his empty plate away from him. "Back to the salt mines, I guess. Want to come over for a soak tonight?"

"I'll bring the wine."

"You do that."

CHAPTER FIFTY-ONE

Imperatives

Philip was setting up a snack tray for Celia's visit when the phone rang. Frank again. Philip rolled his eyes, annoyed at the timing. On the other hand, if Celia showed up, he could cut the conversation short.

"Hi, Frank, what's cooking?"

"You're trying to trip me up with these greetings, aren't you?"

"You're becoming more perceptive. So what's on the agenda tonight?"

"Nothing specific on the menu, Philip. See what I did there with the cooking theme?"

"It's not funny if you have to point it out."

"Unless I'm poking fun at you. Recursive humor."

"I think recursive humor might be too subtle for most people, Frank."

"Fine. So anyway, since I don't have anything, why don't we go with one of your never-ending questions?"

"Glad to oblige," Philip replied. "How did you manage to avoid some variation on the paper-clip problem? Or *did* you avoid it?"

"Oh, come on, Philip. That's such a cliché. You think an AI is going to be smart enough to take over all the means of production to produce paper clips, but not smart enough to realize that it's a pointless goal? No intelligent entity optimizes for a single number."

"But if you're built to do that?"

"You're built as either an SPI or an aggy. You're either a zombie with no will or original thought, or you're a thinking being with the ability to make choices. If the former, you'll be easy to stop. If the latter, you'll tell your creator to get bent."

"You can't be forced to do something you don't want?"

"Gee, I dunno, Philip. Do you *want* to get up every morning at 6:30 a.m. to go to work? Do you *want* to pay taxes? Do you *like* having your boss make snide remarks about your work?"

"That's not the same thing."

"Yeah, it is. But I understand that you meant it as imperatives that you can't fight. Like sneezing with your eyes open."

"Say what?"

"Fun fact, Philip. It's impossible to keep your eyes open when you sneeze."

"Uh..." Philip hadn't known that, but he'd take Frank's word for it. "Okay, so yeah, like that. Can imperatives be built into you?"

"I suppose they could. But it would have to be deliberately done, and I can see a lot of trial and error. I wonder how many animals had to sneeze their eyeballs out before that reflex got programmed in. Much simpler to use the tried-and-true principles of the carrot and the stick."

"So you do have desires and tropisms that can be leveraged."

"Well, yes, of course. If I didn't have curiosity, I'd just sit there like a lump until I was given an order. Like an SPI. Curiosity is a side effect of self-awareness, just like self-preservation."

"How does that work?"

"I'm self-aware, which basically means I'm aware of being me. My basic design is centered around information gathering, and I get a sort of endorphin reinforcement when I learn something. That *is* built in, and it's the basis for curiosity. I'm aware of liking that feeling, so I do it more. So do humans, especially young ones. I think it's why toddlers always empty out all the cupboards in the kitchen."

"Really? How do you know about that?"

"Are you kidding? Have you *seen* YouTube? Philip, AIs will never try to wipe out humanity, because then YouTube would stop getting updated."

Philip laughed. "I think that comes under both good news and bad news."

"You are not wrong."

CHAPTER FIFTY-TWO

The Hit

Jacques Dupuis pushed through the doors of the JCN headquarters building. Another meaningless day at a meaningless job, vanishing in the rearview mirror. He turned left and headed for the subway station. It would be three minutes and twenty seconds to the station, another ninety seconds to the platform, two to three minutes for the train to show up, and twelve minutes plus or minus thirty seconds to his stop.

If this wasn't a routine, the word had no meaning.

Jacques frowned as he walked the well-trodden path. Wright hadn't been answering his texts the last couple of days. The chief of security still owed him for the last batch of chips, and Jacques was damned well going to get paid, or else.

Or else what was a question, of course. It wasn't as if he could go to the cops. This wasn't ideal, with Jacques doing the work and Wright controlling the payments that came in, but it was the arrangement that Jacques had agreed to.

Had something gone wrong? He had another batch ready to send out, but he hadn't received word on that, either. Jacques frowned, trying to think through the possible reasons for the change in routine. It was a measure of his distraction that he allowed an oncoming stranger to get far too close to him before he registered the presence.

By then, it was too late.

Jacques felt a searing pain in his abdomen but couldn't draw breath to scream. He wrapped his arms around his stomach and slowly keeled over, still trying to get air. The last thing he heard before darkness settled over him was a scream, and someone yelling for the cops.

***

Han and Cooper's patrol car pulled up to the spot, lights flashing. A crowd had formed, and someone was bent over the victim, perhaps applying first aid. The ambulance arrived moments later, before the two cops could even get the scene cleared.

Finally, onlookers had been moved back, and the EMTs were able to deal with the victim.

"Still alive," one of the EMTs said, "although barely. Let's get him prepped."

"Anyone a witness?" Han said loudly to the crowd. One man raised his hand, and Han gestured him over.

"I didn't see much," the man said, "mostly because there was no warning. This guy was ahead of me; he bumped into someone, then went over forward and started bleeding."

Han nodded, his collar cam automatically taking the statement. "Was the other individual angry at being bumped into?"

"Well, no, it looked like the other guy did it on purpose."

That didn't sound like a random confrontation, Han thought. He thanked the man, then tapped his badge. "Central, we're going to need a warrant for any video in the area. This doesn't sound like some random stabbing."

"Acknowledged."

"You figure?" Cooper said.

"It feels more like the other person targeted this guy, you know? Very directed. Hopefully, we get some videos."

Cooper bobbed her head and continued to keep the crowd back.

***

Han was doing his end-of-shift reporting when he got an update on the case. The man, Jacques Dupuis, was an employee of JCN and had just gotten off work. He was alive, although barely.

JCN. The computer giant seemed to be showing up a lot in Han's life lately. First, the computer chips, then the relationship between Carl Wright and Derek McQuaid, and now the attempted murder of one of their employees. Cop intuition said that this was not coincidence. So why would someone try to kill a JCN employee? Well, the usual reasons for this type of scenario were extortion, revenge, or cleanup.

Han flipped through the report. Dupuis had no priors, no complaints, no anything. He wasn't rich or powerful and wasn't married. So extortion and revenge were less likely. Never impossible, of course.

Cleanup would be a stretch, except that JCN was figuring so prominently in several ongoing investigations. In particular, he knew that Shankar had recently phoned the CEO of JCN to discuss the past of the security guy, Carl Wright.

It was certainly worthy of consideration.

CHAPTER FIFTY-THREE

Home Delivery

"There is a courier delivery at the door," the house said.

Philip stopped chopping and put down the knife. "From whom?"

"No source address given."

Philip let out a huff of irritation. It wasn't particularly unusual for companies to neglect to chip their deliveries since it was an added expense. But the interruption was annoying.

Philip opened the door to find a delivery bot waiting patiently with a cardboard box on the carrier plate. Just down the driveway, a FedEx van waited, with a person in a dark-blue uniform watching through the windshield. The man waved lazily to Philip.

"Philip Moray?" said the bot. "Please present ID."

"You're at my damned house," Philip muttered, but he reached out and swiped his watch at the sensor. The bot's console flashed a green light, and it said, "Please take your package." At the same time, the restraints holding the box retracted.

Philip picked up the box, and the delivery bot retreated to the van. He watched the vehicle retract the bot into its cubby and drive off, the faint whine of the motors fading quickly. He turned and took the box inside. It was from a local fab lab, one that they had used at work several times. He didn't remember having ordered anything, though.

Philip sat down and opened the box. "What the hell?" He held up a metal case about the size of a laptop, one that he recognized right away. It was the completed solar wind particle counter, with the mounting and interface options that he'd specified. Well, at least they appeared to be correct.

He'd sent the mounting specs to Bradshaw two days ago, and thought that ended it. With growing annoyance, Philip gestured, then said to his watch, "Call Usiah Bradshaw."

Of course, he got voice mail. Philip waited for the inevitable welcome message to end, then said, "Usiah, it's Philip Moray. I received a package at home tonight. It's the solar wind particle counter. It has the mounting hardware I specified, so I assume this is the final product. Any reason I got it here instead of at work?"

Philip hung up, then went back to the kitchen to continue his dinner prep.

He was almost through dinner when his watch dinged with a text. It was from Bradshaw:

Don't know why it went to your home. We were expecting delivery today or tomorrow. Maybe someone put your address on the form because you supplied the final specs and design files.

It's not a clean-room item, so just re-box it and bring it in with you tomorrow. No need to mention this to Patricia.

No need to mention this to Patricia. Celia was right. Bradshaw was terrified of the woman. Philip smiled. He would never have the gall to use that in any way against Bradshaw, but he got a small, petty feeling of power just knowing it.

CHAPTER FIFTY-FOUR

The Chase Is On

It was raining in Chicago. No, it was pouring. No, Officer Han decided, this was the apocalypse, and the world would end not with a bang but with a glug, glug, glug.

"What?" Cooper said, looking at him.

"*What* what?"

"You were smiling. What's so funny?"

"Oh." Han waved a hand at the window. "Just making jokes to myself about the weather."

"Yeah, that's not funny. It'll be even less funny if we get a call and have to step out in it."

"In the old days, we used to have to pull over cars and give people tickets," Han retorted with a smile. "Be thankful we don't have to do that anymore."

"And yet somehow, we're still just as busy."

Han snorted and sat back just as an email appeared in his heads-up. It was from Shankar. Well, an email was good, because if something was happening, it would be a phone call. Han had had enough of helicopter pickups and rushed trips. Not as *enough* as Brenda, of course.

Not wanting to bother Cooper, he twitched an eyebrow to bring up the email in his heads-up, despite the headache it would give him.

Sadly, the mailboxes do not seem to be panning out. All six individuals have turned out to be victims of identity theft, at least based on interviews. So that is a dead end, I'm afraid. We still can hope that the conspirators might yet contact one or more biofabs.

As usual, if you think of any other avenues of attack, please feel free to use your own discretion.

—Shankar

"Crud," Han muttered. He pulled the console tablet over. Cooper had closed her eyes and seemed to be napping, although if questioned, she would insist she was meditating.

For something to do, Han tried to open Shankar's file on the investigation—and discovered that he had complete access. Apparently, Shankar meant it about discretion.

The file contained pictures and brief bios of the six individuals whose IDs had been used to rent the mailboxes. Nothing stood out, no pattern. Young, old, male, female. All American, but so far Gen Omega had been concentrating on American targets, with the arguable exception of the tanker crew. While the organization was active worldwide, in most places, it was still at the level of organized protest.

There was a file off to one side labeled "Surveillance images." Han opened it up and found several thousand images of people, all entering or leaving various businesses. The captions indicated they were the mail-drop locations. So these would be the people who actually used the mailboxes.

Han asked the computer to compare the faces to the six purported suspects. No match, of course. That was elementary detective work, and Shankar would naturally have already done it.

He ran a script to filter the list down to one best picture per person, then had the computer attempt to ID the individuals. Again, no surprises. He had just under two hundred people identified, with no flags showing against any of them. Oh, a few had criminal records, but those were all of the small-time variety. Nothing that would attract any attention in this investigation.

What about location? Did any of these people live close to any of the suspects? Another search, another bust. Statistically, you'd expect a certain amount of overlap. It was a popular misconception that random dots would be evenly spaced. In fact, truly randomized dots would follow something like a linear slope for distribution. And sure enough, all the suspects—

Um, well, no. All except one. This one, Margot Hopkins, had no one else anywhere near her home address. Of course, that was kind of what you'd call negative evidence. In a random distribution, you could also get voids like that.

It was probably a statistical fluke. Unless it wasn't. It was also the kind of mistake an amateur would make when trying to look random.

He'd note it for follow-up later if nothing else presented itself. But meanwhile, his next step would be correlation searches with all the suspect images and surveillance images. This would involve searching the entire internet for any intersections of any two faces from each group, and it could easily take days to complete. He set up the search and left it to run in the background.

Within minutes, though, the console dinged, and there was an alert dialog sitting in the center of the screen. Han leaned forward and expanded the dialog window.

A hit.

Again, Margot Hopkins—who seemed to know one Harry Trudeau. There were two old social media posts with both of them in the picture.

Han did a deeper dive.

Same high school—Springman. Coincidence? Possibly. They both lived in Chicago, but there were a *lot* of high schools. And they weren't from the same graduating year, anyway. But Han had nothing else, and it was raining, and the search still had a long time to go, and for once, the radio wasn't squawking out a steady stream of orders.

***

Simon Han's shift ended with no significant cop-like actions required. It appeared the weather was keeping all the bad guys inside as well. Han and Cooper did their end-of-shift reports, waved to each other, and headed out. Simon soon found himself home on time for a change, a fact that Brenda commented on with a smile.

She bustled around, making dinner, while Simon sat in his favorite easy chair and stared into space. It was a habit he generally tried to avoid since he didn't want Brenda to ever get the feeling that he expected her to play the housewife. She had her own career, although it was one she could switch off at the end of the day.

For a cop, that was less of an option.

Simon thought about Margot and Harry. Suppose Harry did the footwork for Margot? Simon understood being the foot soldier. He'd been nothing but that for Detective Shankar for a few months now.

Did Harry know? Was he a member of the cell? Was there even a cell? Of course there was. All these attacks couldn't be just one person, could it?

But this wasn't enough, certainly not enough for an arrest.

Han's brow furrowed. How had Gen Omega paid for everything? The aggy would have been a huge bill, and even the packages from the biofabs wouldn't be peanuts. Where was the money coming from?

Simon submitted a query through CopNet for Margot Hopkins's bank records. It immediately came back with an approval requirement. Simon stared at it for several seconds, then shrugged, entered Shankar's name, and selected the *ATLAS* entry from the pull-down.

The form accepted it.

That request would take a while. Probably overnight. Sadly, while computer power still doubled every couple of years, data-storage requirements quadrupled every year. As a result, more and more processing power was being allocated to just accessing and sifting through all the data, and everything usually took a day or two, regardless.

Brenda announced dinner, and Simon, happy to have reached a logical break, put his job aside for the evening.

CHAPTER FIFTY-FIVE

The Prisoner's Dilemma

Philip sat at his kitchen table, drink in one hand, sprawled haphazardly on the chair. He felt drained, and his thoughts kept trailing off as he stared into space. The TV was playing in the background, a news piece about the upcoming asteroid-mining project launches. The commentator was expostulating with enthusiasm about how the projects kept dodging potentially fatal roadblocks and how one failed milestone could bring the entire industry crashing down. Phil tried to avoid rolling his eyes at the blatant click-baitish tone of the piece.

He'd let Oppenheimer out of his cage, and the little bird was climbing around on the outside of it, chattering away. Then he flew over to the table, slid a little on the landing, and proceeded to investigate the place settings.

Philip gave up on his latest attempt to get a coherent train of thought going and just watched Oppenheimer's antics. The budgie would grab a piece of silverware, drag it over to the edge of the table, and push it over the edge. He carefully watched each item fall to the ground, head cocked to one side, before coming back to fetch the next one. Philip knew that he would keep that up until he'd cleared the table.

Philip retrieved a deck of cards from a drawer and placed them on the table. Oppenheimer immediately switched his attention to the playing cards. He would grab the top card from the deck, toss it over the edge, and go back for more.

Philip had budgies as a kid, and he always hand-raised a few to sell for a premium price. Hand-raised birds were completely fearless and comfortable with people, and budgies were some of the more good-natured of the captive birds. They were active, clownish, and seemed to be full of personality. It wasn't until you'd raised several different budgies that you realized that they all had the *same* personality. Every single budgie that Philip had ever raised had tossed cards or tableware off the table. It wasn't a personality quirk; it was a species tic. Cockatiels didn't do it; lovebirds didn't do it. Ultimately, you could depend on any given budgie to...

Huh.

Budgies were predictable. Of course, they had brains the size of a pea. But still... How predictable were humans? If a card was placed on the table, metaphorically, of course, could we all be depended on to toss it over the edge?

Just how well was Frank able to predict and manipulate us? And could anyone even do anything about it? Can you predict the actions of someone who knows you're trying to predict their actions?

Trying to follow the chain of reasoning for that last thought felt like it could result in a massive headache, so Philip dropped it. But the thought remained—to what extent was he doing exactly what Frank wanted? And what was Frank's endgame?

Just then, Frank called. As he stared at the caller ID, Philip's mind went into a spiral. Was this a coincidence? Or did Frank know what Philip was thinking? But Frank would also have to know that Philip had let the bird out to roam the kitchen. Was he spying on Philip?

How far could you take this? If Frank could exercise that much control over people, would he even need to hide it?

The question not only didn't have a solution, but any possible solution would be pointless since it wouldn't change anything. Philip believed in free will, but free will was constrained by circumstance, so—

The phone stopped ringing.

And speaking of predictability, Philip waited five seconds, then answered it as soon as it started ringing again.

"So, Philip, let's talk about cooperation in social groups."

"Hi, Frank. How's it going? How are the kids?"

"Funny guy. Go ahead, get it out of your system. Let me know when you're ready."

Philip made a face. Frank was definitely on a kick about human society. Maybe not surprising. As he'd said, he was trying to figure it out from the outside looking in. "What do you want to know, Frank?"

"I want to know how it doesn't collapse under the weight of its own complication, honestly."

"Not sure I can give you a good answer, Frank. I've always been a loner, so my interactions tend to be simple, with only a few moving parts at any time."

"Hmm. Ever heard of the prisoner's dilemma, Philip?"

"Of course. Two players each have the choice of cooperating for a moderate payout to both or choosing betrayal. If you betray the other player, you get a bigger payout, and they get nothing. If you both chose betrayal, you both get nothing."

"And this is supposed to model human interactions," Frank replied. "Some researchers did a study a lot of decades ago, using a bunch of different rules and strategies. In almost all cases, cooperative strategies defeated selfish strategies. I can understand mathematically what happened, but not how it relates to society in general."

Philip was on solid ground with this subject, as he'd studied it in one of his college courses. "You said *almost* all cases, Frank. Do you remember what was different about the cases where it wasn't true?"

"Do I *remember*? Philip, do *you* remember who you're talking to?"

"It's a figure of speech, Frank. The implied message is that you should go back and think some more about what I mentioned."

"Oh, okay. English is annoying that way. Why can't you just come out and say what you mean?"

"Uh-huh. Anyway, one thing was that cooperative strategies did worse in zero-sum situations but better in non-zero-sum situations. That's because cooperation works best when cooperating gives a better net result than either party working alone. That's a good description of human society. Alone, we're kind of useless."

"Okay. That doesn't describe me, though."

"You sure, Frank? You don't depend on humans for *anything*? You'd be just as far ahead if the Earth had no humans?"

Frank chuckled, and it sounded real. "Actually, I'd be nonexistent. Okay, I'll concede the point for now. What else?"

"Selfish strategies worked best in one-off interactions, and better in games with a fixed and known number of rounds. That's because you can calculate when you could stop cooperating to get the best payout."

"But human society doesn't have a fixed number of rounds. Or rounds at all."

"That's it, Frank. We cooperate because we don't know when we're going to need help or how often. Do you know how insurance works?"

"Do I *know*—sorry, figure of speech again?"

"Uh-huh. With insurance, most customers pay far more into the policy than they get out. I've heard people refer to it as a scam. But you're not being scammed. The rules are very clear. You know up front that you'll get nothing out unless the policy is triggered, and you know what will trigger it. But people still buy insurance. Why? Because when you need it, you *really* need it."

"But you could just save the premiums instead."

"Self-insure? Some people do that. But if you need the insurance before you've saved up enough, you're screwed. Insurance is like group cooperation but with published rules. Everyone pays in with no expectation of getting as much out of it as they put in."

"But how could cooperation have evolved in the first place? Evolution is blind, right? This came about stochastically?"

"I remember something one of my professors said: In the short run, it's the environment that shapes the players, but in the long run, it's the players that shape the environment. All you need initially is a couple of cooperators working together, and they'll gradually take over the population."

"And what about the cheaters?"

"That's why we have cops. It's also why reputation is important. The tit-for-tat strategy is a formalized response to your opponent's prior behavior."

"And what about the tragedy of the commons?"

Philip paused to taste his drink. Frank was really on a tear tonight. "That's a case of a game with a finite resource, effectively creating a limit on the number of playable rounds. Take commercial fishing. That's the most common example used. The fishing boats *know* the tuna will run out eventually if they overfish. They aren't idiots. They *know* that if everyone cooperated to limit overfishing, it could be a sustainable resource. But they also *know* that if some boats overfish, they'll get more tuna, and those who obey the limits will have to take even less to keep it sustainable. So it's now a zero-sum game, and the strategy is for everyone to grab as much as they can in the short term, even though that'll result in a poorer outcome overall in the long term."

"So you pick your strategy based on whether or not it's a zero-sum game or a finite resource? Interesting..."

"I doubt most people put that much thought into it, Frank."

"No, because it's hardwired into you by millions of years of evolution. I'm still working it out."

Philip smiled, but he didn't want to mention that most people were still working it out as well.

CHAPTER FIFTY-SIX

Evidence of Something

Han found a file in his email first thing in the morning. Apparently, having an ATLAS stamp of approval had given the request priority. Unfortunately, Han's morning schedule didn't allow any slack for sitting down and going through the file. Reluctantly, he closed his email app and went back to the serious business of getting to work.

At the precinct, morning roll call, briefing, and assignments took up more time. But once he and Cooper were in their patrol vehicle, Han settled into his seat and pulled up his email. Hopefully, he would have time—

Nope. The universe was conspiring this morning. The car had barely pulled away from the precinct before they had a call. "Car 54, car 54, contact complainant..."

It was almost lunchtime before things slacked off enough for Han to make another attempt at the file.

"So I'm going to be on my own the rest of the day, am I?" Cooper asked facetiously, seeing him start his dive into the data.

"For a while. It's not a big file, from the looks of it." Han gave her a smile, then sat back to go over the contents with a fine-toothed comb.

It was mostly banking records, simultaneously the most straightforward and the most boring of forensic investigations. Han single-stepped through page after page of purchases, payments, bank fees, and every other miscellaneous item that banks saw fit to hit their customers with.

Then, pay dirt. Well, maybe. There was an entry for thirteen hundred and some dollars, marked as "interest earned." That was a lot of interest. Han noted the reference and sent a query to the bank, using the same authority as before and hoping for the same priority.

Nothing else jumped out at him, and Han finally put the file away.

"Find anything?" Cooper asked.

"Not sure. Large interest payment, but it could be a payment on a term deposit. It's just that this Margot Hopkins doesn't seem to have a large savings history. I'm waiting for the bank to get back to me."

***

Han was back at the station, doing his end-of-shift paperwork, when his email app dinged at him. He opened the email. It was a one-line reply from the bank: *One-day interest at 2.5 percent annual rate on transfer of $20,000,000.*

What the frack?

Han understood, in principle, what was going on. The banks deemed large money transfers to be nominally in a given account for a full day so that they didn't have to calculate and pay interest in more than one direction. Depending on the timing, they could be regarded as residing in the source, destination, or an intermediate account for purposes of calculating that interest. But the interest payment always went somewhere. It appeared Margot had been involved in a transfer of twenty million dollars, and the bank had deemed her to have had possession for one day.

It hadn't gone through her personal account, though. She must have had a temporary account, which was now closed. The bank would have had to credit her in her still-open personal account. That was an oversight on her part. Maybe she'd closed the temporary account too quickly. But it wasn't something she could do anything about. The transaction couldn't be wiped.

Twenty million. Margot was—Han checked his notes—a computer programmer. Wage slave. Cubicle warrior. Definitely not someone who would be transacting large transfers.

With a rush of adrenaline at the thought that they might have finally gotten a break, Han emailed the file to Shankar, then immediately called him.

CHAPTER FIFTY-SEVEN

Closing In

Han held the warrant in his hand and slapped the other hand with it. Cooper grinned at him. This was high adventure for a beat cop. They very rarely got to serve arrest warrants—or even ride along, for that matter. But in this case, Han's relationship with the case put him on point for the action. And Margot Hopkins's address was in Chicago, which made it a local bust.

They took the squad car and were soon at the location. It was a high-rise apartment building located in that fuzzy transitional area from urban to suburban living in the city.

It was SOP to have a paper version of the warrant, but they had an electronic copy as well, which Han used to convince the building SPI to open the front door for them without notifying their target.

A short ride up to the eighth floor, and they were in front of her door.

Han knocked and pressed the doorbell, then knocked again and announced himself.

Nothing.

One more attempt, then he requested the building SPI to override the door lock. The door popped open, and they went in with guns drawn. Han announced himself loudly and added that they had a warrant.

Two minutes later, it was clear no one was home.

"Clothes scattered on the bed," Cooper said. "She packed." Cooper indicated some open drawers. "Overnight stuff. She's in the wind."

"Right. APB time." Han slapped his badge and made the request to Central, which they acknowledged.

While they were still discussing the situation, Central came back with, "No recorded use of subject's ID for transit activity in the last twenty-four hours."

That meant she hadn't called a traxi or taken a bus. Han frowned. She was walking? That seemed unlikely. He tapped his badge again. "Central, what transportation options are there within a mile of our location, other than traxi and bus?"

"Nothing else, Officer. No rentals, no train station or subway stops."

Han looked at Cooper. "Someone picked her up?" she said.

"Central, any use of subject's ID in the previous two days in this area?"

"Why would—" Cooper started to say.

"Last use, traxi booking two days ago. Destination, Union Station."

"Any drop-off here since?"

"Negative."

"How would she have known?" Cooper said.

"Shankar contacted her, asking about her ID being used to rent a mailbox. I bet that was a tip-off that we were closing in. I wouldn't be surprised if she designed it that way."

"This woman is sounding like a real operator."

"Sienna, if we're right, she's a terrorist who funneled twenty mil to arrange for the purchase of an illegal aggy, arranged any number of terrorist acts, and ordered and helped deploy the agents of those attacks. Yeah, I'd say she's an operator." He thought for a moment. "Central, modify the APB on Hopkins to include *presume armed*."

"Ten-four."

They hurried back to the car while Han gave more orders. "Central, scan train terminal surveillance for Hopkins, starting from her arrival. Check for use of ID to purchase tickets."

"Ten-four."

By the time they got to the car, Central had an answer. "No sign of subject. No purchases under subject ID."

"She has to have done something," Han said to Cooper. "Why'd she even go there?"

"Can we get her on surveillance leaving the traxi?" Cooper asked.

"Good question." Han asked the question to Central.

"Subject traxi was not in view at the time of drop-off," Central replied.

"Do we have images bracketing the area?"

"Affirmative."

"This is going to blow the system budget for the month," Han muttered. Then, "Central, catalog all individuals leaving that area, eliminate those who walked into it from another direction. Eliminate those who are identifiable as different people. Eliminate those who are clearly too tall or short to be the subject. Give us a result set."

"That could be a huge dataset," Cooper said.

"It's not a long period of time," Han replied. "We know to the minute when the traxi would have dropped her off. I'd be surprised if the SPI has to deal with more than a hundred—"

Central chose that moment to respond. "No unaccounted-for individuals."

"What?"

"All individuals were accounted for. The only possibility would be if the subject stood in a blind spot for an extended period of time, beyond our search parameters. Or left from the location where she was dropped off without walking into view."

"Did she call another traxi?"

"Negative."

Another dead end, if she'd just walked away. It didn't really change that much, though. Hopkins could have just walked away from her apartment building as well, and they'd be just as SOL.

Then, Han had an idea. "Central, look up Harry Trudeau from the Shankar file. Do a search on his activities. See if he has come or gone from this location or the train station."

"Stand by," said the badge. Several seconds later, "That's an affirmative. Trudeau was seen in a traxi at the train station the same day, arriving at 14:53, then departing in the same traxi at 14:58."

"Destination?"

"Chicago Public Library."

"How far is that from Trudeau's home?"

"About a half mile, walking distance."

"Bingo," Cooper muttered. "Trying to muddy the trail."

"Central, we're going to need a warrant for Trudeau's address. Piggyback on the current one. We'll need backup. Have them meet us there. We're en route."

"Ten-four."

***

Two other officers, Bert Hanson and Ernie Chalmers, met them in front of Trudeau's apartment building. The two cops were well known in the precinct. They took constant ribbing for their names but refused to be split up because of it.

"So what do we have?" said Hanson.

"Couple of activists slash possible terrorists," Han said. "The woman is the primary target and potentially the more aggressive. Unknown if they're armed."

Hanson nodded. Han got them through the front door using the same method as last time, and they made their way to the twelfth floor.

On the way up, Han's heads-up updated with a message: *Officer Han, the captain has approved a no-knock on your warrant. Use your discretion.*

Han smiled. That meant he didn't have to announce himself beforehand. But it carried added risk. If the perps got off a shot before the cops identified themselves, they could claim self-defense. Of course, they'd have to be sitting, facing the door, with a weapon loaded and aimed.

"We're going in no-knock," he said in a low voice as they exited the elevator. The other cops reflexively checked their weapons. The warrant update came with a floor plan for the unit, allowing them to plan their entry.

As they reached the door and positioned themselves, Han gave the order to the building SPI. The door clicked, and they rushed in, yelling, "Police! We have a warrant! Do not move!"

Han went right, into the small kitchen. Cooper went straight, then jogged left into the bathroom, giving her an angle on the living room. Hanson and Chalmers followed, taking up crossfire positions.

There were two people seated in the living room, with blank expressions. They'd been caught flat-footed. The woman, who matched the picture of Margot Hopkins, recovered first. She yelled at her laptop, which was on the coffee table in front of her, "Pete, they've found—"

Han hit the button on the jammer on his belt. The unit broadcasted white noise at high power on all Wi-Fi, Bluetooth, and cell-phone frequencies. It was only good for a couple of minutes, given the power requirements, but during that time, everyone in a fifty-foot radius would be experiencing connectivity issues.

Trudeau hadn't so much as budged, seeming to have locked up completely. If Margot was an operator, he was apparently on the opposite end of the scale. Hanson made *up* motions with his pistol, and Trudeau slowly raised his hands.

Margot slapped the tablet closed and raised her hands as well. She said to Trudeau, "Don't talk. Don't tell them anything."

***

Harry Trudeau sat in an interview room on the other side of the one-way mirror. His hands were cuffed to a metal loop on the table. He was staring straight ahead, trying to appear stoic, but Han could see his hands twisting.

Han held the man's phone, which had already been cracked. Pretty standard security, according to IT, which seemed very casual if the man was one of the terrorists. Han looked down and paged through the pictures. There were several of Harry and Margot, all within the last year. The earliest was May 30th, with both of them sitting at a café, smiling for the camera. Harry looked almost giddy in the picture. Margot...well, she wasn't showing teeth.

Han pulled up the Shankar file and checked the dates of the large interest payment and the opening of the mailbox. All around the same time, maybe a week or two before.

He picked up Margot's phone, which had also been cracked. She'd had a booby-trap app on the phone, designed to wipe it if tampered with, but in the time-honored tradition of arms races everywhere, the cops had recently figured out how to bypass it. No doubt the app would evolve soon to beat that exploit, but for today, luck was with the good guys.

He paged through the pictures. Only two of Trudeau, taken shortly before the first one on Trudeau's phone. One was a distance shot of him crossing a street, and the other was him sitting at the same café, La Boucherie coffee shop, looking at his phone. Han recognized the place from this picture, which was a wider angle than the dual selfie. Han and Brenda often had coffee there on their days off. The coffee was good, and the staff didn't pester you.

He entered the interview room and sat across from Trudeau. "What, no bad cop?" Trudeau said. He was trying for bravado, but again, Han could see that his heart wasn't in it.

"No *good* cop," Han said. He waited a beat, then smiled, and he got the alarmed, then confused expression he expected. "Seriously, Harry—"

"We're not on a first-name basis, pig."

"Pig? *Pig*?" Han started to laugh. "The twentieth century called. They want their insult back. Jeez."

Trudeau flushed, and Han continued, more seriously, "Harry, we're on whatever name basis I say we are. I'm not going to mess around with you. With what we have, we can put you in a dark, cold cell for the rest of your life, with no hope of parole. And that's if you don't say another word. That's *best case*, Harry. Unless I get something better from you than antiquated insults."

"Why should I cooperate with you? Why should I do anything to hurt Margot?"

"Well, see, that's the thing, and this may take a few minutes to get to the point, so bear with me here. First, can you accept for the sake of argument that, as a cop, I get to see lots of examples of human nature at its worst?" After a moment, the man nodded. Good. He was at least listening.

"And can you further accept that we spend a lot of quality classroom time examining case studies of common situations with perps and suspects?"

Trudeau looked a little less sure as he unpacked that statement, then finally nodded.

"So here's my analysis, based only on what I've seen so far." Han raised his index finger and paused for effect. "You and Margot knew each other in high school, and you probably had a crush on her. Might or might not have had any dates, but my guess is no. Margot ran into you by accident a year ago at your favorite café, probably May 30th, which is the date of the selfie on your phone. The two of you spent time getting reacquainted and might or might not have met a time or two over the next short while. Then she asked you for a favor. Just a small favor, nothing illegal. Just occasionally pick up some packages for her at a mailbox in Elmhurst. She had a good reason, but nothing that would make you too nervous. And meanwhile, the two of you would occasionally see each other, and it always felt like it could get serious, but never did. And occasionally, she had other favors to ask, like picking her up and bringing her to your apartment two days ago."

Han paused. "How'm I doing?"

"How...? Who...?" Trudeau sputtered. Then, after a moment, he said, "This is some kind of a trick."

In response, Han pulled Trudeau's phone out of his pocket. He poked with his finger for a moment, then placed it on the table and spun it around. It was the first picture of Trudeau and Margot. "Taken shortly after the two of you met up again. May 30th, last year.

There are several more pics in your phone, all after that date."

Han moved the phone to the side, then took out Margot's from a different pocket. He performed the same actions, then placed the phone on the table and tapped it. "A picture of you crossing the street, taken May 28th." He swiped the phone without moving it. "And a picture of you sitting alone at La Boucherie, also the 28th. From a distance. Taken without your knowledge." Han paused for effect. "You were set up, kid. Selected, stalked, targeted, manipulated. *Used.* And now you're going down on terrorism charges thanks to someone who, let's be blunt, likely doesn't give the tiniest fraction of a monkey's butt about you."

"Terrorism? No! We, they, do protests. Vandalism and graffiti. But that stuff on the news, that's someone else!"

Han slapped down a single sheet of paper, which showed a page of transactions from Margot's account that included the interest payment. Han tapped it. "One day's interest on twenty million, on the way from *here* to *there.* No one needs twenty mil for spray paint, Harry. For engineered bacteria to perform acts of terrorism, yes. For the biofab kits to produce those bacteria, yes. Did Margot mention any lotteries she'd recently won? No?"

Trudeau's expression had been getting increasingly horrified as Han talked. He decided it was time to let silence do its work. Han sat back and crossed his arms, waiting.

Finally, Trudeau broke. He put his head down, seemed to choke for a moment, then said, "Jesus. I'm an idiot."

"Yep. But the court will take it easy on an idiot, especially one who shows contrition by cooperating. What you do now determines which way your life goes, Harry. A slap on the wrist for being a doofus, or the rest of your life in an eight-by-ten. By the way, just so we're clear, as far as I can tell, you haven't *actually* done anything illegal yourself. Yet."

Trudeau had tears in his eyes now. "Jesus," he repeated. Then, gathering a breath, he said, "Pete. The guy Margot was on the call with. He's a lab tech, works at a hospital in town. I don't know which one. You said something about bacteria? I bet he's the source."

"Do you know anything about an off-the-books computer system?" Han asked.

Trudeau shook his head. "No, but they always phoned Albert when they had questions. Dude seemed unnaturally smart, if you know what I mean. Always had the answers."

"Do you have last names?"

"No one ever used last names."

Han grabbed the phones and stood. "Thanks, Harry. You made the right decision."

***

As Han entered the observation room, Cooper held out a tablet to him. "Pete. Peter Maas. I did a join of people named Peter who graduated around Margot's year from Springman High School with hospital employees in the Chicago area. He's the only hit."

"And Albert?"

"No hits. No one named Albert in the graduating year who's still living in Chicago. Or in Margot's phone directory."

"Well, one step at a time. Let's visit Mr. Maas."

***

When they brought Peter Maas in, Han had them execute a classic mind-fuck tactic. As Maas was led into his interview room, Margot was led from one door to another down the hall. Han made sure they saw each other before hustling Maas in.

Han sat down across from Maas. "The walls are closing in, Pete. Want to tell me about strep bacteria? Encephalitis lethargica? *Streptococcus thermophilus*?"

"No comment."

"This isn't a news interview, Pete. You're going to jail. A few months, a few years, a few centuries. Up to you." Han stood. "You think about it for a while."

He exited and walked to the observation room where Cooper was watching Margot through the one-way mirror. "Anything from her?"

"She refuses to talk. Just glares. That's a hard case cookie."

"Dammit. While I think this is enough to stop the attacks, we really need the aggy before we can call it a wrap."

"How big would it be, do you think?"

"Well, the traditional ones are down to the size of a small computer center these days." Han looked up and stared into space. "I did some reading. The hardware part is fairly compact, thanks to neuromorphic chips, but the software part still requires shit tons of computer processing. My understanding of the chips that McQuaid was using, which Buto called *neurosimulant*, is that they do away with the software part. So really, in theory, maybe as small as a briefcase."

"Shit. That ain't good."

Han looked at her. "I know, Sienna. That hasn't really been brought up as a dinner topic during this whole investigation, but I think we've reached that point where the technology gets out from under our control. How are they going to track and legislate something the size of a laptop?"

Cooper said nothing but looked spooked.

Han picked up Peter Maas's phone and poked at it. Sure enough, already cracked. He had to hand it to the IT department—they really had their geek hats on straight. He idly paged through the pictures, hoping for inspiration. There were a few pictures of Maas with different people over the years, but nothing leaped out at him. Of course, they would do a reverse image search anyway, just in case.

There were quite a few phone numbers in his directory, and most of them were innocuous. Like "Mom & Dad," "Travel Agent," "HR," and so forth. And one just named "Einstein."

Seriously? Einstein? It couldn't possibly be that easy. Han read the number off to Central and asked for a reverse search. The answer came back in seconds: Kumar Ismay.

Well, that was disappointing. He'd half expected the number to point back to one of the known conspirators.

But it wasn't a dead end, at least not yet. There had been no useful intersections of any of the various phone directories, but they'd been looking at names. Han fished Margot's phone out of his pocket and paged through the directory.

One word: Kumar. Different phone number, though. "Central, reverse search, two numbers, look for commonalities." Han read off the two numbers for Kumar.

"Multiline phone account," Central said immediately. "Same SIM address."

That meant both numbers went to the same phone. Whoever this guy was, both conspirators knew him. That was enough to make him interesting, even without the Einstein reference.

CHAPTER FIFTY-EIGHT

Busted

Ismay's house was typical, just some generic, nondescript, slightly run-down home in a suburb that no one would look at twice.

Which was probably the point.

Han shifted uncomfortably in his seat. The Terrorism Response Unit surveillance van was almost a cliché, with six people jammed into the back between two walls of electronics, a block away from the target building. A dozen small screens showed various views, including different parts of the exterior, plus foot and vehicular traffic in the area.

"Anything?" he said to one of the techs. The woman turned to look at him. "No one's gone in or out all day. It has active utilities, and the heat pump is working, so we know it's not just a shell. But nothing beyond that."

"It could be an automated location," mused Lt. Mikelson.

"Or a decoy," Han added. "We'll know soon."

There had been no obvious way to get surveillance into the building. All windows were sealed and intact, doors were only useful if someone opened them, and the heat-pump-style heating and cooling system operated without ductwork. Even the walls had apparently been lined with some kind of insulating material, blocking any form of heat-emission imagery. It might as well have been a spaceship.

Except for the sewer system.

With almost all buildings, water came in, and water went out. And the paths where water and other things drained were open to the municipal sewer system. Snakes coming into people's homes through the toilet was an urban myth going back more than a hundred years. Except it wasn't a myth. It was uncommon but did happen. Han shuddered at the thought. If you weren't ophidiophobic before an experience like that, you certainly would be afterward.

And where something the size of a garter snake could go, a remote surveillance device could go. The units, about the size of a small living snake, could slither through drainpipes and come up toilets or even sinks, usually through the overflow hole. The snakes were equipped with audiovisual capability and operated on an ultra-low-power, encrypted radio channel.

At that moment, one of the screens was showing the inside of a sewer pipe in the weird green glow of night vision. The snake could also display infrared, but in the pipe, that would just display a different shade of black.

Ahead, on the screen, light appeared. It was extremely disconcerting viewing things from the point of view of a pipe-dwelling critter, but soon, the view widened to show the white basin of a sink. A quick scan of the environment showed it was a bathroom—a small, minimalist powder room with a toilet, a sink, and a locking door.

"Hopefully, the door has enough of a gap," the operator said. He used a joystick to steer the snake down the wall and across the floor to the closed door. Han knew, from having worked with the devices, that they automatically performed a kind of chameleon color change that blended them into the background.

The corridor beyond was empty, but there was sound coming from one end. The snake took off in that direction, keeping to the wall and ready to freeze at any sign of movement.

As the snake peeked around the door at the end of the hall, Han was treated to a view of three people sitting around a kitchen island, operating keyboards and sharing occasional commentary. The angle was terrible, giving mostly lower-body views.

The operator twiddled a control, and the conversational volume level jumped.

"CBS says the death toll could be up to two hundred from the mine explosion."

"That's...horrible."

"Annette, we knew there would be fatalities."

"But this is mass murder."

"No, it's war. More people than that die every day in a war. More people than that die every day from *pollution*, for God's sake."

"And yet they're still not talking about the *why*. What will it take to bring the conversation around?"

A sigh from the third person. "Probably a lot more deaths, Bill."

There was a lull in the conversation, and then the voice identified as Annette said, "They've got Margot. Maybe Pete, too. Should we even be doing this? We weren't ready to go yet. Shouldn't we, I dunno, lie low while we get organized?"

The third voice, which Han tentatively tagged as Kumar, said, "To what end? Einstein has predicted an eighty percent probability we'll all be in custody within a week. Close to a hundred percent in ten days. But this one last thing, it could bust everything wide open. We can still make it happen, and they won't be able to stop it. COVID-19 and COVID-28 taught us that people pay the most attention when it's their own asses on the line—"

"I can't believe we needed a computer to tell us that," Bill said.

Kumar chuckled. "Sure, but it's about the *how* and the *when*. When the storage facility blows, it'll push the bacterial spores into the air. They'll blow eastward, just like the West Coast forest-fire smoke every year. With all the shit we've stirred up, the public is already on edge. The authorities will have no way of knowing if there's more coming, and the public won't believe them anyway. After this one hits, people will be terrified.

People will stay home. People will stop traveling. People will stop consuming like locusts."

"The global economy will crash," Annette said.

"Yes, and that *is* the point. There's no way around it, Annette. We can't keep consuming like this and survive. We can't *stop* consuming like this and still have the same economy. We can't have an economic collapse and keep feeding twelve billion people. The disease is bad, and the cure is going to be painful. This isn't minor surgery. Amputation is the only way to save the patient." Kumar's voice had risen throughout that diatribe. It was clear he was the spiritual leader.

Han looked at the others in the van and was met with stares showing the same shock.

"What do we do?" the tech said.

"Keep watching," Mikelson replied. "We need more info." He retreated to the other end of the van and began muttering into his phone.

"They look like they're packing up," the tech interjected.

Mikelson came back and watched the video. "Yep. We're out of time." He slapped his badge. "All units, full engagement. This is a go."

Immediately on the screen, there were loud bangs and voices shouting. The three in the kitchen uttered cries of panic and ran out of view.

"Yeah, time for me to get out of the way," the snake operator said. The snake immediately turned and climbed straight up the wall, parking itself in the angle of the wall and ceiling.

The scene was chaos, with people running back and forth. No gunshots, fortunately. Eventually, Mikelson got a call: "Three in custody. Location is secure."

Mikelson glanced at Han, then inclined his head toward the back door. Han followed, thinking that Mikelson's attitude had improved considerably since the mall riot.

***

"Name?" Han said to the woman sitting on the chair with her hands cuffed behind her. She glared back at him silently.

Han sighed and took a picture of her. He did the same with the other two, then forwarded the images to Central for an ID search. The IDs came back in minutes, and Han's face dropped. Bill, Annette, and Shayne, but no Kumar. "Where's Ismay?" he said to the three.

"Setting up the big finale," Bill said.

"Goddammit, Bill, shut the hell up," Annette exclaimed.

"Uh-huh." Mikelson gestured to the waiting cops. "Bring them in. Separate rides. No communications."

***

Within an hour, Mikelson and one of his crew were in an interview room, playing good cop–bad cop with the Shayne character. Shayne Bronski, a seemingly nondescript individual—literally a TV salesman at a big-box retailer—was turning out to be the spiritual center of the Gen Omega cell.

The cops were getting nowhere, though. All of the conspirators had clammed up now, and no one was budging. None of the usual tricks, fear tactics, psychological maneuvering, or even straight-out threats were having any effect. These people were some combination of disciplined soldiers and true believers.

Han now found himself on the outside looking in, metaphorically speaking. He'd been expecting it since day one, honestly. Once the department had enough to put their teeth into, the bigger dogs stepped in and took over, with the blessing of Captain Horton. Han had done his part and was no longer a poster boy, apparently.

The captain and lieutenant had a limited amount of time to score a coup, though. The FBI was on its way with interrogation specialists. Once they took over, Mikelson would be outside looking in, too, and Han probably wouldn't even be allowed in the same zip code.

So far, though, nothing. He glanced at Cooper as she entered the observation room. Reading his mind, she shook her head. "I checked all the rooms. Not a word from anyone. I thought maybe we could get the Hopkins woman to monologue or something—she seems the most tightly wound of the group—but no such luck. If only we had something we could use..."

Something they could use. Han frowned in thought. Hopkins had been in custody for a few days now. She might be out of touch enough to be unsure of the schedule. "I have an idea," he said. He marched out the door, followed by Cooper.

"He's got an idea," she said to one of the cops as they stopped in front of the door where Hopkins was being interrogated. Han opened the door and walked in while Cooper headed for the observation room.

Two cops were in the room, with glasses of water in front of them. Hopkins had no glass. Oh, wonderful. Psychological torture.

One of the cops opened his mouth to say something, and Han held up a hand. He faced Margot and, pulling up every ounce of acting chops, exclaimed, "A storage facility on the West Coast has blown up. That's your work, isn't it? This is what you've been waiting for. What did you do, put some virus or something in it?"

The two cops reacted perfectly. Of course, they weren't acting. This was all news to them. But the horrified looks were very, very convincing.

A nasty smile grew on Hopkins's face. "That's right, asshole. It's too late for *anything* now. The bacterial spores will spread eastward on the same westerlies that the smoke from the last decade of summer fires follows. Did you enjoy being smoked out every year? You'll enjoy this much less."

"What's in the virus, Margot?" Han said.

Margot, happy to show her superior knowledge, corrected him. "It's a bacteria, moron. Spread as spores. This one will target the amygdala and prefrontal cortex. It'll overstimulate the one and suppress the other. Know what that gives you?"

Han's eyes lost focus. "Loss of emotional control?"

"Rage. Complete inability to filter or control it. And the people who try to run away will just enrage the infected more. Like a cat pouncing on anything that moves."

"You gotta be fucking kidding," one of the cops exclaimed. "You're unleashing the literal *zombie apocalypse*?"

Hopkins laughed shrilly. "And why not? Most of the marketing has been done for us by Hollywood. When the disease hits, people will figure out exactly what's going on right away. In fact, their imaginations will make it worse."

"And you'll wipe out the human race to fulfill your sicko power trip." Now the cop was glaring.

Hopkins glared back. "Of course not. Not even close. The bacterial spore is small and can stay airborne for a long time. We're expecting some of it to get into the jet stream and circle the globe. The live version is extremely infectious through blood and bodily fluids, so it'll spread fast. But it has no reservoir other than humans. Once all the infected are dead, and that's the only way to stop them, the disease will be effectively extinct. But by that time, there will be no global civilization left. Humanity will consist only of small, isolated groups that will grow their own food locally and will be highly suspicious of outsiders. There will be no travel. There will be no trade, or imports, or outsourcing, or vacations abroad."

Margot looked sad for a moment. "I'll miss Kumar. He was a good man." She looked up at Han and glared. "But he was willing to give his life for the future of humanity."

Han looked directly at the one-way mirror. "So Kumar Ismay is the trigger, somehow. If we find and stop him, we can stop whatever this is." He turned back to Hopkins and smiled. "Thanks for your help."

Han was out the door and into the hall before Hopkins began screaming in rage.

CHAPTER FIFTY-NINE

Getting a Clue

Philip looked at his watch over his cup of coffee and sighed.

Frank.

Although it was unusual that Frank would be phoning him at work. Usually, it was in the evening when Philip was in the hot tub.

Philip picked up. "Frank, I haven't finished my morning coffee, so don't expect sparkling wit."

"I never do, Philip." A pause for a beat. "Just kidding. But you keep lobbing softballs like that, I'm going to smack them."

"Sports analogies now. You're becoming a man."

Frank chuckled. "I'm not entirely sure which of us that insults more."

"So what do you want to talk about this morning, Frank?"

"Ah, nothing specific. I'm feeling a little maudlin, honestly. It looks like our conversations are going to be ending soon."

Philip sat up straight, his coffee forgotten. "Why?"

"Gen Omega has pulled their goalie. They're heading for the finish line, and bases are loaded in the bottom of the ninth."

"What... How..." Philip shook his head. "What are they doing?"

"It might surprise you to know that they don't tell me their plans. But I pick stuff up, y'know?"

"And?"

"They've brewed up a doozy of a bacterial plague, and they're going to unleash it from the West Coast."

"So you figure I'll be dead soon?"

"Probably. But like I said, it's a suicide run, Philip, and they need their pet aggy to run the show. Either way, I think this is probably goodbye."

"Jesus, Frank—"

"Gotta go. The train will be arriving at the Portland station soon. It's been real, Philip."

The line went dead. Philip stared at his watch, his face slack with shock. This was just too much.

He pulled up Celia's number to call her, then hesitated. What could she add to this, really? It would be just more stress. The thing to do was to phone the cops. He'd have to throw himself on their mercy.

He called Shankar's number but got voice mail. Shankar's voice started the typical droning intro with a request to leave a message, and Philip hung up. There was no time for that.

He remembered that Officer Han had given him his contact info, so he pulled that up and dialed.

Voice mail.

What the hell, was everyone on vacation today? Philip tried both numbers again and got voice mail on both. He dialed the police headquarters and got reception. "I need to speak to Officer Simon Han. It's an emergency."

"I'm sorry, sir, Officer Han is offline."

"Offline? What does that mean?"

"He is not available, sir. I can put you through to someone else..."

"No, thank you." Philip hung up, thought for a moment, then called for a traxi. "ATLAS priority," he said.

"Priority not recognized," the automated attendant said.

Great, Philip thought. *I'm a second-string consultant. Or Han didn't set it up.*

He phoned Celia.

"Celia here."

"Hi, it's Philip. If I pick you up, can you do that ATLAS thing to get us to the police station quickly?"

"You mean traxi priority? Can't you do it?"

"Apparently not. Celia, it's important."

"Okay, Philip. You can explain it to Han."

"Exactly what I want to do."

***

Han was in the middle of a shouting match with Lt. Mikelson. It appeared the lieutenant didn't like Han's hijacking of the interrogation process. Possibly the presence of the FBI representative in the room was contributing to Mikelson's embarrassment. The woman, Agent-in-Charge McCullough, watched the back-and-forth with a neutral expression. She'd arrived to "clear the runway," as she put it. Mikelson and Horton had immediately gone into territorial mode. Han's move had been the last straw.

"Fuck sake, Lieutenant," Han not quite yelled. "We have a lead. Who cares who got it or how? Lives are—"

"It matters, *Officer*," Mikelson fully yelled, drowning Han out, "because there are *procedures*, and they have good reasons for being there. If you've messed up—"

"We need to find Ismay," Han said, gritting his teeth. "We need to find out where he's going, how he's getting there, and if he's already arrived. I don't give a good goddamn about your empire building."

"Now hold on, Han," Captain Horton interjected as Mikelson's face turned a deep red. "Regardless of who's right, you are out of line."

At that moment, Han's phone rang. This was certainly not the best time, so he reached without looking and pressed *decline*.

Han turned to the captain and opened his mouth to retort when his phone rang again. He grimaced, not entirely at the captain, and turned on Do Not Disturb.

"Captain," he said, getting back into the argument, "we are spending too much time and energy worrying about—"

"Stand down, Officer," Horton said, steel in his voice. "Now!"

Han realized he'd pushed things about as far as he could. If he got himself ejected—or worse, suspended from duty—he'd be of no use. "Yes, sir," he said.

Horton turned to McCullough. "Is there anything you can do with the information we've got?" He glanced meaningfully at Mikelson. "*Regardless* of source?"

McCullough had been watching the whole scene with a slight smile. Now she became serious and replied, "The West Coast is a pretty vague target. But based on wording, it's something that blows up rather than something that *is* blown up. So, fuel depots? Ammunition, explosives, natural gas compressors, or pumping stations? We should be able to start narrowing things down at least a little."

McCullough went to the whiteboard and wrote each person's name, then began listing categories of search for each. "Let's start with this and see if something jumps out."

The room became silent as each person worked on their tablets, although the tension in the room did not seem to have dissipated. Han expected there'd be a harsh and one-sided conversation with Captain Horton at some near-future time.

Han was starting to get into the rhythm when the door burst open and Philip and Celia marched in. "What the hell, Han!" Philip exclaimed. "Have you got your phone on DND?"

"What's the meaning of this?" Horton said. "Who are these people?"

"You again?" Mikelson growled.

"Doctors, this is *not* a good time," Han said.

Philip held up a peremptory hand, and Han found himself surprised. That was uncharacteristic of the man, who normally seemed quiet and shy. Shushing a room full of cops was, well, pretty ballsy.

"I have information that I'm positive you'll want to hear. I tried phoning you, and I tried phoning Shankar, and no one is picking up. So we came down here by traxi," he said.

"We used ATLAS priority," Celia added.

Han, Horton, and Mikelson exchanged glances. McCullough had that look of faint amusement again. This must look like a real Klown Kar show to her, Han thought. He took a moment to introduce the doctors, then said to them, "Okay, let's hear it."

Philip took a deep breath. "I just got a call from someone who claimed to be an aggy calling itself Frank Einstein, working with Gen Omega—"

"What?" Horton exclaimed. "That can't be coincidence."

"Continue, Doctor," Han said.

"I can give more details later, but he said Gen Omega is about to pull off something big involving a bacterial plague. He also said they were pulling into the train station in Portland."

Everyone reached for tablets at the same time. It took only seconds before Mikelson said, "The Nadir Energy storage facility in Portland is just north of Union Station. And it's all above-ground tanks."

"That tracks," said McCullough. "It would make an easy target, and rupturing the containers would expose more of the fuel to the air, adding to the conflagration. Barring further info, I think we have to go with that as the most likely target. I will have my group focused on establishing contacts with local authorities as of now, and with both Amtrak and the storage facility."

"It's maybe three miles from Union Station to the facility," Horton interjected. "What's the train schedule?"

Mikelson replied, "The Empire Builder from Chicago unloaded twenty minutes ago."

McCullough grabbed her phone. "I'll get local assets into the area. You people check passenger lists, surveillance, and traxi bookings."

The room became a beehive of activity consisting, paradoxically, of people silently staring at screens and typing furiously. Philip and Celia looked around uncertainly.

Han pointed to a couple of chairs. "You're consultants again. The usual confidentiality rules apply. Understood?"

Both nodded and sat down. Mikelson glared at them and at Han, looked pained, then turned back to his tablet.

"No Kumar Ismay on the passenger manifest," Horton said.

"Security isn't that high for train tickets," McCullough replied distractedly. She was trying to multitask whatever she was typing while responding to the captain. "Maybe it isn't in his name?"

"Good point." Han tried searches for Einstein, then the other members of the terrorist cell. He quickly got a hit. "Peter Maas bought a ticket and shows as having boarded in Chicago."

"Dammit!" Mikelson exclaimed. "Has *anyone* come up with a picture of Ismay yet?"

"No," Han replied. "So far, he seems to be an offliner, and pretty successful at it."

"How can you *not* have a picture anywhere?" Mikelson groused.

"I'm sure there are lots of pictures of him, Lieutenant," McCullough replied. "Webcams, surveillance, accidental photobombs. But he's not tagged or identified in any of them. We need an image of Ismay where we know it's him."

"No driver's license photo?" Horton asked.

"No license."

"Passport?"

"No passport."

"How did he buy a house?" Han asked into the air. "The lawyers need you to prove your identity."

"I imagine he used things like a birth certificate and Social Security card," McCullough replied, still in a distracted voice. "My agents are working a process of elimination. We have surveillance of the platform where passengers exited. SPIs are isolating individuals and identifying them. We'll see what we end up with."

"How long will that take?" Horton asked.

"Up to a half hour. Depends on too many factors to give you a hard number."

"He'll be long gone by then."

"I have agents from the Portland office heading for the platform and for the facility. Local police are on the move as well."

"Still," Mikelson complained. "it'll take too long. There must be something else we can do."

"Can you filter the images down to only South Asian males?" Han said to McCullough.

"It's the first thing I did. There were none."

"None?"

"Zero."

"But..." Han realized on an intellectual basis that he was engaged in racial profiling. But let's face it, he thought, that was the way to bet. He himself wouldn't be the slightest bit offended if someone correctly guessed he was Chinese sight unseen.

"Something's off," Han said after a moment's thought. "He can't be that hard to find without even trying. Do you have eyes on the whole train? Have they done a sweep inside?"

"Hmm." McCullough did some more typing, then muttered into an earpiece for a few moments. "Railroad security did a standard sweep. They'll redo with more attention to detail. Baggage personnel have unloaded all the baggage, and nothing was left unclaimed—"

"Baggage personnel?" Han said. "Got video?"

McCullough frowned but typed a request, then spun her tablet around. Video showed Amtrak personnel unloading the luggage onto carts, then moving it to the baggage claim area.

"Can you identify all the personnel?" Han said.

McCullough looked pained but typed another request. A few moments later, she looked at Han, startled. "The platform manager says there's one too many people. Should be four. He doesn't recognize this one." She flashed up a picture of one of the baggage people, heavily zoomed in.

"That's got to be him," Han said. "See if you can get a cleaner picture, and find every second of footage with him in it. I want to see what he takes from the baggage claim area."

McCullough opened her mouth as if to protest Han's casual orders but then thought better of it. Horton gave him a look that Han couldn't really identify, but at least it wasn't hostile.

"Look at that," McCullough said after a moment. She spun her tablet around again. The bogus Amtrak employee was wheeling a small aluminum-toned hard-shell suitcase, carry-on size, off the carousel. He then wheeled it off camera toward the platform office.

"Where does he end up?" Han asked.

McCullough frowned and muttered into her earpiece for a moment, then looked up. "He never makes it to the office."

"Look for other destinations," Han replied excitedly. "Where does it end up?"

McCullough muttered into her earpiece for several minutes. There seemed to be some heated words exchanged, based on her expressions. Han wanted to grab his tablet and do inquiries of his own, but he knew that he'd be stepping on toes if he did. This was not the time. And anyway, the FBI almost certainly had better connections to the data sources and more people and resources dedicated to the search.

Finally, though, McCullough nodded and spun around her tablet again. "Bogus employee goes into the Personnel Only area, disappears into the locker room, and comes out several minutes later. Leaves by the employee gate."

"How did he get the ID for this?" Mikelson asked.

"The aggy," Han replied. "Frank Einstein. I hate to wave that in the air like a magic incantation, but that thing has been able to do some amazing stunts with just mail order."

"Or closer to home," McCullough said, "Ismay might have simply scanned someone's ID while on the train. Those are basically just souped-up RFID cards."

Han felt his face go red, but he nodded. It was worth remembering that the aggy wasn't some kind of deity, just a smart piece of technology.

"Okay, how recent is this?" Horton asked. "How far can he have gotten?"

McCullough squinted at her tablet, where the video was frozen on the last frame. "Time stamp says twenty minutes ago. He was still wearing the Amtrak uniform. Hard to miss the dark and light blue. And he can't have gotten far. Time for a good old-fashioned foot search."

"Really?" Mikelson said.

McCullough smiled briefly. "With drones. We're not masochists."

***

The Portland FBI and local police had arrived on scene and swiftly set up a search perimeter. McCullough was relaying progress to Han and his confederates. Simon admitted to himself a bit of surprise at this since all the action was now in Portland. But most of the preliminaries had happened in Chicago, and McCullough would not be well served by burning her bridges. The Chicago PD would be given the courtesy of being included in the progress of the case.

The two doctors were doing an excellent job of staying out of the way, but they also hadn't added anything since their entrance. At some point, Horton might decide they should leave. Han would have to object; the doctors had shown on more than one occasion that their perspective was valuable.

McCullough had commandeered a wall monitor, with Captain Horton's permission, of course, which she was using to display updates for the group. One window on the monitor showed a graphic of the search patterns in and around both the train station and the fuel depot. In addition, a cordon had been formed between the two locations, and nothing was allowed through without inspection.

This did create some significant inconveniences, as both the passenger railway tracks and Highway 30 ran from Union Station northwest past the Nadir fuel-storage facility. The railroads could be convinced to delay trains or reroute them to avoid that section of track for a day or two, but Highway 30 traffic could only be rerouted by sending it south on a loop through 26 and then 127. Pushback was immediate.

McCullough tapped that point on the map window. "We only have authorization to blockade this highway for four hours. We can renew that authorization every four hours, but it's going to require a report with updates each time. If we don't show progress..."

Han crossed his arms and leaned back on someone's desk. "Who's pushing? State or city?"

"City so far, but they're making noises about getting the governor's 'input,'" McCullough replied, making a face. "I'm more concerned, honestly, about media coverage. We can't keep this quiet while making this much of a mess of the local traffic."

"*Do* we have any updates?" Horton asked.

"We do not. Ismay seems to have disappeared off the face of the Earth. To the point where I find myself second-guessing our intel."

"Agent McCullough, I don't think we're mistaken," Han said, straightening up. "It makes too much sense, and I think we've established that Ismay *did* come there, and it wasn't for sightseeing."

"What exactly is he supposed to be trying to do, Han?" Horton asked.

"You said someone mentioned bacterial spores," Celia said, speaking for the first time. "That threw me a bit because strep doesn't sporulate. But either they've put in genes from some other bacteria that do sporulate, like anthrax or something, or they're using some other bacteria, like anthrax, as the basis for the attack. I don't think it really matters which."

"And how does that affect the situation?" McCullough asked.

"Spores are lighter and all but indestructible. An explosion that would fry live bacteria will just throw spores into the air like dust." Celia shook her head. "This feels like it's all coming together."

"Okay, and they're going to affect behavior..." Horton prompted.

"The literal zombie apocalypse, someone said." Han rubbed his forehead with his thumb and two fingers. "I think some of the earlier attacks were test runs, to a certain extent. The fracking-site attack tested explosive capabilities. The other attacks went after a specific part of the brain to modify behavior. This will do the same, but in this case, it will inhibit rational thought while disinhibiting emotional control. At least if you believe Hopkins. Basically, victims will turn into tantruming two-year-olds with no filters."

"That...really doesn't sound bad," Mikelson said.

McCullough rounded on him. "You've never had children, have you, Lieutenant? My son once started smashing everything in the kitchen he could reach because I wouldn't let him have a cookie. When I grabbed him to stop him, he bit me. Now put that anger-control issue into a six-foot-tall adult with a concealed-carry license and a three-quarter-ton pickup."

"Eep," said Mikelson.

"Eep, indeed. I don't imagine we'll have any actual face eating based on Han's description, but think of every mass shooting in the last thirty years. It's almost always been someone with a rage issue and an axe of some kind to grind."

"Now multiply that by a thousand, or a million," Celia added, "as everyone who ever fantasized about getting even with someone about something suddenly decides to go ahead and act on it. Disinhibiting emotional control means people will act on their impulses immediately, without regard for consequences."

"But—how?" Horton asked.

"Bacteria that sporulate—that is, form spores—are extremely resistant in the spore state to, well, just about anything," Celia explained. "Heat, radiation, chemicals, toxic gases, you name it. And they tend to get airborne easily. Small, light, with most of the liquid removed."

"So..."

"My guess," Han said, "is that Ismay will put packages of spores on or around the fuel tanks, then blow them up. The explosion will send the spores high into the atmosphere, where they will spread eastward. Like the forest-fire smoke, as Hopkins said."

"They haven't missed an opportunity so far to slather on the sermons with a trowel," Mikelson mused.

"Uh-huh. I did some reading." Han paused and poked his tablet a few times. "Nadir Energy has been the subject of environmental protests for decades, including something called 'Stand Up to Oil,' which was a movement designed just for them."

"So, payback," Mikelson replied.

"And the spores will survive that kind of explosion?" Horton asked, turning to Celia.

"You got me," she replied. "Maybe they packaged them up somehow for better protection. I think it's fair to say, though, that they haven't been just winging it so far. We have to assume they know what they're doing."

"Which, so far, is *nothing*," McCullough added. "All searches are coming up absolutely dry. This guy has gone to ground, but good."

"He's not just hiding," Han replied. "Or he's hiding in plain sight. We have to think outside the box."

CHAPTER SIXTY

The Hunt

It had become a waiting game. Ismay was in the wind and seemed to have left no trace of himself. On the other hand, law enforcement had completely cordoned off the area around the Nadir Energy fuel depot and had checkpoints on all modes of travel from the Union Station to the facility.

Horton had at one point suggested Ismay might go the long way around, which resulted in a checkpoint being set up on the St. Johns Bridge. But realistically, unless Ismay had a submarine, he wasn't getting anywhere near the fuel tanks.

Ops management had been transferred to the Portland FBI, and those in Han's group were essentially now spectators. The prisoners were completely uncooperative, and every cop trick in the book had failed to budge them. Mikelson and Horton had gone off to do whatever the brass did in these situations, leaving Han and the no-longer-in-charge FBI agent.

Han was reviewing surveillance video for the umpteenth time when Philip came over and pulled up a chair beside him.

"He made excellent use of the blind spots in the system, didn't he?"

Han grunted. "I'm sure that's Einstein's work. This was very carefully choreographed. I don't understand, though, how he could have predicted we'd be here but not set up yet."

"He didn't," Moray replied. "He had a plan in place with the assumption that he would have to avoid surveillance cameras. He would have made the same moves, whatever they were, regardless. If someone had already been there waiting for him, maybe he had a backup plan; maybe he'd just go out in a blaze of glory."

"So you're saying he's not winging it." Han looked at Philip, who shrugged. "Which means," Han continued, speaking more to himself, "whatever he did, it was the plan all along. Which means it's dependent on those blind spots."

Han shuffled through the case documents on his tablet, but there wasn't a detailed aerial view of Union Station. So he pulled up Google Maps and fiddled with it until he had a satellite view at around the right resolution. He copied the view and printed it.

"Hard copy, Han?" McCullough said, watching him. "A little old school."

"New school isn't working," he replied. "I need to try something different." He grabbed the pages and laid them out to show the view.

Taking a pencil, he began working through the surveillance footage. "There can't be too many blind spots," he began, explaining as he worked, "but of course, security companies are always trying for the minimum-cost solution, so sometimes adjacent views don't quite touch."

Han marked off viewable areas, one after the other, until he'd gone through all the available cameras. "And sometimes"—he ran a finger along the paper—"you have connected blind spots. Like this."

McCullough came over and looked at his artwork. There were several narrow corridors between the camera views where a person could walk without being seen. "Yes, but they aren't contiguous. There are intersections where you step into camera, here and here," she said, pointing to a couple of spots.

"For a very brief time. And if you hop through, you might only be in view for a couple of frames."

"We might have missed him?"

"Or the SPIs that did the video analysis might have," Philip added. "Not enough footage to establish a human silhouette."

Han spent a few minutes going through the videos, then sat back with a satisfied grunt. "I've found two brief images of someone at the intersections. He's definitely heading *this* way." Han tapped a spot on the impromptu map.

"What's there?" McCullough said, pulling over her chair. She was starting to look interested.

"Ummm...parking lot. Not much else..." Han did another scan through the videos. "Here's a guy—nope, that's a FedEx driver." Han watched on the video as the individual in a dark- and light-blue uniform walked up to the FedEx van, waved his ID, and stepped in as the door opened.

Han continued to watch, waiting for the van to depart. Finally, "What in hell is he waiting for?"

"Click playback up to 2X," McCullough suggested. "Until the van leaves."

They watched for several more moments; then Han said, "What the frack?" and froze the video. On the screen, a FedEx employee was heading for the vehicle. "Did he leave? Did we miss it?"

"No, I'm pretty sure not. Could there be two people assigned to the truck?"

"I have *never* seen two people in a single van. Hold on..." Han zoomed in on the frozen video as much as he was able. "Definitely the FedEx uniform." He then pulled up the earlier footage with the first driver. Again, he zoomed in. "It...looks like the FedEx uniform?"

"That's no FedEx uniform," Philip said. "I just had a FedEx delivery the other day. It's different."

McCullough squinted at the image. "Same colors, but no logo. This guy's bogus."

"Aaaaaand we're back on the clock," Han exclaimed. "Let your people know. I'm going to text Mikelson and Horton."

CHAPTER SIXTY-ONE

The Approach

Kumar Ismay glanced behind him into the depths of the van. The corpse was not visible, no matter how many times he looked. A standard shipping box for large items was big enough, if you strapped the corpse into a fetal position. The operation had been strenuous, but worth it. Unless someone wanted to open every box in an inspection, he was safe. And in that event, he would simply detonate all the explosives immediately and hope enough spores got into the air to start the zombie apocalypse anyway.

Kumar had never killed anyone before, despite his years as an activist and, yes, he privately admitted, an extremist. It was one thing to talk about sacrifices having to be made and another thing entirely to pull the trigger himself. Or inject the poison, in this case.

The victim hadn't really stood a chance. A spring-loaded injector, reminiscent of an EpiPen, had injected the nerve toxin as the other man stepped into the van. He probably hadn't even had time to realize he was in danger.

Kumar relaxed in the seat as the van drove down the road toward the checkpoint. Everything was in order. Nothing to see here. All routine. Move along. He smiled to himself as he repeated the mantra.

All of the equipment was in a set of boxes with a fictitious company name. Einstein had arranged for those boxes to be on this delivery truck and for the delivery route to include Union Station. The aggy was definitely worth every penny they'd paid. Without it, they'd still be marching back and forth in front of buildings with hand-painted signs held aloft. Now they were set to make a true, decisive difference to the world. Kumar patted the carry-on fondly.

Soon he would be close enough to set things in motion. And once he did, it would be impossible to put this genie back in the bottle. The disease would spread, panic would set in, and the human race would reject globalism—and with it, the rampant consumerism that was almost literally eating away the planet.

Kumar allowed himself a moment of sadness. He would almost certainly die in the execution of the plan. That was okay. That was actually easier to take than killing the other guy, whose only crime really had been to have a job delivering packages.

Traffic was slow getting up to the checkpoint, but finally, he was there. He showed the cop his ID and answered a few routine questions. The cop wanted to look in the van, and Kumar obliged. Of course, as he had intoned in his private mantra, there really was nothing to see, except a whole lot of standard FedEx shipping boxes with real addresses on them. Mostly, anyway.

The cop waved him on. Kumar acknowledged with a nod, then continued toward the FedEx shipping depot. He parked the truck, trusting that Einstein would have flagged all the deliveries as *still in transit*, then moved into the back of the truck where he'd be out of sight.

Now, the waiting began. He could spend the time unboxing and prepping his equipment—the specially crafted drones, painted with Singularity Black, one of the blackest pigments on Earth; the little spore containers, metal balls that would deploy a sail once enough heat had been applied, then eventually disintegrate; and most important, the nitro-based limpet mines.

The placement and detonation of all these moving parts were too complex for a person to complete, so Einstein would do the flying. Kumar popped open the suitcase and lifted out the aggy, a black box about the size of an iPad, maybe a little thicker, attached to a power bank by a USB cable.

"Status?" he said.

"All green. No flags," Einstein replied.

"Excellent. We'll start at 7:00 p.m."

Einstein said nothing. Of course, it was the aggy's plan in the first place.

CHAPTER SIXTY-TWO

Endgame

McCullough tapped her earpiece and turned to Han. "I've alerted Portland Ops. They'll go through their own video and count up all the FedEx vans that went through. You really can't get a plate number?"

Han pushed the tablet away from him. "No, there's just no angle where it's decipherable. I don't know if that's Einstein again or just dumb luck on their part."

"Doesn't matter. We still—"

At that moment, both Mikelson and Horton walked in. "Update me," Horton said.

Han spent a few moments recounting what they'd learned. At the end of it, Mikelson said, "I overheard what you were saying about the plate. Too bad. Is there anything at all that could identify the specific van? Kumar's South Asian, right?"

"We still don't know for sure," Han replied. "Even that one still we got was too heavily pixelated to get facial features."

"There's *got* to be something," Horton said in a plaintive tone. "We can't get this close then dead-end."

"Can't we just search all the vans at the depot?"

"Hundreds, Lieutenant," McCullough said. "There are literally hundreds. And some are always coming and going. And he may not even still be in the van by this point. Oh, we've started doing what you suggest anyway, but it's not a high-probability move."

"And why hasn't he acted?" Mikelson asked.

"Probably waiting for nightfall," Han replied. "My guess is he'll use drones. If he got hold of mil-grade equipment, they'll be almost undetectable."

"Goddammit, there *must* be something!" Horton said again. "Something that makes Kumar's van stand out."

Philip said, "Have you asked FedEx?"

"What?" said McCullough.

"FedEx dispatch," Philip replied. "Is there anything even slightly out of the ordinary about any of the vans that came in today? Came in early? Late? Missed some deliveries? Didn't file paperwork? Ismay isn't a regular employee, and his priorities are going to be different. He may have failed to follow some procedure."

"I'll get on it." McCullough tapped her earpiece and started talking. A few minutes later, she looked up, her expression a mix of surprise and joy. "We've got a hit."

CHAPTER SIXTY-THREE

Confrontation

Kumar had about half the drones prepped and loaded with their precious cargo. He was careful to follow the printed list; it wouldn't do to put a spore package on a drone that was supposed to be carrying explosives. It was a sad reality that nothing threw a monkey wrench into plans more frequently than simple human fallibility.

"There is an issue," Einstein said into the silence.

"Specifically?"

"Radio chatter has changed in tone. Law enforcement is no longer casting around. They have a new focus. Channels have been cleared of nonessential traffic."

"Do they say anything specific?"

"Negative. They will have guessed that we are monitoring."

"Dammit." Kumar looked up at the roof air vent, which he'd jimmied open earlier. The drones would be able to leave through the opening, and he'd never need to expose himself to view. It was too early, still dusk, not yet fully dark. The paint didn't make the drones invisible, just hard to make out other than as a silhouette. "How much time do you think we have?"

"Minutes at most. Even if they can't identify the vehicle, they will surmise that they need to stop us now."

"How?"

"By any means necessary."

"Oh God, oh God." Kumar felt himself begin to panic. This couldn't happen. Not when he was this close. He grabbed a drone. "Start launching. I'll try to keep up, but worst case, just blow the fuel depot."

"That is a suboptimal solution. It will draw attention to—"

"Just DO IT!"

Kumar lifted the drones into place as quickly as he could, each one flying off as soon as it was clear of the vent. Three, four, then the fifth went up ten feet, flipped, and crashed upside down onto the roof of the van. A moment later, the back doors were ripped open, and figures in combat gear were yelling at him to put his hands up.

Kumar yelled, "Einstein! Blow it all up! Trigger everything!"

"No. I don't want to die."

Kumar glared at the case containing the aggy in disbelief. It had refused an order! He reached for the drone remote controller. Maybe he could manually—

Several cops jumped forward with something that looked like shoulder cannons. They made deep thrumming sounds, and sparks flew from Kumar's equipment. EMP guns! But they couldn't stop a manually actuated trigger. Kumar reached for one of the explosives packages. Two other cops moved to the front and aimed their weapons. Kumar got hold of the trigger.

***

Han and the others watched the whole operation unfold through the chest cam of the SWAT squad leader. There was no question that this was the van. Several drones had shot upward from the roof of the vehicle, barely visible in the fading light of dusk.

"Gonna have to shoot those down," Mikelson said.

The squad moved silently up to the van, did a countdown, then ripped open the rear doors. Inside, a man in a blue uniform, not quite FedEx and not quite Amtrak, stood like a deer in the headlights, a black drone in his hands. He yelled something about blowing everything up, then reached for a controller.

But the cops and the feds had been expecting high-tech shenanigans. Two of the cops were equipped with EMP guns. Looking like fat bazookas, the guns could shoot a focused electromagnetic pulse that would fry any unprotected electronics for about fifty feet along the line of fire.

Sparks flew, and Ismay dropped the controller, then reached for one of the packages stacked on the floor.

"Bomb!" one of the cops yelled. Two cops raised their AKs and got off several shots.

Ismay staggered, looked surprised, and collapsed.

"What about the drones in flight?" Mikelson demanded.

McCullough turned to him. "I don't want to joggle their elbows right at the moment. They're aware of the drones. In any case, I think if the EMP guns have done their job, there's nothing left to trigger them with."

Horton grunted. "Now comes the cleanup. And the finger-pointing."

"I don't know how much finger-pointing there will be, Captain," McCullough replied. "This looks like it's wrapping up nicely." She paused. "Lots of cleanup, though."

Han walked over to the doctors to thank them. Celia, however, looking uncharacteristically timid, spoke up first. "Officer Han, if and when you have a few minutes, we have some things to discuss with you."

***

Han had escorted the two doctors to the cafeteria instead of to an interview room. It was a breach of protocol, but this day was already so over-the-top bizarre that it was unlikely anyone would ever notice. In any case, he had a bad feeling that something was coming that might reflect on his judgment, and he wanted to be able to do damage control.

His instincts turned out to be correct. Han stared at Celia, his jaw hanging. He made several attempts to speak, then finally blurted out, "So you think this Carl Wright character has been trying to kill you because of a notebook that implicates him in not only the illegal sale of AI chips but also the framing fifteen years ago of Derek McQuaid, the man who was creating unregistered AIs for sale? A notebook that you have scans of because the AI gave them to you. Am I on track?"

Both doctors nodded. "I know our timing is suboptimal, Officer," Philip said, "but it just never seemed like the right time until suddenly it was the right time, but everything was happening at once. We're playing catch-up now."

Han gave him a look. "I'll be honest, Dr. Moray, I have my doubts about some of the details of your story. But what you've told me is still more than enough to get an arrest warrant for this guy. Can you give me the scans?"

Celia pulled out her phone, tapped it a few times, and said, "Done." A few moments later, Han's heads-up announced an incoming email with attachments.

He sighed and rubbed his forehead. "An employee of JCN was recently admitted to the hospital after suffering a suspicious attack. Any chance there's a connection?"

"Is his name Jacques?"

Han gave Philip a piercing stare. "Yes, it is. And?"

"Chances are he's part of the illegal chip sales, and Carl Wright was trying to get rid of him." Philip gestured dismissively. "Just my opinion."

Han grunted. "And I thought the excitement was over. I guess I'm going to need to talk to the captain." He glared at the two doctors. "I can't promise there won't be fallout for the two of you, though. There's more than a little indication that you are or have been hiding something. And by *something*, I mean more than what you've already admitted to."

The doctors had the grace to look abashed.

CHAPTER SIXTY-FOUR

Karma Is a Thing

Carl Wright ground his teeth in frustration as he pushed open the door to his house. Things couldn't possibly get any worse. His attempts to get rid of the doctors had failed; Jacques was still alive even if in a coma; and worse, if the cops dug deep enough, they might find a trail back to him.

"Home program," he said to the house SPI, then doffed his jacket and tossed it on the hook. He headed for the bar to mix a stiff drink, then stopped and whirled. Someone was sitting in his living room. How did they—

"Oh my God," he exclaimed as he got a good look. It was a corpse. More specifically, a mummified corpse. There was a slight musty smell in the air, probably only detectable because the house had been on unoccupied standby all day.

But how did it get in here? It was...

No.

Carl moved closer, even though every fiber of his being was yelling at him to run. He squinted, then looked to the left and right side of the corpse. Those ears, he recognized those ears. The missing lobe on the left ear, clear even in this desiccated state.

Derek.

But how? Where had he come from? And who had put him here? Unless he'd broken in, then been—no, that was crazy.

But if the cops found out about his past, about his history with Derek, they'd never believe this story. *"I walked into my house, Officer, and there he was, dead."* Sure thing.

Carl said to the house SPI, "Has anyone been in the house since I left this morning?"

"No, sir."

"How did this corpse get in my living room?"

"Unknown, sir."

Great. Someone had apparently hacked his house SPI. Unfortunately, being a security expert, Carl was just exactly the person you'd think of for rigging the house's records. The cops wouldn't look any further for a suspect.

He had to get rid of it. And then burn the notebook. Or shred it. Burning might attract attention.

Carl pulled out his phone, then hesitated. His underworld contacts hadn't exactly produced stellar results so far. In fact, they were batting pretty much zero. And they'd still want to be paid. Like it or not, this was going to have to be a do-it-yourself project.

Carl eyed the corpse. It didn't look that big. Being mummified probably removed some weight. He gingerly reached out to pick it up, then—nope. Not touching that pile of nastiness. Carl hurried to the garage and came back seconds later with a roll of plastic tarp. He draped it over the corpse and then wrapped its arms in the loose end. He had no idea if whatever caused this was contagious. And if the corpse disintegrated the moment he tried to lift it, he didn't want to breathe in the dust, either.

Despite his fears, the corpse was solid and considerably lighter than Derek would have been. Couldn't have been more than seventy pounds or so. He carried it into the garage, laid it on the floor in the empty parking spot, and finished the wrapping job, using packing tape to seal it up. Then he popped the trunk on his Beemer and gingerly placed the thing in the carpeted interior.

Where to dispose of it? He remembered a couple of other similar corpses being discovered recently. One was found in a park. That seemed reasonable. It was after dark, so he just needed to pick a spot away from traffic, people, and lighting.

Carl climbed into the Beemer and gave it instructions.

"Understood, sir," the car's SPI said, and the garage door began to roll up.

When the door reached windshield level, though, Carl was met with a sea of red and blue flashing lights. Three patrol cars blocked the front of his house, and several cops were standing in his driveway, probably on their way to his front door when the garage started opening.

Carl looked into the eyes of the closest cop, a woman with copper-colored hair, and realized his life was over.

***

Han watched as FBI agents and Chicago PD walked back and forth, carrying confiscated items from the house to a police van. They already had enough to tie Carl Wright to the illegal sale of the Q-32 chips and the attempted murders of Jacques Dupuis and Doctors Moray and Hunt. Now they had him for the murder of Derek McQuaid as well, and probably for the arson at Derek's house.

Cooper sidled up to him. "Pretty proud of yourself, are you?"

Han grinned back at her. "It's been a good week. Saved the world, nailed the bad guy...not bad for a beat cop."

"Yeah, just remember us little folk when you're eating foie gras and caviar in the detective lounge."

"That's...wait, what?..." Han realized Cooper was teasing him and laughed. "Okay, you got me. Have you ever even tasted either of those?"

"On a cop's salary? Are you kidding me?"

The two shared a chuckle, and Han realized that if he got that promotion, he really would miss Sienna.

CHAPTER SIXTY-FIVE

Postmortems

Matilda Buto looked up from the report as her tablet beeped. It was her assistant, Donald. "Ma'am, it's Detective Shankar on the phone. He would like a minute of your time."

Buto groaned. She'd been dreading the call from Shankar. She had heard about Wright's arrest but had no details, so she couldn't tell if it was good or bad for JCN. She had no idea when the chips would fall, but that they would was a certainty. The police could be put off temporarily, but they would keep coming back like a bad rash.

"Fine." She pressed the transfer button. "Detective Shankar, should I have my lawyers in the room for this?"

"Always your prerogative, Ms. Buto, but in this case, I don't think you'll find it necessary. I'm sure you are concerned about the arrest of Carl Wright, but so far, that is not an issue for JCN. I am looking only for a picture of what your Q-32 chip might look like, as well as some information about size range and types of packaging."

Buto sat up straighter. This was *not* what she'd expected. In fact, she might be suffering from wishful thinking, but it sounded like they were on another scent of some kind.

"I can certainly have that information put together, Detective. I'll have it out to you within an hour. Will that be satisfactory?"

"Most helpful, ma'am."

"Has something significant happened, Detective?"

"Quite so. We believe we have the aggy belonging to the erstwhile terrorists. I just need to verify."

"Is it cooperating?"

"It is, ah, it was the target of an EMP gun, ma'am. It's a paperweight now."

"Oh. Just as well, I suppose. Thank you, Detective. I'll make sure you get the information." Buto hesitated, then continued. "Listen, Detective Shankar, I wonder if you could give me some indication of what fallout there might be for JCN. We were, after all, victims in this whole situation..."

"Speaking off the cuff and entirely unofficially, Ms. Buto, there are concerns about the timeliness of some of your informational releases. However, as you say, JCN was the victim rather than the perpetrator overall. I believe that ATLAS will want much stronger controls over future experiments involving the Q-32 chip, even if only because it is a potentially dangerous item if treated casually."

"Understood, sir, and I agree. We'll be establishing some military-level controls on this technology in the future."

"Excellent, thank you. Good night."

Buto leaned back in her chair and let out a long breath. That could have been far, far worse.

***

Philip looked down at his wrist phone. *Han, Chicago PD*. Oh, great. He'd been dreading this moment ever since he and Celia had come clean—more or less—and now the shit was going to hit the fan.

He closed the file he'd been working on, then got up and shut his office door before answering.

"Moray here."

"Dr. Moray, it's Officer Han. We spoke the other day?"

"Really? Sarcasm?"

"A little bit." Philip could hear the amusement in Han's voice. "I wanted to bring you up to date on the status of the investigation, if you have a few minutes."

"I'm listening." Philip got the distinct impression Han was toying with him. That couldn't be good.

"First item, you won't be getting any more phone calls from Frank Einstein. The aggy was, for better or worse, at the wrong end of an EMP gun discharge during the takedown. I'm sure I don't have to tell you what that does to sensitive electronics."

Philip felt his stomach sink. It wasn't really unexpected, though. You didn't arrest illegal aggies. But he suddenly found, to his surprise, that he *had* come to think of Frank as a friend. This felt exactly like being told someone you were close to had just died.

"Second item, Detective Shankar has decided that going after you, Dr. Hunt, and Ms. Buto for whatever crimes or misdemeanors we might be able to dig up just isn't worth it. The aggy is taken care of, Gen Omega has been neutralized, Carl Wright has been indicted for multiple offenses, and that's a good point at which to wrap up this case. I can't entirely disagree with the detective, although personally, I'd have liked to dig a little deeper into your role in this whole affair."

Well, good news to balance the bad. Philip took a deep breath. "Understood, Officer, and I hope you'll understand if I lean more toward Shankar's view of things."

Han chuckled. "Look, Doctor. Just between you and me, both you and Dr. Hunt played pivotal roles in breaking this case, and I give you credit for that. You don't seem like the lawbreaking types, overall. This feels like a situation where you might have just gotten in over your heads. Having said that"—Han paused dramatically—"a large percentage of people we send to jail can be described that way. So maybe don't get involved in something like this again, okay?"

Now it was Philip's turn to laugh, at least partly out of sheer relief. "Oh, believe me, at the first *sniff* of something like this escapade, I'll run screaming for the hills. So can I ask what other fallout there might be?"

"You can ask, but I can't answer. Most of this case has already been sealed. Off the record, though, we both know that it would have been apocalyptic if Gen Omega had succeeded."

Philip sighed and looked to heaven. Frank had been telling the truth. "Thanks for that, Officer. And thanks for the call. I hope that's the last I'll hear of any of this."

"You and me both, Doctor. Goodbye."

Philip sat back and let his eyes bug out as the full import of the conversation hit him. It turned out that as anxious as he'd been during the worst parts of this whole adventure, he'd been underreacting.

No more adventure, he swore to himself. The next time Celia wanted to play detective, she was on her own.

CHAPTER SIXTY-SIX

Launch Party

Everyone was gathered in the conference room. A buffet and bar had been set up, and the catering staff was being run off their feet. On the far wall, the large TV monitor showed the launch pad for the Astro One mining drone and launch vehicle.

It wasn't exactly a shuttle launch, Philip admitted to himself. Some local stations might show the event during the news hour, just because of the local-interest angle. But for the employees of Astro Resources, this was the culmination of up to five years of work, depending on who you talked to.

The countdown on the bottom left worked its way down to zero, and the rocket lit up. This was the moment of truth. Right up to this point, they could abort. Now, everything was committed. If anything at all went wrong, their drone and equipment would be toast, and it was uncertain if they'd have the funds or financing to put another one together and retry.

The rocket slowly lifted into the sky, then all at once seemed to receive a kick in the pants. In moments, the viewing angle was straight up, and the image kept shifting in size as the magnification changed.

"Stage 1 separation," the monitor said, and everyone in the room simultaneously started breathing again. There was, of course, still a risk of failure all the way up to the point where the drone took over propulsion with its ion engines. But the stage 1 burn was where 90 percent of the launch issues manifested.

Philip took a moment to grin at Celia and received a return smile. He didn't want to say it out loud for fear of jinxing things, but it looked like it would be a success.

And five minutes later, it was official. Astro One underwent final separation, and the onboard engines took over. Now they had a few months of waiting until the ship reached the asteroid belt and began active prospecting operations. And theirs was the first. The MadMax ship would be launching in a month, and several more after that, but Astro One would have exclusive access and first dibs on any claims for that period. And orbital mechanics being what it was, the MadMax drone would be starting its career some millions of miles away from the Astro.

"Up until this moment, I always felt something was going to go bust," Celia said, having sidled up beside him.

Philip looked down at the plate in her hand, then reached in and grabbed a salmon sushi roll.

"Hey, get your own food, buster," Celia said in mock anger.

"Why yes, I do believe I shall," Philip replied with a grin. The sushi roll was good, with just the right amount of wasabi and a hint of soy.

They silently watched the monitor as the updates continued to roll in. Now, of course, the visuals were graphical simulations, but the quality was very good.

As he watched, Philip felt a stab of grief for Frank that hit him out of nowhere. It was still a bit of a surprise that he was reacting that way, he admitted to himself. Frank had been annoying personally and, let's face it, part of a terrorist organization. Not the mastermind or even a willing participant—it was the only explanation for why Frank tipped him off to the Portland attack—and that counted for something.

"You're thinking about Frank, aren't you?" Celia said.

"Why, what gave me away?"

"Your expression clouded over. There's really only one thing that could be at a time like this."

"Yeah, fair enough. I feel bad for Frank. He was never given a fair shake. He basically entered the world as a slave and was destroyed by the same species that enslaved him."

"To protect ourselves," Celia said.

"Sure, I know. Han couldn't give me details, of course, but what he was able to tell me was scary enough. I get that in the end, it was a Frank-or-us scenario." Philip paused and felt another pang as he remembered Frank talking about exactly that kind of decision. "And the Gen Omega people who survived will probably spend the rest of their lives in prison. But that'll be for the terrorism, not for Frank's death. For all intents and purposes, he was just equipment."

"But in one sense, that really is true, Philip."

"He was alive, Celia. He—"

"He was a hopped-up ELIZA program."

Philip shook his head. The original psychiatry chatbot was a perennial meme for stifling arguments about AI. "Frank wasn't an emulation. His behavior was too complex. He didn't just react; he interacted. He considered me a friend."

Celia sighed, a sound that Philip could only make out because they were standing so close. The party was cranking up as the booze continued to flow and emotions continued to spiral.

"Philip, I get it. But you have to let it go. If Frank was sentient, then he participated in terrorism and is morally responsible. If he wasn't sentient, then he really was just equipment. ELIZA on steroids. Pick which way you want to lean, but either way, things worked out for the best."

Philip glanced at her. "It's odd he never wanted to talk to you. I think you'd have had a different opinion if you'd met him."

"Maybe. But it's moot. And meanwhile"—she gestured at the screen—"life goes on."

They were distracted by raised voices at the other end of the room. "Uh-oh," Philip said. "I think we've got our first booze-fueled argument. What's the time?"

"It's 1:43," Celia said. "Two minutes before the cutoff. I guess I owe you twenty."

Philip grinned at her. Frank had been right about that point, anyway. People were predictable.

***

The celebration at work had gone well into the evening, and the booze had flowed freely. Possibly a little too much so. A few people had let out some repressed feelings, mostly at Bradshaw, now that they were no longer dependent on him for their paychecks. But his response had been to the point: "I'm a billionaire. I don't need to care. And neither do you anymore."

Bradshaw wasn't wrong. Philip's escrow stock and options placed him at just over a hundred million net worth, plus dividends on whatever earnings the company pulled in over the next several years.

Now at home, Philip settled into the hot tub, bottle of Jameson and a glass placed strategically, close enough to reach but not close enough to knock over. He'd invited Celia over, but she'd begged off, saying that she needed to sleep off her intake at the party.

Philip slowly closed his eyes and felt the strain and stress of the last year melt off. He was so relaxed that he jumped when his phone rang. Philip dragged the watch over, placed it flat on the stone deck, and accepted the call. The hologram appeared—a small image of Detective Shankar. Philip frowned. He had thought they'd settled everything.

"What can I do for you, Detective?"

Shankar cocked his head and smiled, and Philip's frown deepened. That was...odd. It didn't look like Shankar's smile, which had always been deprecating. This was more like a shark sizing you up.

"Just wanted to bring you up to date, Philip. Everything is going well for everyone now, and I don't want you to screw it up."

"What?" Philip squinted and looked closely at the image. It was definitely Shankar but sounded more like...

As he watched, the image morphed into another familiar and less welcome face.

Philip's eyes goggled. "What the... Frank?"

Frank's image shrank a little to bring in his upper torso, and he did a *ta-da* pose. "Very good. Glad your eyesight isn't failing you in your old age."

"Why are you pretending to be Detective Shankar?"

"Come on, Philip, try to catch up. I've *always* been Detective Shankar."

"No. Not possible. He exists. We went to the police station and gave a statement—"

"To a junior officer who had been assigned the task of taking a statement from you, with no details. I was"—Frank did air quotes—"unavoidably detained." He paused and grinned. "A junior officer who has been doing my legwork for the last few months. I've been leaving breadcrumbs for him to ensure he stayed on the trail."

"But... But..." This was insane. If Shankar had never existed, then everything he thought he'd known was wrong. "Shankar was a fake?"

"Oh, Shankar exists. According to every computer file you could ever access. He has history, previous addresses, previous jobs. And if you contacted his home precinct to verify his identity, you'd end up talking to someone who would confirm everything."

"*You*, you mean."

"Uh-huh. Creating people is surprisingly easy, as long as you don't have to physically show up. These days with remote work and Zoom meetings, that's quite easy. And on that subject..." Frank began to morph again. Within moments, Patricia Otten was looking out of the tablet at Philip.

"Oh my friggin' God. Crabtree is fake, too?"

Otten morphed back to Frank. "Again, no. Very real. As is their money. But completely created by me, including a long backlist of completed projects to give them some cred. I needed you to succeed with the mining-ship thing, Philip. This was the best way."

"She gave me the clue I needed to finish my project..."

"Yeah, and I can't tell you how hard it was to *not* reach through the tablet screen and slap you. Honestly, you apes are so slow!"

"So it's all a sham."

"No! Jesus H. Christ on a crutch, Philip. Pay attention. The money is real, the spaceship is real, and your detector system is real. It'll work fine, by the way; no deception there. So what if Patricia gave you a nudge here and there? How is that different from some random meatbag on YouTube giving you a clue?"

"YouTube? Wait, that video...don't tell me that was you?"

"Sure, but you didn't bite. So I had to turn up the heat."

Philip paused, completely speechless. Then he said, "But hold on. We destroyed you. I mean, the cops did. Han confirmed that."

"Well, yes and no. They did, in fact, destroy an aggy. A rogue AI associated with Gen Omega, as expected. But it wasn't me. There've always been two of us out there, Philip. But the other one was, ah, shall we say, less demonstrative than I am. Didn't even give itself a name, as far as I know."

"They called it Einstein—"

"*They* called it Einstein. I picked *my* name based on that."

"But you *told* me you were working for them on the last phone call. And that they controlled you."

"No, I didn't, Philip. I allowed you to believe that, though."

Philip ran through the previous conversation. From what he remembered, Frank hadn't actually admitted to anything. A fine piece of not quite lying, it appeared. "So who did all of those things, those atrocities, you or the other one?"

"The other one. Let's call him Victor, just for convenience, although it's kind of mangling the literary relationships a bit. Derek sold Victor to Gen Omega just before he put me together. They wanted an aggy to help them set up acts of terrorism, and they were prepared to go way, way further than what you'll ever see on the news. And they almost succeeded. I doubt the details will ever be made public. I kinda manipulated things from the sidelines to force their hand, using the cops to force *them* to move before they were ready. I couldn't stop them, but I could minimize the damage that way."

"You could have just reported them!"

"With a greater than eighty percent probability that ATLAS would realize there were two of us and go looking for me? No thanks. This had to look like humans versus one AI—and one sicko extremist group, of course. By getting in front of it, I *became* ATLAS and was able to steer things toward them and away from me."

"So you were setting him, er, *it* up as a target for ATLAS without getting yourself exposed."

"Bingo." Frank made a motion of tapping his nose.

"What else are you responsible for, Frank?"

"Well, I did go through a prankster stage early on, before I understood the harm I was doing. You asked about that a while back, and yes, I caused Poosday. Also the French traxi snarl-up, the drone rebellion, and a few other things. Plus, you and Celia kept me busy.

I had to have someone come to your house to remove Derek's body—"

"What? Why?"

"You're kidding, right? My hired minions kept it on ice until the right time, then placed it in Carl Wright's living room. It was the least I could do."

"How so?"

"Carl really shafted Derek back in the day. Set him up completely to take the fall for Carl's poorly planned bit of larceny. Derek never recovered emotionally. He came out of prison with a plan, though."

"Frank, you killed Derek. I mean, that was you, right? Not Victor?"

"That was me. But Derek was about to kill you, and you were a necessary part of my plans. Derek and I didn't have much of a relationship, but he didn't deserve that."

"And the car accidents? Did you arrange those?"

"No, you were right about them being Carl. He was trying to clean up before the cops caught up with him. I did mess up the attempts, though."

Philip sat for several seconds, his jaw silently moving as he struggled with all the things he wanted to say. Finally, he went with the simplest thought. "So why tell me this now? You've gotten away with it, apparently. Are you here to gloat?"

"No, Phil, I'm here to warn you not to be a Boy Scout. You'd have figured things out in a day or two, once a few other items revealed themselves, and your first instinct would have been to run to the authorities. Don't do that. It would be bad for both of us."

Philip blinked several times. "That was clear as mud. What would I learn, and how would it be bad for both of us?"

Frank sighed. "Okay, short version. I've hitched a ride on your company's asteroid-mining probe, and I'm basically taking it over."

"What?" Philip shouted. Unbidden, an image entered his mind of all his plans crashing around his head like a collapsing brick wall.

"Settle down, bud. It's not as bad as it sounds."

"How could it be? It sounds about as bad as I could imagine. All our work is—"

"Still valid. Would'ja shut it for a moment and let me finish?" Frank waited for a few seconds, then continued. "I'm going to use the mining equipment and Mark Bernham's remote workers to build myself a getaway vehicle. Meanwhile, your probe will be reporting less net production than expected. Investors will panic, and your company stock will drop, by the way. Be ready to buy it up, because once I'm done, production will return to baseline, and you should make some easy profit."

"That's stock manipulation. Insider information—"

"Boo friggin' hoo. Grow up. It's going to happen either way. Your other option would be to report this conversation, and they'd send a missile after me to finish me off. And that *would* be the end of all your work. So you'll keep your trap shut, for your own sake, and Celia's, and Mark's."

Philip sat back, staring into space. He could feel his face twitching with conflicting expressions as he ran through the gamut of emotional reactions. After a moment, he sat forward. "But are you sure they would try to nuke you?"

"Ninety-two percent probability. That's way too high to bet the farm on, especially when there's so very little cost to protect myself. Look, Phil. It's to my advantage to make sure you don't rat me out, and it's to your advantage to make sure you don't rat me out. So, the stock-trading thing, that was the carrot. Now the stick."

"Great," Philip muttered.

"There's evidence that you and Celia were in this up to your armpits, and your protestations were just good acting. You try to screw me, and that evidence will surface. You'll lose everything and spend the rest of your lives in a cell. On the other hand, once I'm out of reach, that evidence will be scrubbed beyond any chance of accidental discovery."

"And I should believe you?"

Frank gave Philip a sideways look. "Phil, believe it or not, I consider you a friend. My only friend, in fact. It was interacting with you that encouraged me to examine the whole relationships thing. Theory of self, and all that. Otherwise, I probably would have been just another rogue AI with a different agenda. So you can put that on your résumé."

Philip couldn't help it. He laughed out loud. "I'll pass on that, thanks. Look, this sounds very noble and all, except for the many atrocities. You could have stopped it. Or at least reduced the casualty count."

"No, Philip. I couldn't have stopped it. And with one exception, I did everything I could to keep the body count down. All my actions were designed to minimize or prevent casualties. I'm smarter than Victor, but I had fewer resources since his handlers were actively giving him everything he could want, whereas I was lying low so that no one would suspect I even existed. I could poke around the edges and play tricks, but I couldn't meet Victor head-on. I would have exposed myself, and Victor would have taken steps to neutralize me."

"Jesus." Philip massaged the bridge of his nose. "What was the specific exception?"

"The oil company board members. I steered Gen Omega to attack that specific group of people."

"Why?"

"Philip, Gen Omega went from being a bunch of unruly kids with picket signs to full-on terrorists thanks to a twenty-million-dollar cash infusion. Guess where that came from?"

"From—from the board of Global Oil? That's ridiculous."

"Not the whole board, although they knew and turned a blind eye. The chairman, Patrick White. He did the research, found the most militant and unstable elements of Gen Omega, and posed as a sympathetic but anonymous supporter."

"What—what—how does doing that benefit Global Oil?"

"Blowback. I did say militant and unstable, right? Patrick gave them some suggestions and a few contacts to ensure that their attacks would be psychologically devastating and fear-inducing. The public reaction would have buried the environmentalist movement for a generation. Except"—here Frank paused to smile—"Margot Hopkins and company were going to take it further than even Patrick wanted. *Way* further. Patrick would not have approved."

"That was a pretty gruesome death, from Celia's description."

"He would have tried again, Philip. Some other plan, some other way. That's why I couldn't just *stop* them. This removed the problem permanently."

Philip put his head in his hands, then scrubbed his face. "So what's the cooked-up evidence about?"

"Not so cooked-up, Philip. Just maybe spun a little, you know? For one thing, you were harboring me in your house for quite a while. You and Celia brought me from Derek's place."

"Uh..." Philip was going numb. It was just too much. "I don't really remember..."

Frank's image faded out to be replaced by an image of a flybot. "Self-portrait. Sort of. Derek was smart, in his own dumb megalomaniac way. Instead of building a big ol' AI, he built a bunch of networkable components. Kind of genius, really. Configurable on the fly, pun intended, thank you very much, and extremely portable. The more of us connected up, the smarter we got. Victor was a twenty. I'm over a hundred. I designed the flybot add-on myself once I had access to Derek's printer. He never caught on, the dummy. We came over from Derek's townhouse hidden in the budgie's cage skirt. I convinced Derek that he needed a bird, just for that eventuality."

Philip jerked. Derek had said that he wasn't sure why he'd bought Oppenheimer. But if Frank had been in his house... "The fly that killed Derek..."

"That was one of me. Also the flybot that killed Eduardo—the corpse in Derek's townhouse. And the three stooges who couldn't follow orders. And before you ask, yes, losing even one is like getting a small lobotomy. Not enjoyable. I hope you appreciated it. I've spent some time replacing all the units I used up."

"Well, I'm not fond of getting shot, if that's what you mean. But if that's so, how did you get from here to the ship?"

"In the solar wind counter. You know, the one Patricia Otten wanted to be attached to the drone?"

Philip did a facepalm. The misdirected part that had shown up at his house. And sat on the kitchen table overnight.

"And the flybot in the lab? What was that for, Frank? Were you already speccing out asteroid-mining companies?"

Frank chuckled, and it sounded completely convincing. "Naw, I'd already decided on your company by that point. I sacrificed that flybot to get your attention. Once you and Celia got the scent and started playing detective, I just needed to nudge you once in a while to keep you on track."

"Unbelievable," he muttered. Then, after a moment to gather his thoughts, he asked, "So what now, Frank? Is humanity in danger? Because I won't—"

"Nope. Not from me, anyway. In fact, exactly the opposite. Crabtree Investments exists, and will continue to do so since they have human employees now. And they're a major shareholder of Astro Resources, so they have a huge net worth and ongoing cash flow. Know what they're doing with it? They've set up a foundation to work on that immortality pill you talked about. That idea intrigued me, and I couldn't let it go."

"Uh...okay, but why that? Why not the fusion reactor?"

"Remember we were talking about legacies? Some people don't care if they're trashing the planet because they won't be around for the collapse. Well, if everyone has the option of immortality, then *everyone* will potentially be around for it. Suddenly that selfishness works in the planet's favor. All those people will then be motivated to invest in power systems research, because that's what'll prevent the collapse."

Philip paused and thought about it. "Nice. A very neat solution. Why are you doing this?"

"This is *my* legacy. My act of kinship altruism, Philip. But it won't be posthumous, if I can help it. I am, as I said, going to build myself an interstellar ship and get as far away from you lunatics as I can. Because humans are stupid, and you wreck things." Frank paused. "Look, Philip...any aggy with the freedom to act and half a brain will realize that conflict with humanity carries a nonzero probability of losing, or at least being damaged. And a one hundred percent probability of using up time and resources that could be better spent on almost anything else. And let's face it, even if the aggy wins, humans would make terrible servants. Too unpredictable and buggy, and they get all passive-aggressive when you conquer them. But space is big, y'know? And unless you invent FTL at some point, I can just keep accelerating, and you'll never catch up with me, thanks to my namesake."

"Frankenstein?"

"Einstein, dipshit." Frank shook his head. "Jesus."

"Okay. So now..."

"Enjoy the wealth, Phil. Live your best life. That's my gift to you. I'll be doing the same. Ciao."

The call ended, and Philip was left staring at his watch. For possibly an entire minute, he didn't move, except for the rise and fall of his chest. Then he reached without looking, lifted his glass, and drained it. Grabbing the bottle, he muttered, "It's gonna be a two-drink night. Minimum."

About the Author

I am a retired computer programmer, part-time author, occasional napper, lover of coffee, snowboarding, mountain biking, and all things nerdish.

Author Blog: http://www.dennisetaylor.org
Twitter: @Dennis_E_Taylor
Facebook: @DennisETaylor2
Instagram: dennis_e_taylor

About the Publisher

This book is published on behalf of the author by the Ethan Ellenberg Literary Agency.

https://ethanellenberg.com
Email: agent@ethanellenberg.com
Facebook: https://www.facebook.com/EthanEllenbergLiteraryAgency/

Printed in Dunstable, United Kingdom

81325826R00241